Praise for Cynthia Pelayo

"A dreamlike modern fairy tale full of grief, longing, and murder, *Forgotten Sisters* is Cynthia Pelayo's best yet. Like the best hauntings, this one will linger in my head for a long time."

—Christopher Golden, *New York Times* bestselling author of *Road of Bones* and *The House of Last Resort*

"Aspects of *Forgotten Sisters* glide past each other like ghosts as Cynthia Pelayo adroitly juggles past and present, reality and the supernatural, in this elegiac gothic novel. You'll be haunted long after you've finished turning the pages."

—Alma Katsu, author of *The Fervor*

"A gritty murder mystery about a house that drips with haunted histories and a river that carries dark secrets and dead bodies in its current, *Forgotten Sisters* is a mesmerizing, propulsive read that doesn't just bend genre, it transcends it."

—Rachel Harrison, national bestselling author of *Cackle* and *Black Sheep*

"Personal, historical, and heart-deep. *Forgotten Sisters* captures the complicated sense of being stifled by home yet lost without it. From the eerie start to the unforgettable ending, Pelayo brings the chill of crime stories, grim fairy tales, and the gothic into a haunting mystery that will drag you into dark waters and never let go."

—Hailey Piper, Bram Stoker Award–winning author of *Queen of Teeth* and *A Light Most Hateful*

"Guaranteed to make your heart thump and skin crawl."

—*The New York Times*

FORGOTTEN SISTERS

OTHER WORKS BY CYNTHIA PELAYO

Chicago Saga Novel

The Shoemaker's Magician

Children of Chicago

Stand-Alone Novels

Santa Muerte

The Missing

Poetry

Poems of My Night

Into the Forest and All the Way Through

Crime Scene

Collections

Lotería

Writing Poetry in the Dark

The Hideous Book of Hidden Horrors

Slash-Her

Diabolica Americana

Were Tales

This World Belongs to Us

Poetry Showcase Volume VII

Poetry Showcase Volume V

¡Pa'que Tu Lo Sepas!

Lockdown

Both Sides

Campfire Macabre

Snow White's Shattered Coffin

Far From Home

Halldark Holidays

Twisted Anatomy

We Are Wolves

FORGOTTEN SISTERS

A NOVEL

CYNTHIA PELAYO

THOMAS & MERCER

Text copyright © 2024 by Cynthia Pelayo
All rights reserved.

Published by Thomas & Mercer, Seattle

www.apub.com

Amazon, the Amazon logo, and Thomas & Mercer are trademarks of Amazon.com, Inc., or its affiliates.

ISBN-13: 9781662513916 (paperback)
ISBN-13: 9781662513909 (digital)

Cover design by Olga Grlic

Cover image: © zef art / Shutterstock; © mikesj11 / Shutterstock; © golubovy / Getty Images

Printed in the United States of America

To my father . . . you will not be forgotten.

*The rays fell warmly and gently upon the deadly cold sea foam,
and the Little Mermaid did not feel death.*

—*"The Little Mermaid," Hans Christian Andersen*

Prologue

Under the sea.

The house.

The house is quiet and still. Yes, quiet and still, but I am not quiet, and I am not still, because inside there's this great circular current, an eddy, or maybe it's a storm.

I push the front door open and stumble inside, falling forward onto the hardwood floor.

I cry because that is all I can do. Infinity as tears. I accept that this is all I will ever do, now and forever inside this house, my prison. There will be grief, and there will be silent suffering for eternity, struck from the moment I close my eyes to sleep, sweeping across my dreams, and emerging with me in the day.

Sorrow will be my constant, because they died.

They died.

Today, they died, and where does that leave me?

Alone. I'm alone. Wondrously and pitifully alone.

"Jennie!" I scream my sister's full name, and it's as if my call casts a mighty hook out into the sea, because I feel something within me splinter. I scream again and again, for this will know no end. My unending and desperate pain.

I want all the fish in the waters on Earth and all of the birds in the great blue sky above to hear my call. I need her here with me right now, because I cannot do this by myself.

"Jennie!" My throat is raw, and I taste blood now. Sound fades from my body as her name rips apart my vocal cords, breaking free from the current that erupts in this house, rattling everything within. Chairs and cushions and the antique telephones I keep throughout the house to hold memories seem to shift an inch here or there. I hear the silverware, forks and knives and spoons, clack together as they bend this way or that.

I open my eyes for a moment, and it seems as if nothing is the same, yet everything remains. I close my eyes tight. *This is still my house. This is still our house*, I think to myself, as my entire being aches with a longing for everything to go back to the way it was just a few hours ago.

"Anna." Her voice is small at first, a tinkling bell.

And like that, with pain, the line was cast, and she is here.

I hear footsteps approach, and there are hands on my shoulders. I feel her warm breath on my forehead. I can taste the salty sweet air on my tongue. I smell the hot sand on the beach and the fresh breeze dancing off ocean waves. In the distance I hear the high-pitched whining call of seagulls.

I can't speak. I can't think.

Words are water, and everything melds into this sea of suffering, except her, my beautiful, enchanting Jennie. She is my fairy tale. She has always been and she will always be.

"I'm here, Anna." She puts her arms around me, kisses me on the cheek, and holds me tight. "I'm so sorry I was gone for the briefest of moments. I'm here now, my darling sister, and I promise never ever to leave you again."

Even though deep within me I know this to not be true, I force myself to believe.

Chapter 1

Bodies are decomposing in the Chicago River. People don't like to think about that, to think about long-submerged bloated corpses sinking to the riverbed, but it's happening. It's happening even now, and I wonder if we're happening now with it.

Once a submerged corpse rises to the surface, water continues to be absorbed into the skin. Liquid overwhelms the underlying layers, and the result is that the flesh peels away and slips off, carried by the current. Adipocere, a waxy, soapy substance produced from one's fat, then forms all over the body. In time, bacteria, birds, and other small animals begin to peck and poke, nibble and gnaw away, at the remains.

And once all remnants have been consumed by creatures, and once the surface of skin and fat sloughs off bone and turns into foam, then there's no longer fibrous connective tissue to hold on to, and so the skeleton sinks to the riverbed piece by piece. A complete set of bones then comes to rest atop fine sediment, clay, dirt, and topsoil.

What was once a person is now a part of the river, a body of water that was formed hundreds of millions of years ago, when what is today Chicago was covered by the vast sea.

Decomposition is slow.

I know a lot about the river, perhaps too much. My sister, Jennie, and I live in a coveted Craftsman bungalow along the river in Chicago's Ravenswood community on the North Branch of the Chicago River.

Recently I've committed to discovering the source of an incessant dripping noise that has caused me to lose sleep. Perhaps it's coming from the kitchen, or one of the bathrooms, either the one on the first floor or upstairs on the second floor?

Each of those spaces deserves a bit of a refresh, and I'm fairly good with a can of paint. In fact, this entire house deserves all of the love that I can give it, because the house is sad. I suppose I will get on with it and do some light remodeling, as that will cheer me up, and it will especially cheer up the house. I'm not sure if it will cheer up Jennie. It's been harder and harder to get her to smile since the accident, but I will try to do my best.

This is an important house, and the house likes to be cared for in the most appropriate ways.

I will make the updates myself. Why should I summon strangers into my home who would scrutinize each of my requests and then send me a quote for three times what it should cost me when I could very well accomplish it myself? I don't want people hammering away at the walls of my beautiful home. I don't want work boots dragging in dust and dirt into this house. I certainly don't want anyone disturbing Jennie any more than she has already been disturbed. The only person I trust to fix things, to set them right, is me.

There are, of course, luxury apartments and condominiums pressed along the river's edge downtown in neighborhoods like River North, River West, the West Loop, and the South Loop. Those are steel-and-glass boxes, with no historical significance. A true house has history. A real home lives and breathes, watches and waits. Each birth into a home is energy that charges doors and windows, floors, ceilings, hallways, and rooms. A rare historic home kissing the Chicago River isn't just unique, but extraordinary. These homes seldom hit the real estate listings, and if they do, they demand millions of dollars.

Grandmother took great pride in this home, so much so that she even framed the page from the Sears catalog from which it came and hung it in the entryway. It took her months to track down the original listing from the early 1900s, but she found it and took pleasure in telling us it would serve as our reminder that this home deserved care, as it has cared for us.

The house was built in 1912, and that's how Jennie and I are able to explain away the odd noises and strange sights we experience regularly within these walls.

Jennie said it's an old house, and old houses remember.

Old houses store memories snug within cracks of floorboards and embedded in grains of wood. All of these moments, and more, seep into the very building material of the home, imprinting it with memories. Old houses are time capsules, but also living records. They are keepsakes that archive the celebration of wedding days and the coos of a newborn baby. The electrical work is lined with the laughter of children running across the kitchen floor, and the wooden beams that support the very structure we live in store away all of the screams and cries mourning the deaths of family and loved ones.

A house is alive, as we are alive.

In many ways a house is always recording, and when ready it will recount to us images and sounds, maybe more of the secrets it holds. A house always watches, waits, and listens for its caretaker, but it also recognizes when a new tide is coming, and it will warn us.

I wonder if the dripping I hear is a warning that change is coming.

I know I must be good to this house because it has been good to us. I'll remove a few old plaster walls, paint them, and buff the floors. Maybe I'll even refresh the kitchen cabinets and fixtures as I search for that drip.

The house is often predictable. During the day are the expected knockings and murmurs, footsteps and taps. There's always tapping, the fluttering of two or three or four quick, successive tap-tap-taps or tap-tap-tap-taps when I'm seated alone in the living room or reading a book in my bedroom. The house wants to be sure I know where I am. That I am aware of the present.

Grandmother once called these noises "settling." A soft groan over my shoulder. A light bulb hissing, vibrating, or bursting after my name was whispered at my bedside at night. Or the creaking of floorboards feet from me, as if someone were approaching, but there was no one there. When these things would occur, Grandmother would remain still, poised, and softly say, "The house is settling."

I wondered if when I settled, I would glow and then burst with intensity, like one of our ghostly, touched bulbs. Perhaps I already did glow and burst, but I just didn't know it yet.

Near the end of Grandmother's life, she would laugh off these settlings as the house being foolish. She said the house was like a stubborn child, upset it wasn't getting what it wanted. She never did elaborate as to what the house demanded. Whenever I brought up the noises to my parents, they would tell me the sounds weren't being made by ghosts but that the house was old and that's what these old houses did, moaned and groaned at times.

There is no denying the activity in our home. Jennie and I never refer to it as a haunting, or a collection of specters, or a poltergeist. That seems too simplistic. We know what is happening here is much greater, much more complex than we can explain. We know that there is no word in our reality or the next to thoroughly communicate what it is we are experiencing here.

Our house is itself an entity, a being, and we both accept it. Jennie and I often don't share what we hear or see unless we are both in the same room. We each experience occurrences that are specific to our realities. Our own custom haunting. When I'd find Jennie in the hallway or the kitchen, her stare fixed on a wall or her hands trembling at the kitchen sink, I'd ask what happened, and she would give me a weak smile and say, "I was just thinking of that song I do love so much."

The fear would strike most when I'd hear knocking on the front door. One day, I wondered aloud what was trying to get in, and Jennie spoke softly behind me, "Ghosts are recordings reliving moments of their life. They cannot move off course from their routine unless there's a disruption to their path."

"What kind of disruption?" I asked.

"They must be remembered by someone living. Or, when a place they lived and walked in is shaken up and dust particles that hold pieces of their memory shift and move, it awakens them."

I learned to accept these settlings, the activity in the house, the result of the movement of things and the occurrence of sounds, sights, and smells I could not understand or yet explain. It was like the rattling of windows during a gust of wind. You couldn't see the force of air, but you knew it was there, and you knew it was something you could not control. This house has seen so much over the years, and recently no number of measurements or calculations could make this structure make sense.

When Grandmother died, Jennie and I were still little girls. The house was left to my mother and father with instructions from Grandmother that when my parents died, it would be passed on to Jennie and me.

And so, here we are, without Grandmother, and now without Mother and Father. With the greatest ache in my heart, I accept that the house now belongs to my sister and me.

I've rarely left the house since the accident, except for necessary errands. Jennie leaves for twice-daily walks, one in the early morning and the other in the evening, which she takes great pleasure in. Jennie appreciates the seasons that move and sway in this great city, never fully remaining fixed until they do.

I am the caretaker for my sister, even though she is twenty-six, and I am younger than she is at twenty-three. The younger caring for the older. Yet she is my sister, and this is my duty.

My life is simple.

I care for Jennie. I care for the house.

I clean the house daily, sweeping and mopping, dusting, polishing, and vacuuming. It was important to Grandmother that the house serve as a jewel along the river. My mother and father made sure of that, and I will make sure of that as well. I will make sure this home gleams, no matter the gloom that rests within. Even though I will keep myself busy with the scrubbing and the polishing, I know the house will always need more. I know that Jennie will always need more. And I fear one day soon I will come undone.

Grandmother had once said, "Think of the house as an oyster, and you and your sister live within as two pearls—rare but not impossible."

"A house under the sea, like 'The Little Mermaid'?" I recall asking. She smiled. "Of course, Anna. Under the sea like 'The Little Mermaid.' Anna and Jennie, my enchanting mermaids."

Grandmother, like my sister, spoke in nonsensical phrases, offering wisdom when no advice was asked, but I suppose that was part of their charm. Grandmother's musings were constant, forever lessons about this world and our expectations for existing within it. Her most urgent request, however, was that as the house changed hands, from Mother and Father to Jennie and me, that we remain living within it, caring for it. Not selling it. Never to discard it but to remain living here, in this special house, in this world-class city.

When I pressed her on why, to explain the importance of this house and the river, she would brush it off and sing a little melody she often hummed to herself:

> By the sea
> By the sea
> By the beautiful sea
> You and me, you and me
> Oh, how happy we'll be

Right before Grandmother died, I begged her again to tell me everything she knew about the house and the river. At first, she ignored my pleas, telling me how much she loved us, Mother and Father and Jennie and me, telling me to continue reading the books we loved so much, and for me to continue telling stories and for Jennie to continue making music. Those were our loves: stories and music.

I pressed Grandmother again to tell me, and she finally said, "A lot of sadness happened in this home, a long time ago, and your grandfather and I made a promise to this house that we would fill it with nothing but joy, and in turn the house would bring us magic and love."

The house is paid for, and Mother and Father left us with a sum to live comfortably on. We are not wealthy but live without major financial burdens. There is money for groceries and utilities, and if the house needs repairs, there is money for that as well. We care for the house as lovingly as the house cares for us.

After cleaning the house and preparing our meals and spending time outside, I still had so much time left in the day. Jennie rarely emerged from her room, except for her walks and her meals, but other than those few times throughout the day I would see her, I remained largely alone.

Loneliness is silence.

I have a voice with which to speak, but there is really no one to talk to, and I am reminded of that every day here. I very seldom speak with Jennie, and the only noises that ever arise in this house are its movements and the moments in which it must make itself known.

And so, now seated here on the living room sofa, I admire the rays of golden sunlight flooding in through the floor-to-ceiling windows of the french doors that open out to a little deck. From the deck there is a little gravel path that twists and curves down to a wooded area of bushes and trees, a couple of benches, and the river that commands this house. Sitting here, I notice again the sounds of a drip.

Steady and constant.

Deep within this house.

I move to the french doors, turn the handle, and push, and I am overcome with the smell of spring in the city. I step outside onto the deck and walk down the wooden stairs to the path arriving at the frontage of the river. I sit down on a little bench in front of a great tree whose branches twist and bend and reach over the water. At its base I admire the pretty fairy garden I planted long ago as a little girl.

There are pink and blue and yellow and red stones. There are colored buttons and glass marbles and flowerpots that grow golden alexanders, white Queen Anne's lace, and bright-red cardinal flowers. When I was little, I'd come here and write letters to my fairy. I would fold up the letter, kiss it, and cast it into the river, hoping my messages of love would reach the magical creature. The sweet imaginations of a child. I wish I had enough imagination and hope today to believe in a real fairy that could take this heaviness from my heart and replace it with peace.

I sit for a moment and admire the stillness of the place, of all of this—the trees that surround me, peony bushes, and hanging roses, and within the silence something stirs. A whimpering.

I stand.

It is as if the whimpers vibrate from deep within my chest, because I understand the meaning of sorrowful songs too well.

The cries grow clearer, and then I see a gray plastic grocery bag floating along the surface of the water. It flows down and then turns toward me, as if it were meant for me, and then it catches in a tangle of gnarled and knotted river birch roots.

I climb down and reach for the bag, which moves and groans. I tear it open, and inside I find two gray puppies no larger than my fist. I press the little creatures to my chest and snuggle them, falling instantly in love. "Thank you, fairy."

I bring the puppies up to the house and set down a dish of water, and my heart is bursting with emotion. My eyes are filling with tears because the river has answered my calls to soothe my loneliness.

I think of the river, and I think of Chicago, and I think of the sea, wondering which names would best suit these little ones I've saved from a watery grave. I think of the beauty along the river, of trees, vines, ferns, grasses, and shrubs. I think of prairie flowers, brilliant and bright butterfly-attracting milkweeds, purple-and-pink shooting stars with their slender branches, and of bright-yellow sawtooth sunflowers.

I know these darlings deserve something more.

The bull thistle has large spikes and invades prairies and woodlands with its spiny leaves. The red clover is also an invader of prairies. Each a dreamy, rich pink tone, a color with a touch of magic. They were birthed from the river and would be named after ornamental flowers that line the river.

I kiss one. "You're Clover," I say. I kiss the other. "You're Thistle."

As the two puppies tumble about me, licking my hands and arms and cheeks, I can feel the house looming behind me. A shadow that is forever an extension of me.

Inside, I find Jennie standing at the top of the stairs in a black satin floor-length nightgown. My sister is beautiful, much more beautiful than I can ever be. I am plain and short, with brown hair that rests just above my shoulders. Freckles are dotted across my face, a reminder of the chaos of the cosmos and the constellations above. My voice is soft and small. Jennie's voice is deep and alluring. I wear cotton housedresses that fit comfortably so, and black loafers. Jennie wears form-fitting black satin and black silk, which clings along her breasts and hips.

Jennie is the night.

Jennie is moonlight and midnight.

She is taller than I am by a foot. Her hair is thick and long and black, cascading down past her waist. Her dark eyes are black holes that want to swallow you. I admire her long neck and high cheekbones, her full lips and her smooth, pale skin. She is the point of all attraction, and I wish I could be as mystical and magnetic as she is some days. Jennie is the desire of all humans. She could have anyone she wants, but instead she chooses herself.

She chooses loneliness.

Her nostrils flare. "What is that?"

"They're puppies." I hold one up in each of my hands.

Her eyes flash to the back door that leads to our river walk. "The news announced they've found another body in the river today."

"Another body?" I say. I take a seat on the sofa, overcome with the news of yet another person found dead. With the spring thaw, there was the discovery of a body just a week ago, and now, another. "That is so awful."

The puppies squirm in my hands, and I look up to my sister. "Jennie, perhaps it's not safe for you to walk along the river at night anymore."

Jennie laughs. "Do not worry about me, my sweet Anna. All of the bodies that have come to the surface are men. No one is going to harm me along the river."

"I'm sure that's what all of those men believed too, right before they disappeared."

She ignores me and starts making her way up the stairs to her bedroom "Get rid of them," she says. "Those puppies do not belong here."

"No! I'm not getting rid of them. They're a blessing. They would have drowned if I hadn't saved them."

I look at the puppies in my hands, their eyes now closing, drifting off to sleep. I hope after so much terror they can finally feel safe in knowing that they are in the hold of someone who loves them. And after experiencing so much terror of my own, and so much heartbreak and loneliness, I need them as much as they need me.

Jennie says from the shadows at the top of the stairs, "Maybe they were meant to drown. It's not wise to interfere with the way things should be, no matter how tragic the circumstances."

I hear the door to her bedroom shut, and then music begins to play. It is an old, dreary song that speaks of a life long ago, one that Jennie could not let go of, and one that haunts us both.

I once again hear the sound of the drip. It has returned, but now I hear something else: the gushing and running of water. "Jennie?" I call.

I walk up the stairs and peek into the second-floor bath to be sure, but there is nothing there.

I look at the tiles and the sink, the dry showerhead, but still, I hear water racing all around me now in this small room.

I think of the river outside and all of the secrets this house holds. I suppose it is time to tear up these walls.

Chapter 2

This is the guy they give me? I eye him as we stand on the Irving Park Bridge looking over the Chicago River. The Marine Unit boat is stationed below us. The divers have been under awhile now. Detective John Rodriguez has got his arms crossed over his chest, and he's moving from side to side. His eyes dart all over the place, but no place at all. I don't know what the hell I'm supposed to do with him. He's like some kid's toy that's been wound up, and the only way to stop it is to slam my hand down on it, but I know I can't do that.

"It's cold," Rodriguez says.

Of course it's cold. It's Chicago, and even in spring it's cold. "What the hell do you want from me? A blanket?"

"Training's going great," Rodriguez mutters under his breath as he rubs his hand through his hair.

"You're the one pointing out the obvious," I say.

Sergeant Flanagan says Rodriguez is a good recruit for homicide, so for now I'll keep my mouth shut. I trust Sarge. He's a good guy and spent a lot of time in homicide, so if he says the kid's good, then maybe the kid's good. Still, let's see how he does. This isn't vice. It hasn't been easy on me, and I know it's not going to be easy on Rodriguez. He's going to have to get used to screams, blood, and body parts real quick.

I chose this job, and he chose it too. You just don't raise your hand one day in roll call and tell Sarge you want to work in homicide. You had to have been a detective in another department at least a few years, and be good, real good, at your job. And it's not just being good at surveillance, report writing, interrogation, and closing cases; you have to have good instincts to bring all of that together. Yes, I can teach this kid everything I know. I'm going to, but there's something else to detective work that can't be learned. It's that hunch, that feeling inside like an alarm blaring when something isn't right. It's also that feeling like a blinking arrow pointing you to an answer. If you've got it, you just know. You either have the gift of investigating or you don't.

"Hey! Rodriguez. You all right?" I'm clapping my hands together inches from his face, and he gives me that look, that look that tells me if I clap one more time, I'm in trouble.

He shakes his head, shoves his hands in his jacket pocket, and keeps his eyes fixed on the water. A woman with a small child in a stroller stops in front of us on the bridge. I know how this is going to go. These people are all the same. Predictable.

"Did somebody get killed?" she asks.

"No, I'm just standing here taking in the scenery."

She gasps and continues on.

"Every single time the yellow tape goes up, someone asks that."

Rodriguez glances my way, and if he looks at me one more time like that, it's not going to end well for him.

"It seems like you're the one not all right, Kowalski," Rodriguez snaps.

I nod toward the water. "Of course I'm not all right. We got another body in the river. We gotta focus."

He rubs his hands together to keep warm. "There's been a lot of those lately. Anything about the body from the Clark Street Bridge accident?"

My lower back is beginning to ache. We've been standing out here too long. "Nope. Nothing. But we got one here."

My hope is that we can figure out who this is at the Medical Examiner's Office and alert their family. Then we can piece together what the hell happened.

No one wants to be told that their loved one was found in the murky river. The river isn't kind to anyone in death. No body of water is kind to anyone in death. I learned that early in my career, and sadly later in my career too.

I remember the very first time I saw someone like that, oozing with liquid, bloated, and bruised. It was my very first week in homicide.

The medical examiner smiled as she pulled on her gloves.

"Welcome to homicide, Detective Adam Kowalski," the ME said.

I remember the room was cold. It looked and smelled like a hospital operating room, all metal cabinets and drawers, surgical equipment laid out, some sharp-smelling disinfectant. The large metal table in the center with the black bag on top screamed that this place was different. The ME pulled down the zipper, and there it was, a gelatinous, swollen mass. The mask over my face helped some, but I was still almost knocked back by the stench from the corpse. It smelled like rotten meat and dank river water.

I'll never forget that person's skin. Skin shouldn't look like that, ballooned and shiny, like if I pressed down on it, then my finger would push straight through, breaking past skin and blood, down to bone.

It was the face that was the most jarring of all. The lips were nearly gone, washed away, and what remained was an exaggerated toothy grin. The flesh was dissolved in parts, and in other sections appeared slimy. The material of their eyelids was all doughy and looked like some thick, pink, fleshy-colored paste. And what peeked out from that pinkish material were those cartoonish-looking eyes, bulging from its head in a shocked stare, as if saying, "I can't believe this is my body now."

"This isn't what they looked like when they went in," the ME said. "This individual was probably in the water for just a few days."

"A few days?" If that was a few days, I couldn't imagine what a few weeks or months would do to someone.

"Did you expect them to look better? We're lucky rapid skeletonization didn't take place. It's been humid outside, and the temperature reached ninety-eight today."

"Skeleton . . ." I couldn't even produce the word.

"Skeletonization," the ME repeated. "Determining the manner of death for those recovered from bodies of water—lakes, ponds, the river—is a challenge. The progression of decomposition is altered with the current, how the body interacts with the physical environment, or any structures it may come into contact with, animal predation, and temperature."

I looked at the corpse's hands. Patches of purple bruises, cuts, and abrasions covered the knuckles in blooming swirls.

"Dragging along the river bottom contributes to these injuries," the ME said, noticing where my focus lay.

I looked the cadaver up and down. "How'd they'd get in the water?"

The ME gazed at me. "That's your job to figure out, Detective."

I'm trying to tune out Rodriguez's movements. He's bouncing like some track-and-field runner about to sprint in the Olympics. There's no sprinting here. All we can do now is watch and wait and listen.

We're standing on the bridge looking east out over the Chicago River. It's getting dark. Afternoon rush hour traffic behind us is moving along at a crawl, and it's probably not going to get any better now that the ambulance has arrived and is blocking off a lane. An ambulance arriving at a crime scene with its emergency lights off is never a good sign. There's no one here to save.

"Are we going to hang out here all day, or are we going to get to work?" Rodriguez asks.

I eye him. "We're waiting for Sarge for our briefing." And just as I say that, Sergeant Flanagan approaches. There's no missing him. He's the tallest person I've ever met. He's holding a notepad, and he's already shaking his head side to side.

"All right, this is what we got," Flanagan says, getting right to it. "Male. Early twenties. Jogger called it in."

"Sounds familiar," I say, and Flanagan closes his notepad with a sharp snap. There's no such thing as a coincidence. He knows that and I know that.

"The jogger?" I ask.

"He's over there with Officer Rodan."

"Good. We'll talk to him," I say.

Flanagan looks from Rodriguez to me and then says, "I've got another stop. We'll talk at roll call."

"Yeah, we're going to talk at roll call about how this is now the, what? Fourth man we've fished out of the river this season?"

Flanagan's eyes blaze. "We'll talk about it at roll call."

No one wanted to talk about what was happening, but I didn't care. I had retirement upcoming. I didn't need to play nice. Hell, I never played nice. I always did things my way, and I was going to keep doing things my way to the end.

"And, Kowalski . . ."

Here we go.

"If the ME says it's an accidental drowning, it's an accidental drowning. You've gotta let it go," Flanagan says.

"Oh, I'm never going to let it go. You better believe that."

I turn to see Rodriguez smiling.

"The hell you so happy about?"

"Nothing. Maybe we will get along, after all."

I clear my throat. "Oh, most definitely not. Come on," I say, and start my way down the river walk. We make it as close as the paved path will allow. I step off the concrete and onto the muddy patch of land leading down to the water. There are broken branches and empty beer bottles scattered across the uneven land all the way down. The banks of the Chicago River are eroded in many places. The wooded sections of the river have trees falling into the water, and this section is no different.

"Careful, don't fall or anything," Rodriguez quips.

"You'd love that!" I shout over my shoulder. "Then your partner would be Boyd, and I don't think you'd want Boyd to be your partner."

"Anyone's probably a lot nicer than you!" Rodriguez shouts from behind.

I turn around. "Nice?" I can feel what is left of my eyebrows lifting off my head. "Boyd accidentally shot his partner a few years back," I say, putting air quotes around "accidentally." "Plus, my job isn't to be nice to you. You know why? Because homicide isn't nice. Last year I had to tell a mother we scooped her baby's body parts out of the Garfield Park Lagoon. We later figured out it was that garbage boyfriend who had killed and dismembered the child. He'd fallen asleep playing video games after putting the baby in a running bathtub. Makes sense? Of course not. People's stupid and deadly decisions don't make sense. And here we are. Someone else's baby." I gesture over to the forensics tent set up at the base. "An adult, but still someone else's child is dead in a Chicago waterway. My job isn't to be nice to you, or to anyone else, for that matter. My job is to figure out who killed them, make sure they don't kill again, and give their families some closure."

"I get it," Rodriguez says, closing his eyes and shaking his head as if that movement could brush away the decades of cruelty I've seen people do to other people.

I turn back around and continue making my way slowly off the paved walking path, pushing past dead branches and stepping over empty plastic bags, water bottles, and potato chip bags.

"This is going to mess up my new boots," Rodriguez says.

"They were going to get messed up eventually," I say, careful with my steps, making sure not to slip in the mud. The last thing I need is to lose my footing and fall into the water.

"Anyone ever clean this place up?" Rodriguez asks.

"Friends of the Chicago River visit a few times a year, cleaning up all of the trash people throw from their car windows or drop in the street. You should reach out to them to see if they've seen anything suspicious along the river recently."

"Me?"

I stop. "Yeah, you. Don't you get it? You wanted this transfer to homicide from vice. You're not running around with your little gang-banger friends anymore. Your job now is to understand the how and why, and that includes talking to whoever can help fill in the picture for us."

"The how and why of what?" He throws his hands up. "The only how or why I'm seeing is you got us trudging through mud." Rodriguez lifts his foot and looks at the bottom of his boot caked in mud. It's useless scraping it off. We've got at least another ten yards of mud to trudge through before we get close to the dive team.

Rodriguez continues. "The guy probably drank too much at the clubs and fell in the water and drowned. That's not a homicide."

The problem with Rodriguez is he thinks killings and killers are always going to be big, that they're always going to make a huge statement. Not everyone's a William Heirens who's going to cut up the torso of a little girl, shove bits and pieces of her in a storm drain, and leave a scrawl on a wall with red lipstick behind for investigators:

FOR HEAVENS
SAKE CATCH ME
BEFORE I KILL MORE
I CANNOT CONTROL MYSELF

Not every killer is a John Wayne Gacy, who murdered nearly thirty people, that we know of, and buried them in a crawl space of his home. Not every killer is a Richard Speck, who broke into a home occupied by eight nursing students and killed them all. And not every killer is an H. H. Holmes, who retrofitted a brownstone building into a murder castle in Chicago's South Side, a home equipped with secret passages and sound-proof rooms, and with a basement rumored to have a crematorium, and be full of vats of acid. We'll never know what was inside Holmes's house, or how many people he killed. He confessed to killing twenty-seven, but the actual number's been estimated to be into the hundreds.

Chicago's got a long, complex history with killers.

"Some killers operate methodically, quietly," I say as I take in a deep breath. The air smells fishy and stale, and if we weren't waiting here for the dive team to swim a body right over to us, then it'd be a pretty decent spring night in Chicago. But what was a decent night in Chicago, for me? I don't think I've had a decent spring night in years, and every time I get close to this water, I remember what it took from me, and I don't like remembering. The winter gives us some relief; crime dips a little. People's movements slow, but when the thaw comes, so does the anger, and so do the bodies. "You're going to have to check your impatience, Rodriguez. Where were we last weekend?"

Rodriguez chews the inside of his cheek as he rolls his eyes. "The Adams Street Bridge."

"What'd we find there?"

"A drowning."

"What'd you see then?"

Rodriguez rubs the back of his head. "Male. He'd been in the water, what? Maybe three days, the medical examiner said—"

"No." I cut him off because he wasn't paying attention.

"What did you *see* when we arrived at the Adams Bridge? When you get to a scene, you have to take in all of your surroundings, no matter how small. You also have to be able to recall it just as easy."

"There were people outside, sitting on the steps in front of the City Winery."

"Good. What else?"

"Lot of people out, even for a cold day on the river walk."

"It wasn't that cold," I say, remembering back to that day.

"Right, it was one of those teaser days we get when the city feels like we're deep in spring after a tough winter. A few people were standing on the platform under the bridge, just staring at the water."

"And?"

"There was a tour group, of kayakers. The guide and about six people in his group. They were stationed right at the steps. They were the ones who spotted the body. It was caught right beneath that platform."

"What does that all tell you?"

"If he hadn't been caught beneath that platform, he probably would have floated up this way."

"Maybe," I say. "And what else?"

"No one really cared or took too much notice."

"Why's that?"

"People thought it was an accident."

I nod. "Right, people thought it was an accident. So if we think something is an accident, the assumption is we're not really going to take notice of the details, right? We're not really going to keep a close eye on things, and how many drownings did the report I gave tell you we've had just these past few months?"

"Four."

"You think those males, between the ages of eighteen to twenty-five, are all . . . an accident, because if that's what you think, maybe you need to reconsider homicide and head back over to vice, where you can stand on street corners undercover chasing down drug dealers."

Rodriguez blows into his cupped hands to warm them. He gives me a side look and nods. "Yeah, you're right."

Above us I hear cars honk and the sounds of the city. Here at the water, I watch as two officers in diving gear emerge with a bloated mass, the water splashing as they move toward us.

Before they reach the bank, Rodriguez gets my attention. "What's that over there?" He points over my shoulder, right beside where the tent is set up. There's a large painted blue mark, a diamond, on a tree.

I scratch at the stubble on my chin and exhale. "Doesn't that look familiar." There's a flurry of activity around me: forensics, uniforms, members of the Marine Unit. I shout over to CSI, who is sweeping the scene. "I'm going to need some photographs over here of this symbol!"

It is springtime in Chicago, but winter still has a grip on us. Yet, things are in motion. Things are heating up a little bit. Things are churning in the city and in the water, and my intuition has never been wrong in all of these years, and what my gut tells me is we have a killer on our hands.

Chapter 3

Our home is called the Avondale.

Sears debuted the Avondale around 1911 with a promotional post-card at the Illinois State Fair that year. The very top of the catalog announcement framed in our entryway reads:

SIX ROOMS AND BATH

Followed by a black-and-white illustration of the brick bungalow on a manicured lawn. On either side of the house illustration are two large planters with lush flowers. The single-level home is wrapped in windows, and two chimneys jut out from its sides.

Farther down, the advertisement reads:

> At the price quoted we will furnish all the materials to build the six-room bungalow, consisting of mill work, porch ceiling, siding, flooring, finishing, lumber, building paper, eaves trough, down spout, sash weights, buffet, colonnade, medicine case, pantry case, hardware, painting material, lath, shingles, screens for rear porch, and mantel. We guarantee enough material to build this house. Price does not include cement, brick, or plaster.

The Avondale, No. 17006 "Already Cut" and Fitted.
$3,098

I imagine that the house once vibrated with the energy of children, laughter and dancing, games of hide-and-seek and more, and of course the hushed joy of being told stories that filled their heads with wonder.

Grandfather worked his entire adult life at the Western Electric Company, which manufactured telephone parts. Its campus, the Hawthorne Works, was Western Electric's largest facility, a space that spanned two hundred acres, a city within a city, with its own hospital, railroad, fuel storage, fire department, and other resources for employees. They supported their workers with a company store and restaurant, social club, gymnasium, baseball diamonds, bowling alleys, and a library where Grandmother volunteered when she had time.

While the commute from the North Side of Chicago to the far South Side was long, Grandfather never regretted his decision to purchase this house in the Ravenswood neighborhood because being on the river always felt like home, Grandmother would say.

I miss Grandmother and Grandfather tremendously. Like Grandfather, Mother worked in developing telephones, working at Motorola in Schaumburg and later in tech consulting. Father did the same.

At times, I try to remember my mother and father, but each time I try to recall their features or the tone of their voices, a great flash of undulating grief consumes me. So I continue to put them out of my head. Some memories are far too painful to resuscitate, and so they remain floating somewhere in the depths of our hearts.

The dogs take to the house with ease. Clover and Thistle slip across the floor as they chase one another or tumble down the first step of the stairway leading to the second floor in their attempt to go upstairs. Each time they see Jennie on the first floor, they want to follow her up to her room. They find her curious, as do I, given her shifting moods.

My bedroom is located on the first floor off the kitchen. In the morning I can step out of my room, make myself a cup of tea, and look out into the open living room and dining room and out those french doors and admire the river.

After tea and breakfast, there is always a bit of cleaning to be done to be sure the house remains a sparkling gem. Grandmother, and later, Mother, took great pride in the midcentury clean lines and furnishings of the house, and that is the aesthetic I've worked to maintain. Both Grandmother and Mother were fond of Frank Lloyd Wright's designs, which worked in harmony with their environments, and that's the feel we aimed to replicate with this home.

After cleaning the house, I put on a light jacket and walk the dogs down to the river. Springtime in the city offers some unpredictability, but still, there is the relief that we have emerged from the deep frost. I take a seat at the little wooden bench and scoop up both puppies and set them beside me. I gaze upon the shimmering surface of the murky, deep-green water and how it reflects the bright sun above. The water is peaceful, but constantly in motion. Each time I spot a ripple, I picture largemouth bass, bluegill, catfish, and more traveling in their little colonies below.

Our house is a special seat that witnesses the river's daily movements. This is our little oasis in a bustling, electric city that pulsates all around us. Our home is one of only thirteen Ravenswood Manor houses with an exclusive easement to the river. We have lower-bank access, with a private high bank surrounded by several large trees: an American elm, a majestic maple, two sycamore trees, an eastern redbud, several ash trees, and then the dreamy sassafras tree with deep-red leaves that shield my fairy garden.

Along the edges of our property are old doors that I collected from visits to antique stores with Grandmother. We later painted these doors bold and bright colors: reds and yellows, blues, purples and greens. I then took to decorating the garden with small mirrors and old, empty picture frames, discarded birdcages, and large wooden chests I'd later fill with soil and seeds that served as planters. I collected the discarded, but beautiful, items and incorporated them into this magical space bursting with color and life.

This is what I did most mornings. I'd come down here and search for herons or owls, turtles, and migrating birds. The experience is different each day, a new scattering of leaves, their shade different from the previous day and, of course, new growth around the fairy garden.

It was Grandmother who encouraged me to create the fairy garden. She once told me that within every tale there is a thread of truth or a great lesson woven within the fabric of the words. She said that this truth and this lesson were guiding lights. She could see I did not quite understand what she meant. She then asked me what my favorite story was, and I told her, "The Little Mermaid."

She said, "Of course, as it should be."

It's thought that a fairy garden brings cheer and good luck. This also means that a fairy garden is in essence a door leading to that other world, *their* world. Fairies, with their ethereal glows and gossamer wings, wave their magic wands and can grant us our wishes on their whims. Yet I know all too well that it is dangerous to anger a fairy. It's very important to keep fairies content.

I enjoy the soft lapping of the water nearby, until it's disrupted by the sound of a television blaring. Once again, Jennie's watching the evening news with the volume as high as it can go. The sound is so loud and crisp, it's as if they are reporting live from our home. The report from the newscast inside is carried outside.

After a night out in Chicago on Friday at the Riverwalk Wine Garden, twenty-three-year-old Andrew McGrath told his roommate that he was going home, but he never arrived.

Late this Monday evening, Chicago police detectives identified the remains of McGrath recovered from the Chicago River. The body was located at about 5:00 p.m., a mile from where he was last seen.

His friend Stephen Falk said McGrath, a Naperville, Illinois, native, attended the University of Illinois at Urbana-Champaign and moved to the city this year, where he worked in marketing.

In early March, McGrath went to the Riverwalk Wine Garden with friends, Falk told NBC News. McGrath then called a car service to take him to another bar in the River North neighborhood. That was the last time he was seen.

Falk said he is the one who broke the news to McGrath's parents, describing the call as "devastating."

The police said that the Marine Unit recovered McGrath's body near Irving Park Road, at the North Branch of the Chicago River.

The medical examiner said that McGrath's cause of death is pending.

After my walk outside with the dogs, it's time for lunch, and then planning, lots of planning as to where the work on the house would begin to find the location of this drip. There is the added pressure of managing my own work with the housework, but I know I can balance both, given that I work from home.

It makes the most sense to start in the kitchen, especially since the dripping continued throughout the night, and I can at least check carefully if the noise is coming from this area.

I take notes and measurements, looking over every now and then to check on Clover and Thistle, who have settled into the house rather quickly. Even in the short time they've lived here with Jennie and me, they've already doubled in size.

The dogs have learned which rooms are sealed off, which floorboards creak and moan, and which don't. Soon too they will learn to ignore the steady and now seemingly constant drip-drip-drip, the rattling of doorknobs by spectral hands, and the disembodied voices that speak in low whispers in the night and laugh brightly in the day.

Still, even though I try to brush these things aside, I can never quite shake the fright of a door being swung open or cups and plates clacking within the kitchen cabinets. A house lives in us too, in many ways. I am confident that with each inhale and exhale, this house exists inside me. I hope that somehow, by adding a new countertop, a fresh coat of paint, perhaps replacing a few worn floorboards or sagging plaster walls, I can disentangle what has become knotted within me.

Maintaining this house was important to Grandmother and Grandfather, and later, Mother and Father. Each of them taught me a little bit here and there about all things related to home repair and upkeep. It has always been enjoyable work, because I love this house so much. And now with them gone, I want to show the house how much I love it. I hope that in making these updates, the house will continue to love me too and give me what I want, what I have always wanted—to simply be loved.

I spend the afternoon clearing out the cupboards and moving all of those items into the living room. I locate a few curious items, deep in the back of some of the cabinets, wrapped in newspaper. I carry them to my room, where I will inspect them further later. I then go to check on Jennie in her bedroom. Hours have passed, and normally she would have been down for lunch by now.

I knock gently on the door, but there is no answer. I turn the doorknob and peek in on her. She is asleep in her bed. I close the door and note the time. It is unlike her to sleep at this hour, but I can only assume she is as tired as I am. After everything she has gone through, it is expected that she needs time, lots of time, to heal.

Usually at this time, she busies herself in her room with her musical devices. She collects, buys, sells, and repairs vintage records and turntables. She is somewhat of an expert in antiquated sound systems, from the phonograph, later called the gramophone, to the modern-day record player or turntable. Packages arrive for her in the mail from all over the world with devices she can repair. I take them up to her room, and she in turn leaves packages beside the stairs. I take those to the post office, and then the cycle continues.

Jennie's favorite quote is by Thomas Edison:

"Of all of my inventions, I liked the phonograph best. Life's most soothing things are sweet music and a child's good night."

I find the quote beautiful, but macabre. It is the pairing of the words "sweet music" with "child's good night" in the same sentence that evokes sadness and grief, a final lullaby ushering in a forever night.

Regardless, it is work that pleases my sister. So I never speak ill of her interests to her, because I hoped that she would never speak ill of mine, even though she still does. She is also not pleased with what she calls my "disturbing the house," just because I want to make it fresh, to gleam and glow and feel refreshed. The house needs that. We need that now more than ever.

Jennie loves stories of evolving technology, and she was fascinated to learn that Grandfather was behind the short-lived department at Western Electric that invented the loudspeaker and successfully brought the magic of sound to motion pictures.

Both Jennie and I know too much about the way old things worked.

Western Electric eventually abandoned all manufacturing efforts in film to audio to municipal energy to focus on their core business— the production of telephones that was concentrated at its massive Hawthorne Works facility. And that is where Grandfather worked until he retired in 1983.

The house holds a few items that are now considered antiques that were manufactured at Hawthorne Works. We have several Western Electric candlestick telephones, the Model 20 that made its debut in 1904. The metal parts of the phone are made of brass. Earlier models were nickel plated. After World War I, the Model 40 was introduced, and we have a few versions of this as well, in which the base is made of steel. Both have their signature black finish. We have a Western Electric rotary dial telephone on display in the kitchen and one in the living room on the coffee table.

I keep a candlestick telephone at my bedside, and there is one in the living room on an end table. They serve no purpose other than as decorations and beacons of the past, reminders of how we once communicated in a time where not everyone had access to a telephone in their pocket and instant communication.

Mother once joked that none of the cell phones she had developed were on display because there really was no competing with the beauty of the devices Grandfather had contributed to creating.

Grandfather knew everything there was to know about telephones. He told us how in 1915 the first transcontinental telephone call was made by the same two men who had made the very first telephone call forty years earlier in 1876, Alexander Graham Bell and Thomas Watson. Bell, in New York City, spoke to Watson, who was in San Francisco. They were three thousand miles apart and were pioneers of communications.

Grandfather marveled over the magic of landline telephones. It was not your actual voice being heard on the other end, he would say. Your voice would be converted to energy that traveled over wires to another phone. Then, that electrical energy was converted to sound waves so that the person on the other line could hear you. This wonderful instrument, the telephone, made it possible for people to talk to loved ones and communicate urgent business matters.

I suppose it's because of my family's history with telephones that I was destined to be drawn to technology in the realm of communication. I live with an ever-present urge to talk, even if no one is listening, and there really is no one listening. I have my sister. I have my dogs. And that's all I really have. Even with all of this technology with which to communicate, I feel so dreadfully alone in this drafty house.

I return to my room, and today I suddenly find it to be so cramped with the bed and the desk and my computer and headset and all of the things I need to record my podcast. I realize I will certainly need more space. I need room to work, to plan the updates to the house, a place to store material, and maybe it would be nice to not work in my bedroom anymore, to have a proper office.

My intention with my work is to continue doing what my grandparents and parents said I did so well, which is to use my voice to tell stories. The stories I enjoy telling are ghost stories about Chicago.

I tuck my pencil behind my ear, pinch my notepad beneath my armpit, and gather my two dogs, sweet and soft little bundles, in my arms. We walk up the stairs and turn right in the dimly lit hallway. The floor shines like glass. It smells of wood polish from my cleaning this morning. The cherrywood crown molding and wall sconces remain without a speck of dust. We walk past the bathroom, and then we stop in front of one of the empty bedrooms whose door has been draped in black cloth.

I set the dogs and my notebook down on the floor and then reach for the black cloth, tugging at the material until it releases from the pins on either side of the door. The heavy fabric cascades down, in a blooming black mass, and gathers on the floor in a heap. I place my hand on the doorknob, turn it, and push the door open.

"You're disturbing the dead."

I turn to see Jennie standing behind me. Her eyes flash from me to the empty room. Her face is twisted, and pained, as if a part of her had been unintentionally unwrapped.

I study the room. It's bare. Four white walls. A floor and ceiling. A large window looking out over the river. I don't remember this room having been cleared out, but so much has become muddled in such a short time.

"Jennie, we can't keep these rooms sealed off," I say. "Plus, I need more light and more space. I don't feel well some days, and this room will help bring me joy. It has sat here empty for what feels like forever."

Jennie is in another black nightgown. Satin with lace trim along the wrists and collar. I admire her long black hair, how smooth and shiny it is. She prefers it loose, like the river at night, mesmerizing and endless.

"They used it once," she said.

I remain standing in the doorway, with Jennie just a few feet away.

"They are not here now, and they are not here anymore," I say.

Jennie bites her bottom lip, perhaps holding herself back from saying anything that would cut. It doesn't matter, since her sharp words often feel like daggers, all because she could just not forget. She refuses to forget, and so she carries this cold and biting pain within her that extends outward and injures me whenever she reminds me that they are no longer with us.

Some people believe that forgetting is a part of the healing. I don't know what I believe. I only know it is better not to think about the way things once were so that I can remain aware of what I need to do.

"I'm going to use this room as my office. For my podcast, and as a space where I can store some of the materials for the work I plan on doing on the house."

She laughs. "Your work? You mean where you talk to nothing, to air, about what? Haunted houses?"

"Sometimes I talk about haunted houses." I feel my throat tighten. "Not always, but I always talk about haunted Chicago."

Jennie folds her arms across her chest. "We should be grateful to be here, existing, and not preoccupied with meddling and disrupting."

"I'm not disrupting anything," I say.

A smirk spreads across her face. "Then explain the dripping. It's starting. It's inching its way toward us. If this continues, then one day there will be no hiding from it, because we will both remember, and we will both be consumed by waves."

"But we are here." As soon as I say those words, we both fall silent because I know we each hear it.

A woman's voice downstairs.

The voice is saying something, but I cannot make out the words. It's a steady, high-pitched drone.

Speaking. Speaking. Pause. Speaking. Pause. Speaking. Speaking. Speaking. Moaning.

"She's back," Jennie whispers. Her eyes wide.

"It's nothing . . ."

Some things are meant to be shaken and awakened, while other things are meant to be forgotten, wrapped, and stored away within the folds of time.

"It's nothing," I repeat, trying to convince myself.

We stand there silent for what feels like years, until the voice stops.

"I'm bored," Jennie says. "I'm going to my room. You know, my sister"—she stops, turns, and looks me up and down, inspecting me like it's the first time she's seen me in ages—"Chicago is an October sort of city, even in spring."

"Those aren't your words," I say. "Those are author Nelson Algren's words. You're quoting him."

"Am I?" She glances upward dreamily. "It doesn't matter that he once said that, because I am saying it now. Maybe we are saying these words together at once, in our same points in time. Which came first? Does anything matter? No, my sister. Nothing matters. Time does not matter. Maybe it meets at no point. All of the possibilities are tangled, or perhaps we're all existing together. We're all preparing for a great collapse of the cosmos, and I welcome that." She takes a deep breath, exhales, and for a moment I suspect a sob deep within her chest, but she straightens herself up. Jennie turns away from me and retreats to her room.

Her bedroom door shuts, and I hear her humming. It is the song Grandmother often sang to herself:

> By the sea
> By the sea
> By the beautiful sea
> You and me, you and me
> Oh, how happy we'll be

With Jennie gone and the house quieting, I step into the room, the puppies following me, two small, cheerful creatures bounding across the floor.

The room is radiant in the sparkling sunlight streaming through the window. I look down to the glittering river beneath us, shimmering and bright. Clover and Thistle are at my side now.

"We'll tell them everything from this room. We will tell them about all of the bodies, and how it took days to find them all. We'll tell them how some bodies were misidentified and went home with the wrong families, only to be exhumed and reburied. We'll tell them of all the tears cried for those who never returned home."

The dogs walk over to the window, where they peer down, bare their teeth, and growl.

Out on the river, I can see it floating across the deep-green surface.

A nude plastic doll.

Chapter 4

"Welcome again to The Chicago Vault, where I talk about all things related to haunted Chicago history. I am your host, Anna Arbor. Before we begin this evening, I would like to thank you, listeners. Because of you, I have reached my twenty-fourth show. When I began this podcast, I just wanted it to be a space where I could talk about the things that interested me, and I'm overwhelmed that so many of you are listening.

"I did want to give you an important update. I will be taking some time off for research and to prepare a special series for you. Just know that I have recorded a lot of content, so you will not miss me, but I will technically be off. Still, I just wanted you to know what I was doing. And yes, for those curious, the work is coming along wonderfully on my house. I've spent quite a lot of time at the hardware store, and it seems that everyone there now knows my name. The workers have all been very kind and thoughtful, answering my questions, down to the orders of supplies being promptly delivered to my home. I'm almost done. The kitchen has been updated, and the first-floor bathroom. I've repaired a few loose floorboards, and so all I really have left is the upstairs bathroom. I'm quite surprised and impressed with myself that I was able to complete these little projects all on my own."

I pause the recording to take a deep breath. What I've yet to mention to my listeners and to Jennie is what I've been finding in the walls: small, rusted metal pieces.

I stand up and cross the room over to the worktable. There's a box on top of the table, and beside it a notepad where I've been carefully documenting these tiny motors and gears, wheels and pinions, cranks and shafts. Each time I take another sheet of plaster wall down, or pull up a floorboard, or remove an old cabinet, there it is, another newspaper-wrapped bundle and one of these tiny pieces within.

Or maybe they were not hidden. The house always knows what it is doing.

Maybe they were where they were meant to be this entire time, and they were just waiting for me to find them. My own personal Easter egg hunt for parts that made up some whole to which I did not yet know.

I walk back to my computer, hit record again, and continue.

"I have spoken previously here about how the Chicago City Cemetery was originally located at the site of what is today's Lincoln Park. The oldest part of the cemetery is along North Avenue, where today you can see the last remaining tomb, the Couch Mausoleum, the only standing remnant of the original Chicago City Cemetery.

"Just a reminder that the Chicago City Cemetery no longer exists. It was the final resting place of thirty-five thousand Chicagoans. The use of the location as a cemetery ceased around the 1860s, and many of the bodies were moved to surrounding cemeteries: Rosehill Cemetery, Graceland Cemetery, Calvary Cemetery, and more. It's still thought that thousands of bodies are buried in the Lincoln Park area.

"The location of the original Chicago Cemetery overlaps a bit with the current site of Lincoln Park Zoo, but in the 1890s, the overall park was believed to be the most haunted location in the entire city.

"There were entire newspaper articles devoted to the strange activity in Lincoln Park. The *Chicago Tribune* once wrote:

"'There have been violent deaths enough in the park to furnish a ghost for every shadowy nook.'

"Around this time, the park was also the location of multiple suicides. Many people took their own lives up towards the north end of the park. Just a little bit south of Fullerton there was a forty-foot bridge that stretched over the lagoon that connected the park to the lakefront.

"The name of the bridge was High Bridge, and it was built between 1892 and 1894. The bridge would eventually become known as Suicide Bridge. There were even postcards that referred to it as such. There are estimates that dozens of people killed themselves in Lincoln Park at that very bridge.

"Now, jumping off the bridge was not particularly fatal, given that the water was shallow. It was a bridge one would either shoot themselves at or hang themselves from. I imagine it must have been quite a grim scene, seeing bodies swaying from the bridge so close to the lakefront where families gathered to picnic.

"After thirty years of accumulating rust and blood and tears, the bridge was torn down and, like many of the city's tragedies, was forgotten.

"Today, there are many ghost stories that surround the park and the zoo. The one that clings to me, however, is one I was told about two sisters.

"One zoo employee told me they could hear the cries of a little girl in the area where Suicide Bridge once stood. The employee was so upset by the crying that they resigned.

"At first, I assumed maybe they were mistaken. They did work at a zoo, after all. The voices of children should be normal, but not after the zoo closed at night.

"After looking into this account further, I learned that two girls did indeed go missing in the area of Suicide Bridge.

"In 1907, Emma and Clara Pontius were ages twelve and ten years old when they disappeared from the bridge. Later that night, the body of one of the girls was found.

"By the next morning, the story was carried throughout the city newspapers, and soon the body of the second girl was found in the lagoon.

"The family was devastated, but their father and stepmother believed that it must have been an accident, that perhaps the younger sister fell into the water and the older sister tried to save her. However, the grandmother believed the story to be much more tragic than that.

"Earlier that morning the two girls were seen at Rosehill Cemetery, visiting their mother's grave. Their grandmother assumed the girls went to the bridge to kill themselves to be reunited with their mother. Their grandmother's account was dismissed, and the girls' death was ruled an accident.

"At first it was assumed that there were no witnesses, but a young boy appeared and said he'd seen it all unfold. The boy claimed that neither of the girls screamed before falling into the water. He added that a man was there as well, who rushed to save them, but that man didn't emerge from the water either. His body was discovered later and was identified as a local man who had saved a little boy from drowning in Douglas Park the year before.

"I posted a scan from the *Chicago Tribune* from June 21, 1907, when the story first broke. I was not able to locate images of the girls, unfortunately. I wish I had. I can only imagine what they looked like: The stiff, well-positioned posture of people being photographed at that time. Their faces serious and staring into the large, black, round camera lens, this great contraption that in many ways did not make sense. It must have been frightening to be photographed at that time. I also wonder what it was like for them to visit their mother's grave that morning, and the fear they must have felt venturing into the great

Chicago City Cemetery, a place thick with gloom that smelled of rot and death.

"Did they hold hands as they approached the bridge? What were their thoughts as they gazed down into the lagoon knowing that they would be drowned?

"Were the cries heard by the attendant at Lincoln Park Zoo those of the ghosts of Emma or Clara, two sisters, falling to their deaths? Or was it something else?

"Now, the fact that I found this story does not necessarily mean that if you hear cries at the north end of Lincoln Park that what you are hearing are the wailings of a ghost, of Emma or Clara Pontius—two little girls who drowned long ago. There's no way to know what the attendant heard, if anything. Perhaps they were the sounds carried across the wind from nearby apartments or condominiums? Or maybe someone told the attendant this story one day, and they could not shake the possibility that maybe there was some truth to it.

"Maybe late one night, a car driving past, or a dog barking, or the murmurs of a great city began to sound like something else. And, like a game of telephone across the years, something was told to one person and then another and another. The story bent and stretched and became reshaped until noises heard in the darkness were believed to be those of a long-dead girl.

"It's a ghost story, yes, but like all good ghost stories, this is based on fact. This is based on historical truth. And the reality that this story is based on something real adds weight to it, because otherwise it would just be purely fiction, and how frightening can fiction really be?

"Well, thank you, friends, for joining me. It's nice to know that you are listening. Again, I will be away for two weeks researching this next series for you that I'm excited to talk about. Like the story of Emma and Clara, I will share with you a ghost story based on a historical tragedy that's unique to Chicago.

"Talk to you all soon."

I end the podcast and glance down at Clover and Thistle nestled beside my chair. I look behind me to the large wooden table that has turned into my workstation. There are swatches of paint pinned to the walls and samples of crown molding and pieces of baseboard from the hardware store. The kitchen is complete, with a new sink and countertops and cabinets. The colors and style match the spirit of the home— clean, but classic. No leak was detected in the kitchen, and so the steady drip-drip-drip continues. Sometimes it's there and sometimes it's not. Sometimes I wonder if the sound has always been there, but maybe I'm the one who tunes it out. Maybe I should have been tuning it in this entire time. Almost like turning the dial on an old radio, searching for a clear station through all of the static.

Before I play back my recording to begin editing, I hear Jennie in her room. Once again, she's watching the news. The volume is so loud I can hear every word clearly in my office.

A Columbia College student has been missing for more than a week after having last been seen at the CTA at the Roosevelt L stop.

Joshua Martin, twenty-six, was last seen at Roosevelt Road and State Street.

The Chicago Transit Authority station serves the Green and Orange Lines on the elevated tracks and the Red Line underground. A missing persons flyer did not specify at which exact station Martin was last seen, but family and friends say he was last spotted taking the CTA train.

Anyone with information is asked to contact Area Three detectives.

Another missing young man.

The circumstances are always familiar: an evening out with friends, at a bar or two, a lounge or music venue. The night dances close to early morning. Parties are separated from one another. The young man decides he'll call a car to take him home. Or maybe he chooses to take public transit, or walk to the next social gathering, or better yet, he'll just end the night and head home, all the while the intensity of alcohol is still racing through him.

It's happened enough for me to take notice and worry. I know that feeling, of being unsure where one's loved ones are. Of the minutes and hours ticking by, a great clock of anxiety. I write his name down, *Joshua Martin*. I want to think about him, in the hopes that my thoughts of a safe return can somehow spin the universe in his favor so he can be returned to his family.

I look up from my notes and find the door open and Jennie standing in the doorway.

"I'm going for a walk," she says hurriedly.

"It's too late for your walk, Jennie," I say, consulting the time. Jennie often loses track of time. "And it's not safe outside. Another person has gone missing."

She sighs. "Another *man* has gone missing"—she rolls her eyes—"and maybe he wanted to go missing. Has anyone thought of that? Maybe he left his house searching for his life's true love and failed to find them. There is no happy ending for him. Maybe there's no happy ending for any of us," she says, pouting.

Tension grows in my shoulders, and I can feel my jaw tightening.

"Jennie," I snap, "that's an awful thing to say. They're someone's family. Children. Siblings. Partners. I doubt that person just wanted to go missing." To go missing, it's awful. For your loved ones to not know where you are is a loop of terror, worries folding in and out.

She raises an eyebrow. "How do you know? Maybe their intention was to step into the river and slip away, to disintegrate and never return. We do not know these people. They are just names on a screen. Words spoken on the television. Those people do not exist . . ."

"That isn't a very kind thing to say." My voice sounds very small against hers. "Someone's missing. They have family and loved ones that are likely very worried. It's ghoulish to dismiss them like that. What if someone dismissed us like that, or you like that?"

And when I say those words, I know that I've already made a mistake. I have summoned mishap and misfortune.

Her face goes blank. She remains unblinking. Stone. And just when I wonder if she will ever speak again, she does. "Life has already dismissed us, Anna. That's why we're both here. I know you like to pretend, to remain occupied so as not to think of things. We both allow ourselves to be consumed with distraction. But we never really forget. Now, I'm going to go for a walk."

I push Jennie's words out of my mind.

"I don't feel comfortable with you going on your walks. There's barely anyone outside right now."

She throws her head back, sounding exasperated. "That's the way I like it."

"What if something happens? You don't carry a phone with you. You refuse. If something happens, how am I supposed to know?"

Jennie's body stiffens. Her gaze is fixed on me. "Something's already happened and is already happening, and we both know what."

I once again ignore her ramblings. Jennie speaks in riddles, word puzzles, and cryptic stirrings all meant to upset me, and I will not allow her to hurt me any more than I've already been hurt.

"Why must you be so difficult? I'm just trying to protect you," I say. "There are threats outside. We can't trust anything or anyone. You know everything is so brittle, and we're dancing on the edge of the shore here."

Her eyes darken and her nostrils flare for a moment. Jennie is beautiful, fiercely so. I was afraid of what anger brewed in her mind. I feared all her possibilities. I know what she wanted to say. I always know what she wanted to say, but she knows if she utters those words, glass would shatter, or maybe it was more like the waves would crash all around us, and if that happened, there would be no life vest and we'd both sink.

Her eyes narrow. "Don't you think I know of impermanence? We are evanescent. Every single person who lives and breathes is fading, and so are we." She laughs. "Everyone believes they'll never end. The ego! That each day will usher in another, morning dewdrops and a bright gold sun. One day there will be nothing, not even a memory of what once was. But we're so consumed with the insignificant disruptions of our day that we're too afraid to let go and see that those silly inconveniences do not matter. That's the great tragedy, that we live never truly appreciating the present. And so, people believe in the lie of their bad thoughts, their actions then become muddled—unsure of their purpose—and they wander the world ignoring that the very next moment in which they exist could be their last. They are all so wrapped up in the troubles of a tomorrow that may very well never be. They're caught in the snare of worry. Yet we exist here. We exist now. We should be desperate to feel everything we can in this moment, but we don't. Instead, we distract ourselves from the now. It's utterly heartbreaking."

Her voice intensifies, and Clover and Thistle open their eyes, four black spots against gray fur on a cream-colored dog bed beside the door, pleading to know what is going on. I wish I could explain it then, and now. These poor little creatures. Maybe Jennie was right. Maybe I should have allowed them to drown. Perhaps that would have been a better fate than being brought into this house seething with sorrow.

"Jennie, please," I plead, looking at those numbers in the upper right-hand corner of my computer screen indicating the time. I turn and look out the window. It's so dark outside. The sun has yet to make its lazy way up over the lake. Even still, I know Jennie will not listen. She does not fear the night. She does not fear anything or anyone.

"We are weak, all of us, because we would rather busy ourselves with others, with things, with duties, with fairy tales and lore to temporarily slot in answers we believe are solutions, but it's nothing. We are nothing. We're just water, Anna. That's all we are," Jennie says.

Jennie moves to take a step forward, into my office, but she catches herself and looks around at the doorframe. She steps back, into the hallway, and into the shadows in which she prefers to hide. I know she will never step into this room.

"We are nothing. We are just a single flash of a dead star that no one will remember, that no one wants to remember." She looks to my computer and points.

"You will quickly come to regret all of the things that you have shared and will share. No one should know the things that you speak of. Everything is empty, and that's how it should remain."

I feel my stomach twist. "What things?"

She takes a deep breath and then releases that single word that's the greatest villain in this house.

"Memory."

Before I can say anything, she's turned down the hallway and is gone. I listen as she walks down the stairs and as the front door opens and closes. I could go after her, but something tells me that if I follow her outside, it will not end well for either of us. She will return safely. I have to believe that. Just like I want to believe that Joshua Martin will return home safely.

I return to the audio I have recorded, and I listen and edit, cutting out any unnecessary words, the ums and ahs, the stutters, all of those small things we do with speech that we are unaware of unless we are forced to listen and to take in the sound of our voice and to sit uncomfortably still with it.

I add in the proper intro and outro, and music. I adjust the volume and equalization throughout. I stand and stretch and check on the dogs, who are still asleep.

I walk over to the window, and there she is, floating in the water on her back, her eyes open, looking up to the sky.

Jennie.

Her body is bloated and black and gray and blue, but that's my Jennie.

My voice is trapped deep within me. I don't even remember how to scream. I race down the stairs, and as soon as I open the door, Jennie is there standing. Her face serene. The sunlight shining on her hair.

Sunlight. How? How long was I editing?

"What are you doing?" she asks. "You didn't have to wait for me. I told you, I'd be fine."

She's holding something in her hand, what looks like a folded-up sheet of paper.

"What's that?" I ask.

"Nothing, just scraps of paper I collected along the way."

She walks past me, her long black skirt swooshing back and forth.

Her bare feet leaving wet footprints across the wooden floor.

Chapter 5

A few days later, I wake to find Clover and Thistle still asleep in their beds. I put on my house slippers. I was up too long reading and researching, and overcome with anguish over all that I had learned. It felt like I sat there, reading, the light out my window growing dark and once again burning bright, a cycle of days and nights elapsing, yet me hypnotized by the cruelty of loss. I would certainly need these next few weeks to prepare for this upcoming podcast series. I required hours and hours to understand the magnitude and the pain of the story. This was a very real ghost story I was not only consuming but willfully allowing to grow, twist, and stretch across my heart like seaweed.

I'm sure many people will not care about this tale. No one wants to think of the long dead. No one wants to remember their story, because their story has no impact in the immediate. I know this all too well, because I spend so much of my time thinking about my parents and how they died. The tragedy of it all is a heavy weight, and if I allow myself too long to rest in that misery, then I'll feel like I'm drowning. There is no one to talk to about any of this, because there is no one, other than Jennie.

No one wants to mourn ghosts.

But I do.

I want to mourn them. I want to think about them. I want to go to Newberry Library and find all of the pictures I can of them, digging through old archives, family records, and long-shuttered newspapers. I want to make copies of their photographs and pin them to my walls, and before I go to sleep at night, I want to tell each and every one of them good night, and that they are not forgotten. That they are still loved by someone who exists in the world today. They died an agonizing death, and they have been forgotten. And so, their suffering continues. What I hope I can do is alleviate that sadness somehow with my thoughts of them and with my words.

So many lives were lost here on a single gray-cast afternoon. It's like they were washed away with that morning rain. Hundreds were killed that day, including entire families. How can one come to comprehend that? Perhaps that's why it was easy for people to forget. Perhaps that's why they remain forgotten. People can't process a single victim and the impact they had on reality, let alone hundreds. We cannot fully grasp those figures. We cannot understand that loss. We just can't. Those names become ink on a page, numbers on a glowing screen. So, what then does it mean to read about one person dying tragically, or three, or three hundred, or more, if there's no name attached? Even then, to most people it's just a name. A picture of the deceased isn't even enough. We see an image of someone recently killed and we keep scrolling, change the channel, and move on to the next exhibit of useless information. Perhaps we need their story to be overcome with emotion. Perhaps it ultimately doesn't matter, since some people either would never care or could never comprehend the weight of that human suffering, unless of course they themselves were in that very position. To really understand someone else's suffering, you must have suffered.

I didn't just want to understand their pain. I wanted to experience it. Multiple families, their histories and legacies, were extinguished within minutes one morning. Their deaths came and went with a flash of summer rain. We very often forget the humans behind the human tragedy. Sometimes that forgetting is intentional.

Clover paws at the door, and then Thistle rises from her bed.

"Tea first," I remind them, and we are a tangle of energy as we burst out of my bedroom. The dogs rush along the hardwood floor, their nails clicking across the surface.

It is unlike my sister to wake before I do. But there she is in her black silk nightgown, without a single crease in the fabric, looking as if she had not slept.

"Good morning," I say, startled.

She takes a sip from a teacup in her hands and then sets it down on the island with a clink and crosses her arms over her chest.

"You were in Grandmother's room last night."

Before I can say anything, she reaches for an object on the counter and brings it over to me at the island and sets it down. Her face is anything but gentle. Her features are tight.

"I found this on the sofa." She taps the inside cover. "Put it back in her room."

I open the front cover and point inside. "Did you ever notice this? This says it belongs to—"

Jennie cuts me off. "I know what it says!"

I look back to the page. "These are our names . . . but not."

"Do not speak of it again," Jennie says. "Put that book back!"

I run a finger across the golden letters on the leather-bound cover. "She said all of her books were mine."

"Ours!" Jennie growls. "This house is ours, and so is everything in it. This house does not exist without us, and we do not exist without this house. It is an intrinsic fact. We breathe because this house breathes, and nothing here is yours alone. Everything here is ours, and I'm asking you"—she closes her eyes, her long midnight eyelashes fluttering—"no, I'm telling you to put this book back where it belongs."

She opens her eyes, studying me with intensity, waiting for my response. Before I can say anything, she continues.

"No matter how many times you read it, that story will never end differently. There will always be water. There will always be rain. There will always be chaos. There will always be screams. There will always be a great roar of shrieking, bent and twisted metal. There will always be those who lived. There will always be those who died, and there will always be those who refuse to forget."

I examine the book that comforted me then and now, *Hans Christian Andersen's Fairy Tales*. Grandmother displayed the book prominently on her bookshelf. The book is old, from 1894, but the pages within are still bright and the colors vivid. The cover is a faded baby blue, well worn in the places where Grandmother held it open as she read to us every night for so many years. The patina of time wears on all things. She read that book cover to cover years ago, and still, each time she spoke those words, it was as if she were speaking them for the very first time.

I can hear her voice reading from the book now . . .

"Far out in the ocean the water is as blue as the petals of the loveliest cornflower, and as clear as the purest glass. But it is very deep too. It goes down deeper than any anchor rope will go, and many, many steeples would have to be stacked one on top of another to reach from the bottom to the surface of the sea. It is down there that the sea folk live."

In Hans Christian Andersen's story, the mermaid emerges from the ocean one day and spots a prince and falls in love with him. Given she can only come to the surface once a year, she visits with a Sea Witch. The Sea Witch is captivated by the mermaid's beautiful voice. In exchange for her voice, the Sea Witch gives the Little Mermaid a potion that will make her sprout legs and shed her fish tail. Before the mermaid ingests the liquid, the Sea Witch warns her that she will never be able to return to her ocean home, and if the prince does not fall in love with and marry her, she will die and dissolve into sea-foam.

The prince does go on to fall in love, but with another, and not our Little Mermaid. The distraught and brokenhearted Little Mermaid leaps to her death. Her body disintegrates into a frothy, pale-white broth. Yet she is immediately resurrected by earthbound spirits who witnessed her suffering and death. They grant her a human soul so she can rest for eternity, not in the sea, but in the absolute place of stillness where all human souls return after death.

The story is tragic because of everything the Little Mermaid had given up—her voice, her family, and her life—all for someone whom she loved but who did not love her back. I very much wished that she had found someone to completely love her. So much suffering happened in the pursuit of love.

I connect with this story because I feel like the Little Mermaid somehow, as if I am destined to serve—serve my sister and serve this house. Like the Little Mermaid, I want to have the opportunity to use my voice, to emerge from this house, and to perhaps find love, and having Clover and Thistle and the podcast feels like the beginning of that possibility.

Still, like the Little Mermaid, I worry if breaking free from my family will be my undoing.

It is the story Jennie and I wanted read to us again and again. Words on a page. Read by Grandmother, her voice animating each and every letter, breathing life into each word, imbuing each sentence with magic. It was alchemy. Those words in that book went beyond an obsession for Jennie and me. The words in this book are blueprints, the schematics laying out the trajectory of our lives.

It is a fairy tale, yes, but fairy tales store sparkling glimmers of truth between their lines, and it is up to us to pluck out glowing golden apples, talking gilded mirrors, bewitched seeds, magical lamps, enchanted carpets, and all of the marvelous items that punctuated a great metamorphosis within the heroes of our stories.

That's what "The Little Mermaid" is: a reverse transformation, a story full of wonder, adventure, cruelty, and death. And death was initiated by renouncing what made her magical. She relinquished what made her special in pursuit of the mundane, but the mundane broke her heart.

We think often of Disney's *The Little Mermaid*, of Ariel's flowing bright-red hair and her eyes gazing upward out of the sparkling ocean and over to land in wonder. She believed that the world above the sea, where humans lived and walked and breathed, offered the promise of possibility. What was possibility but freedom to exist? For now, she existed within a deep-blue depth from which she could not escape, because air promised death. Yet she did not realize that the opposite would be true, that for those who lived in the world above the sea, inhaling water led to shock, convulsions, and then death.

In the original Hans Christian Andersen fairy tale, like many original fairy tales, there was no true happy ending for our heroine. Andersen's own life reflected this sadness, as he never really felt as if he belonged or that his love—his writing—was accepted. In the story, there was the belief of what the land could offer; comfort, adventure, and love were all a myth. Because maybe the only real comfort occurred down in those depths.

What's often unsaid is that the story of "The Little Mermaid" stretches further back than the original Hans Christian Andersen version, first published in 1837. Hans Christian Andersen likely adapted "The Little Mermaid" from "Undine," a story first published in 1811. Still, "Undine" itself was an adaptation from the much earlier "Mélusine," which appeared before 1496.

In all of these tales, a female water spirit, often depicted as a mermaid, seeks the love of a human. Each version varies, but in most variations the mermaid marries a man, very often with the aim of gaining a human soul. In the original "The Little Mermaid," "Undine," and "Mélusine," nothing ends well for our water spirit. Our mermaid always ends up alone, betrayed, heartbroken, and then dead. Their remains are cast back to dissolve into the home they tried desperately to escape. Yet all they wanted was to be loved.

Maybe all of our homes are like that, places we are desperately trying to leave because we know if we stay too long, we'll just wither away, fading to dust and settling along window ledges and within cracks in the floorboards. Each day I wake and rise, the first thing to greet me is this house, and I fear this will be the last place I will see when I close my eyes and settle into my own forever sleep. I don't want the final thing I look upon to be a haunted memory. Our own homes threaten us each day with the possibility that this can be the last place where we ever take a breath.

We're all just bright-orange senseless goldfish swimming in our bowls.

"I'm not putting the book back in her room. This is my book. I can read it whenever I choose. All of her books are ours. That's what she wanted."

Jennie eyes me. A smile crosses her lips, as if I am a naughty child and she is catching me in a great deception. "Not this book. You know that. I know that. Never this book. This book is not just a book. This book is special. This book is a rainy-day sort of book."

We both grow quiet for a moment, our eyes falling on the cover and the title mocking both of us. Every book, every single one, is a book of spells, because the words within have the power to create a physiological or emotional effect in the real world. Words have the power to shift, to change, to move, to bend our reality, and isn't that what magic is? Magic is the manifestation come to fruition, and words hold that energy. Each and every fairy tale is a spell.

Jennie smiles again, and the way the corners of her mouth turn up in sharp points worries me so. It reminds me of how icicles form all along the gutters of our house in winter. While they look pretty and otherworldly, I know if I stood beneath them and looked up, at any time one could dislodge, shoot down, pierce my eye, and stab through deep into my skull.

Jennie is taunting me, poking me, and twisting my emotions, all with her smile.

"What is that supposed to mean? Rainy-day sort of book?"

She looks down at her nails and sighs. "Anna, one day you will stop pretending."

The teakettle whistles, sending a long line of steam behind Jennie. She walks over to the burner and turns it off. "Tea?" she says with her back to me.

"Please," I answer.

She reaches into the cupboard for my favorite porcelain teacup with a ring of pink flowers.

There's the clattering of cup against plate as she sets and pours. I look back to the book in front of me, that great punctuation that I know must be quieted.

"I'll return the book to Grandmother's room," I say reluctantly. After all, I do know the story. I have each word of the tale memorized. I merely wanted the book with me for comfort. I believed it served as a guardian somehow, a protective amulet, especially with news of the recent drownings, and now another missing man, Joshua Martin, whom I worry about so.

I often stay up late at night thinking about them all. I think of the great terror the first two missing and found men must have felt as they succumbed to the river, the very river that exists as my backyard. It carries both the living and the dead.

Jennie turns around, and her features have softened. She seems at peace. "Good. It's important that the things in this house are maintained where they belong. Order—the house craves it by its very design. Everything in its place. This is for the sake of a pattern. We all must follow the pattern that has been designed for us, because the moment we shift away from our intentions, we settle into chaos, and from chaos who knows if one can ever return."

"I'm doing research," I add. "That's why I've been in Grandmother's room reading her books. That's why I needed this book in particular."

Jennie places my cup in front of me and pours herself more hot water. She blows gently over the hot liquid. "Research for what?"

"You know . . ." I did not want to speak of it too much because I know it will upset her. "What we had talked about . . . the accident."

The porcelain cup rattles in her hands. Her expression shifts once again. She sets the teacup down and folds her hands on her lap and stares at the surface of the counter for a moment. Her eyes fall away somewhere else, not here, to a place of steel locked doors.

"I . . ." she begins, but her voice catches in her throat. She stands, grabs the teacup, and moves to the sink.

"Jennie." I follow her, but I know it's too late. I know she's upset. "It needs to be told."

My hand brushes her shoulder.

"Don't touch me!" she shouts, and before she can place the cup and saucer in the sink, both slip from her hands and shatter. Bits of white splintered porcelain cover the floor around her, sharp confetti.

"Don't move," I say, reaching for the dustpan beneath the kitchen sink. I can feel her growing more and more upset. I should not have mentioned the accident. I should not have pushed so much on the book. Whatever would come from this I now feared would be my fault.

I quickly sweep up the broken bits, but I feel the gentle tugs of this and know we can easily unravel.

Jennie shooshes me. "Do you hear that?"

I pause and listen. There it is, the steady tinkling of a drip-drip-drip coming from somewhere in this house.

Jennie turns to the sink, but the faucet is dry. She opens the cabinet beneath the sink and looks inside, but the noise is coming from somewhere, just not there. Jennie closes the cabinet door and then walks to the closest wall and places her ear against the surface, listening. "It's there, somewhere in between the heart and the rib cage," she says.

The sound of the leak intensifies. That incessant drip echoing throughout our house, vibrating down the hallway. I don't want this. I want her to remain calm, to know it is all right, even though I know that things are unstable. We are all always teetering at the end of our story.

"People just watched them die!" Jennie screams. "All of them." She clutches her chest. Her lips tremble. Her breathing comes in deep, heavy gasps. "That cursed leak will make sure we'll never forget. It stalks us. We're never free from what happened."

I take her hand and quickly drop it. She feels like a block of ice. "Jennie." I place the back of my hand on her forehead. "You're freezing. Let's get you to bed."

"No," she says, trying to push me away, but she's so weak that she makes no impact on me. It's as if her hand reaches right through me, as if I'm just an essence of what once was. I am mist. A single spray of floral perfume.

I place my arm around her back and lead her to the living room, where I help her sit. I reach for a throw blanket and cover her arms and shoulders. Jennie's eyes are fixed on me as I do this.

"You want to put this story out there? For what? For entertainment? The dead and dying are not to be consumed. People drown in the river. It's a violent end. I've seen it happen. You've seen it happen too, Anna."

I take her hand in mine. "Jennie, this isn't for entertainment. This is history. People need to know what happened."

She raises her voice. "What happened?" Her eyes widen. "It is happening. It's happening now. It's all folding in on itself. Time. We're its reluctant passengers. It's not a circle. It's the weaving of things in and out, of things collapsing. But all existing in parallel. Just listen to the house. The house hears everything, and we're floating above it all." She looks down at her hands folded on her lap. "Or are we swimming in the water below? Perhaps we're doing both. All things existing simultaneously. All things waning and waxing, cycles of the moon, tides of the ocean. We're all being taunted, Anna, with that great question."

I sigh, not understanding my dear sister. "Which is?"

"Are we unsinkable?"

"Jennie . . ." I say, taking one of her hands in mine. I look out the french doors. It's night outside, but even so, in the distance I see the city streetlights aglow. I'm surprised that Jennie's teeth are not chattering with how cold she feels to the touch. I want to say something, to pluck the right words from the air, to make sense of what it is she's saying, but this is how she often becomes when she grows upset. Her words speaking along the edges of a riddle only she can comprehend. Her sentences dotted with meaning that only she can decode, and so I sit. I listen, and I nod in a quiet stillness so as to assuage her mood.

That is what this is, another one of her moods, or what Grandmother referred to as my sister's "episodes." Grandmother had warned me that over time, Jennie's episodes would increase in intensity. I love her so. She is my sister, but I know that no matter how hard I try to pierce that thick layer of melancholy, I cannot reach her in the black pool that is her mind when she is gripped by these states.

Jennie presses the palms of her hands to her eyes and begins to sob. "No one cares. They're all dead out there."

Chapter 6

Each of them disappeared near a Chicago waterway. Missing persons reports were filed, and shortly after, their bodies were discovered in the water. A few calls came in claiming some van was in the area of a recent disappearance, asking young men if they wanted a ride home. When we asked the callers if they could provide more detail, everyone refused. No clue why.

I don't care what Sarge or upper brass thinks. The similarities are screaming at us. The markers are all there. Young men who had gone missing after leaving different bars, most of which were located in the River North neighborhood. River North is loud. It's popular. It's the neighborhood lots of young people like to get all dressed up and go to. It's where they'll pay way too much for overpriced beer and cocktails in loud and cramped clubs. But I guess there are also fancy art galleries there they like visiting, music spots like the Redhead Piano Bar, and restaurants that serve all sorts of weird fusion stuff for way too much money.

I'd rather get a burger at Portillo's any day.

Still, what River North has besides the bars and clubs and restaurants is the river just a short walk away. And if you are a killer who likes young men, it is the perfect hunting ground.

"I'll let Sergeant Flanagan know we'll get to the ME's office soon," I say as I'm parking the car outside the station. "You been to an autopsy before, right? You're not going to throw up all over the place or anything?"

Rodriguez narrows his eyes. "Yeah, of course I've been to an autopsy."

"Someone pulled from the water, though?"

He starts tapping the tops of his knees like he's playing a drum and looks out his window. "Nah."

Great. Floaters aren't pretty to look at, the first time or any time. "Just get a couple of masks on and don't throw up and you'll be fine," I say. I already feel bad for the kid. This is an image that's going to stick with him for a long time.

My mind goes back to the crime scene. "What else you think of the jogger?" I ask.

Rodriguez stops his drumming and then goes silent for a moment. "Nothing special. Afternoon jog before they go to pick their kid up from school. They see something in the water. They get close. Figure out what it is and they call 9-1-1."

"Anything else from the crime scene that stands out?" I ask.

"I mean, that graffiti. Something's up with that, I think. It looked fresh. The placement seemed pretty on spot with the location of the body."

Guess Flanagan was right. The kid's got a good eye.

"Why are we coming back to the station and not straight to the ME's?" Rodriguez asks.

"Because we're going to check on that graffiti."

One thing about Chicago, people just don't take a dip in the river. It's never going to happen. Fine, you'll get some suburban kids and maybe a drunk friend dares another drunk friend to jump in, but that's not happening every day. So people aren't really hanging out around the river access points, not much anyway. If someone is tagging specific symbols around the water, then that's something we need to look into.

A few years back I put on a life jacket, signed a waiver, and along with other local, state, and federal officials jumped in the Chicago River. It was a training exercise I did because of my only child, Bobby. Rescue boats sat in the water nearby, and while I looked down at the rotting leaves floating along the river, I knew this must be an awful way to die. I thought it would help give me some peace, maybe even some closure. All it did was make the nightmares worse.

Much of the river is man-made. It's never going to be as clean as a swimming pool. It's a moving body of water with organisms and wild-life, and enough bacteria, like fecal coliform and *E. coli*, to get someone really sick if they swallowed the water. There's always going to be shit in the river. Any heavy rain is going to overwhelm the city's sewer lines, and that slop is going to run down regional drains, get backed up, and flow into old pipes, emptying into the river.

I took the hottest shower of my life after I jumped in that water.

"Most people aren't stumbling into the river accidentally," I say.

"But they're drunk. Maybe they didn't realize where they were going."

"I've lived here all my life. I've never known anyone to accidentally fall in that water," I say.

I park the car, and Rodriguez is already unbuckled and waiting for me outside my door. He moves fast.

I push my car door open and climb out. "The case back in February. What do you remember reading in the report?"

"I remember the pictures. The water was icy. Huge blocks of ice were floating in the water."

"Our victim from February was only missing a few weeks before they were discovered," I say as we push past the front door. "The depart-ment said it was an accident. I doubt that."

"Why's that?"

"Call it intuition. A hunch. My gut."

We're in the crowded lobby. People are standing in front of the desk, cell phones in hand, ready to file a report. Others are on the phone, making frantic calls about car accidents, stolen property, and more. Two different people are recounting why they're here. Sounds like one is reporting a burglary and another a domestic violence incident. Just another day in Chicago.

I've been here long enough that it's all a routine, muscle memory, as we slip past the front desk, the room ablaze in CPD insignia, the heavy smell of burnt coffee permanently hanging in the air. I can't remember a time when the precinct didn't smell like burnt coffee. There are old cops and new cops, and cops who have seen every range of misfortune out there, and some who brought that misfortune upon themselves.

No one talks to us. No one looks at us. I'm here a few more weeks, and then they've got to deal with Rodriguez when I'm gone. He's young. He can work the late nights and the overtime and try to process those images that don't go away even after you close your eyes.

"You got a family?" I ask.

"Wife. Lisa. She's pregnant with our first."

The center of my chest grows cold. This job isn't good for a young family.

"You?"

I want to stress to Rodriguez that this isn't vice, but I know he won't listen. We take this home with us every day. These cases grip us. Even when we're off duty, it's still in our head. We're still thinking about what we should be doing, even when we should be doing something with our family. This work is time consuming. These terrible things wear us down.

"Married thirty-three years this summer. Meredith. Mer. We had a boy. The city took him. His name was Robert. Bobby. We get by."

Rodriguez hangs his head. "I'm really sorry to hear that. I can't imagine."

"Yeah," I say, because there's really not much that can be said.

One day you're new on the job and in your twenties and you notice how people look at you. Like you're some baby just learning to walk. They don't take you seriously. You open your mouth to say something and they're already rolling their eyes before you can get a word out. Maybe they envy your innocence, or maybe they just think you're really stupid and are in way over your head on patrol. You're mad and frustrated because you have things to say and things to contribute, but they'd rather you just stand there and observe, because you're too young and don't have enough experience yet, kid.

Then your thirties roll around, and people listen a little more, and by the time you're in your forties, you're the one doing all the talking. You're the one taking on so much overtime, not because you want to but because there's a home invasion that left six people dead or a gang hit that went wrong and killed a little kid. You're working all night and all day, and you can't remember when you last saw your own wife and kid.

Then your fifties roll around, and you don't even know who your kid's friends are, and by the time you start to care, it's too late, because he was at the wrong place at the wrong time, a story as old as time in Chicago. Mix a bunch of people at a party who are upset about something stupid, add alcohol and firearms, and things are going to go bad. Too bad things went bad for Mer and me. Now that my sixties are here, it doesn't really matter. Retirement is coming soon. They put me where they need me, and that's fine. They need young people with energy and a good eye who can move fast and sacrifice their lives to their careers, because it's already sucked all it can outta me.

Two uniforms walk past us with a woman in handcuffs. She tries to kick me as they move past. The uniforms yank her back.

I throw my hands up. "Come on! I wasn't even the one who got you in those cuffs."

"Go to hell, cop!"

I shrug. "I'm already there." I turn back to Rodriguez.

He's smiling. "Seems like you're a ray of sunshine everywhere you go."

I got to admit, I'm starting to like this kid. Now I see why Flanagan has me training him.

"You've got jokes, Rodriguez."

"Can you go a few minutes without fighting with people?"

I place my hand over my heart. "I'm not fighting with people. She almost kicked me. I'm old. I got bad knees. What if she would have kicked me in my knee?"

"You could have filed for worker's comp."

"Look at that," I say and laugh. "Missed opportunity for early retirement."

We get to our desks, and I look over at the whiteboard beside mine. It's blank, and I'm ready to start plotting. I don't even take my jacket off before grabbing a dry-erase marker, uncapping it, and starting to write.

John Doe, age 20–30
Recovered: Irving Park Bridge
Witness: Marshall Booth
Graffiti

I circle the word "graffiti" and take my jacket off and hang it over my chair. "This is where we start," I say.

Rodriguez is leaning against his desk and nodding. Then he points at the board. "We need to figure out when that graffiti appeared. Was it before the recovery in February or after, because that makes a difference."

"We're going to figure it out," I say.

I look back at the board. "One, maybe I can see. Sure. Guy has a few too many drinks, looks over the railing at one of the bridges, slips, and falls. Sure, but when we've now got four, across a pretty steady number of weeks, I don't care what Sarge is telling us, or anyone. These are not accidental drownings."

Rodriguez raises his eyebrows. "What are we going to say in roll call tomorrow?"

"We're not going to roll call. We're going to take a drive down to River North. Ask around about what people have seen, what they've heard, and most importantly, take a look at any entrance points along the river, bridges, walking paths. Anything."

"How many bodies does it need to be? Four? Five?" Rodriguez is bouncing his knee.

"Three," I say. We're past that threshold. I take a seat and turn to my computer and start clicking away.

Rodriguez stands up. "Good. We get the feds in then, right?"

I laugh. He's got a lot to learn. The first being that proving we've got a serial killer working in Chicago is going to be almost impossible. "They don't like the 'S' word around here."

"I don't get it. What do you mean?" He's pointing at the board. "We got four guys across a short span of time. All in the water. You said yourself: How'd they get in there?"

I lean back in my chair and put my hands behind my head. My lower back feels stiff. A reminder I gotta stretch more. "Yeah, you'd think that. These guys, however"—I motion with my head behind me—"don't want to hear none of that. We can dress it up however we want. Hell, a serial killer can walk right in here and claim to have killed dozens, and our bosses will still take pause and be like . . . let's think about this. No one wants to admit they have a serial killer working in their town, especially people in Chicago. We're already the boogeyman of the national news. Our politicians don't want another reason out there that gets our name dragged."

"All right, so what do we do?"

I turn back to my computer, punching in a few keys, initially ignoring Rodriguez, who's hovering behind me now. "Can you at least give me some room here?" I ask when I can't take it anymore. He takes this as an invitation to sit on my desk. I groan and keep looking.

I'm searching for that specific person and date in February. We've had a couple of carjackings that didn't end well, then there was that home invasion that turned deadly. We hadn't been assigned to too many cases since.

"Early February," I say. "It was cold as hell. We had one of them arctic blast days. Thirty below. My old partner had his eyelashes freeze. It was wild."

"You never talk about him," Rodriguez says. "Your old partner. Martin. That was his name, right?"

"Yeah . . . Martin. There's nothing I need to say other than he was with me for twenty years, and now he's not and that's it. That's life." The cruelty of this job is that retirement sometimes seems a possibility, but for some of us, when we get there, the quiet and stillness is deafening, and the body and mind start to fall apart wondering why they aren't being used, and well, for too many who retire, they don't last long into retirement. Something comes and sweeps them away. A stroke, a heart attack. Maybe even cancer.

At least for now, it looks like I'm one of the lucky ones, but what's lucky? I get to retire soon, but what did I lose in the process? I have Mer. Martin had nobody. But still, even then, Mer and I are entering retirement without our boy.

Rodriguez presses his palms into his eyes.

"Don't tell me you're tired already? We're not going home for a while."

I'm clicking on crime scene pictures. There's the surface of the water. There are the banks on either side, patches of mud and snow, and dead leaves. Now the surrounding area. A collection of bare trees. The bridge.

"Right there." Rodriguez taps my screen.

"Hey, what'd I say about personal space?"

"Can you not be an asshole for a few minutes so we can get through this?" Rodriguez says.

"Yeah, fine," I agree.

"Look." He points at the screen again. "It matches exactly."

He's right. It's identical to what we'd spotted today. A blue diamond on one of the bare trees. "What do you think it was drawn with?"

"Spray paint," he says.

"Tagger?"

Rodriguez starts tapping his index finger against his chin. "Not a tag I know of or seen before. It's messy. See here?" He points at the drips of paint against the tree. "Still, these are swift movements, but they're not good with precision. So it's not an established tagger, that is."

His experience in vice is already paying off. Rodriguez knows the streets and what blends in and, in this case, what stands out.

I lean back in my chair and look up at the ceiling. "Let's just say we have a single killer. They're bold. They're comfortable going back to the site where the body was recovered. That also means that—"

"They're local," Rodriguez interrupts.

I point at him. "You got it. If we have a killer who is local, that explains so much—the growing frequency, and the ease with which they operate." This person knows the city. They know the river. They know how to avoid people. They know how to avoid security systems and police cameras. They also know where and how to find people who easily fit their victim profile.

"Their victim profile seems pretty broad," he says.

I disagree. "Take it to the board. What do we got?"

He takes up a marker and jots down:

Male
White
Ages 20 to 30

"Yeah," I nod. "What else?"

"They all left a bar or club alone and went missing late at night or early-morning hours."

He's right, but there's more happening beneath the surface. Most murderers know their victims, and I'm sure this killer does not know these people. We don't know why repeat killers choose certain individuals as their victims. Studies among murderers often turn up a range of answers regarding the motive. Experts tell us that these killers have a fantasy victim, the ideal person based on a series of markers: age, race, physical characteristics, or other qualities. And it seems like that's what we've got with these men.

"So the killer knew the body was recovered, went to the recovery site, and left behind this symbol. Why? Why risk it?"

"That's part of the game," I say.

Most killers want to cover up their crimes, and many do, successfully evading authorities for years, with many never being caught. Murderers even often aim to fool detectives by obscuring their DNA, and sometimes that of their victims, at the crime scene. If there's a killer operating around the river, they're not covering up the DNA of their victims.

"Criminals often conceal their victims' identity," I say. "Sometimes removing hands or feet, or even their head—the most identifiable part of the body."

Rodriguez flinches. "How often have you seen that?"

"We're always finding somebody's something in the Humboldt Park Lagoon, torso . . . something. I've seen it enough times around here. Marine Unit fished out a head by Lake Shore Drive just last June."

"Thanks for the detail."

I laugh. "Doing our entire job right hinges on detail."

If we have a killer, their aim is to make sure the person enters the water, full and intact.

I wonder, then, how they mark their victim. Is the killer frequenting bars and clubs and music venues and selecting who they are going to kill there? Are these men's drinks being spiked without them knowing? Maybe they are being followed after leaving the bar drunk? Or is the killer just waiting outside, near bridges, and selecting their victims there?

Or are they outside these spots, waiting for someone to leave alone? Or do they pick a point near the river, along a bridge, a walking path, to meet their victim? Do they talk to these men? Is there something that they ask them? Is there something they need to know from them before they move forward with their task? Or is it all a surprise? Are there screams?

"And there've been no distress calls?" Rodriguez says, holding the marker to the whiteboard. "People hearing people call for help from around the river?"

"You're free to check the records, but there's been none that I know of."

That river scares the hell outta me. That's why I volunteered to jump in, hoping it would ease my fear, but that didn't help much. I just thought of Bobby, hurt out there at night. Sucking in that foul water.

I stand up, placing my hands on my lower back and stretching out the kinks that have been coiling there for the past few years, begging for me to retire and take it easy. "What we do know is that there's been nothing on any of the recovered bodies that points to anyone, which is why the department continues to push for cause of death to be listed as 'accidental drowning.'"

On the surface, there is nothing that raises an alarm that something strange is happening. None of these cases have shown any signs of trauma, beyond what was caused by them going into the river and being in the water for a prolonged period of time. The local media has kept oddly quiet, but I know that independent media had been murmuring a bit about the cases.

"Most killers will return to the scene to relive the crime. They like marking the occasion. Celebrating it. They don't want it to be forgotten," I say.

Rodriguez backs away from the board, shaking his head.

"What? You think perfectly well-adjusted people kill people?" Kowalski says.

He huffs and walks back to his desk, where he takes a seat.

"This isn't a normal killer," I say. "Your by-the-book killer commits a crime in an area and moves on. This is how so many of them evade capture, but this killer doesn't operate like normal killers. This killer sticks around. They like to see and savor their results, coming back to the crime scene to leave their mark. That blue diamond."

"Then why not tell the sergeant and get the feds to look at this?"

The last thing anyone in upper brass is going to admit is that we've got someone out here targeting young males in one of the trendiest and upscale neighborhoods. Hell, they kept Martin and me so far from the Chicago Strangler case because they knew I know what I'm talking about when it comes to behavioral science. I've closed the most cases in this department. When I say something's up, it's because I *know* it. That case got me suspended and almost fired when I went around Flanagan interviewing witnesses and talking to confidential informants in the area I'd worked in the past. Another set of detectives were pulled onto the Chicago Strangler—both had little experience and were incompetent as hell. Nepotism got them their assignments, and we still haven't begun piecing together that case.

"If Sergeant Flanagan hears any of this, I'm out on early retirement and you're going to patrol."

"Wait, so what are you saying?" There he goes bouncing his leg again. "We're going rogue or something?"

"I didn't say that. You didn't say that. All I'm saying is we're going to turn over a few rocks we probably wouldn't have thought about turning over before, just because we're doing our due diligence."

Rodriguez stands up and starts pacing from the whiteboard to his desk. "I like this. This is the work I want to do."

I spin my chair around and give the kid a good, long stare.

"What?" he shoots back at me.

"Nothing," I say, and laugh to myself as I spin back to my computer.

"You're being an asshole again," he says.

"Always," I counter. I like that Rodriguez is eager. That's always a good sign in a detective. I pull up another screen, the names and dates missing and recovered of the other men. I write those down on the board, and then Rodriguez and I are standing side by side, reading and rereading what we've written down thus far, staring into it like it's some damn crystal ball that's gonna pop out some answers.

"What's the signature?" I ask.

"What?"

I groan. "Come on. Keep up. The killer's signature is different than the modus operandi. A killer's MO is learned behavior. A signature is like a ritual, something that's unique to the offender."

"Drowning victims in the Chicago River, and potentially this, the blue diamond."

"Why a blue diamond?" I ask.

Rodriguez shakes his head. I'm with him. I've got no clue, not yet anyway, but it'll come. Something always does.

"Let's look into any potential meanings." I close my eyes and rub my temples. "All we need is to prove we have a pattern."

Rodriguez is silent for a moment. I've been doing this long enough to know his brain is on fire, thinking, putting pieces together. That's how we do this, our hunch, our intuition. We analyze everything and everyone. Everything is a puzzle, and we just got to start putting it together to make that full picture appear.

My phone starts ringing, and it's the sergeant, and he's going to want to know why the hell we're not at the medical examiner's office yet. I ignore the call. "Let's go. We got an autopsy to attend."

"And after?" Rodriguez is right behind me.

"Make sure you got a flashlight. We're going to be up all night visiting everywhere these bodies were discovered to see if we missed anything else."

"Why not wait until morning?"

Makes sense in a way. Morning would give us more light. Morning meant safe, but we didn't do things because they were safe. We did things now, because everything we did we needed to do with urgency. There was no telling if our killer would strike again, so we needed to be ahead of them before they got ahead of us.

Chapter 7

Why do we need to keep alive the memories of victims, survivors, heroes, and those affected by tragedy? Why should we resurrect the sorrow that overshadowed all of the good moments of their lives? What does this do? What purpose does it fulfill? Why do we need to reach into the past and pluck out images of vomit and bloodstained floors and mangled corpses?

I often wonder what purpose this serves, peering into a brutal past.

What purpose do I serve in wanting to disrupt the dust that rests on heavy leather-bound photo albums that haven't been cracked open in decades? Of seeking out curled black-and-white photographs that sit lost in antique stores that other people pick up and purchase for novelty? What purpose does any of this serve?

I do not yet know.

All I know is that I am pulled by the desire to tell this story, just like Grandmother was compelled to read "The Little Mermaid" to us and did so frequently until the day she died.

I'm standing in the first-floor bathroom now.

I left Clover and Thistle snug in the living room in their little bed as I stepped away to work. Plastic sheeting covers the white porcelain clawfoot bathtub, the sink, and the toilet. I was extra careful to protect the black-and-white porcelain honeycomb mosaic floor tile. I finished the wall against the tub a week ago, removing the old plaster, installing drywall, and then measuring, cutting, and laying down white subway tile. I am proud of myself that I have been able to become proficient at learning new skills.

In preparation for today, I laid down a foam pad, followed by more sheets of plastic. Before I moved to the final wall to complete the update in this bathroom, I had carefully pried off the original wood trim molding, including the baseboards. Those were moved to the basement, where I would later sand and restain them. I would do the same with the door, but for now I keep it in its place to remain as a barrier and keep in all of the construction material, dust, and debris that didn't needlessly need to spill into other areas of the house.

Jennie had expressed anger over this light remodel of the home, and while I did much of this work on my own, I still relied on the hardware store to deliver materials on a regular basis. Larger pieces were also brought inside by the hardware store employees, and having strangers in the house for even a moment caused Jennie to be quite agitated.

To her, the house lived and breathed, a great organism that existed, in many ways, as we did, with eyes and a face. Jennie claimed the house could hear, and stressed that we should be cautious to never speak ill of our home. I wonder, then, what the house thought of all this noise I was making as I pulled sheets of old plaster down to make room for new drywall.

Jennie also claimed that the house could feel our joy. She then stressed that the house felt our pain. I suspect the wiring and pipes that ran behind its walls served as its veins and arteries. What, then, was its brain, I wondered? Where, then, was its heart located? When I'd asked Jennie where to find those two organs, she laughed. She placed her hand on my cheek and said, "Her heart thumped with fear and she nearly turned back."

I didn't know what she meant. Jennie's nonsensical speech increased with time. I attributed it all to our parents.

Of course, I can't be firm with her. Jennie is unwell. Her behavior and moods shifted after the accident. Her ideas became more fantastical. Her thoughts spiraled into great twists and turns of fancy, and all I can do is be patient, because I myself am unwell too. How can I hold us both together if I allow us to each fall apart? And so I push my torment away into a cavern I cannot easily access. I tell Jennie how much I love her, but no matter how often I repeat these words or how often I hold her as she erupts in tears, it's as if her mind drifts away into a place where I cannot find her, and when that happens, the house vibrates, and Jennie's moods only intensify.

When I woke in the morning, I didn't want to believe that this house could hear and sense my every movement. But I knew that the impossible was always within reach. I could not explain the soft footsteps we heard on the stairs late into the night. Or the creaking of doors. I thought of what my grandmother called it long ago—settlings—but this was not a house settling. This was a house firmly making its presence known to its occupants. This was a house communicating, and what it was trying to tell me I wish I knew.

If the house could feel, then what emotion was it trying to signal as cabinets flew open and windows slammed shut? When I asked Jennie, all she said was, "Within this house dwells the music of melancholy. So be careful when the walls come crashing down around you, for you may disrupt something that should never have been discovered. And once that dismal music begins to play, once it fills the house, then there's nothing that can stop it. It will be as if a great tide has torn us apart."

That was no clear answer. All I could do then was kindly suggest that Jennie get some rest as I took to tearing down the walls in the bathroom.

These old houses were constructed not with drywall but with plaster and lath. To create a plaster wall, first lath needs to be secured to a frame. Lath is constructed of thin wooden strips, and it's what the sticky plaster can adhere to. A dry plaster compound is then mixed with water, and once it's the right consistency, it's spread across the lath. After the first coat dries, a second coat is applied, followed by a final layer. Because of the multiple coats and the lathing, plaster walls tend to be thicker than those made of drywall. These sheets are already prepared and ready to be installed. The plasterboard is made of gypsum mixed with water, and the material is spread between two sheets of paper. The drywall is placed by lifting the pieces and screwing them to wall studs.

Newer houses are made with drywall, but nearly all older houses in the city were constructed with the old method, of plaster.

Old houses hold hazardous surprises, like loose wires threaded in walls without insulation. Before I get to work, I turn off the circuits at the fuse box and check the outlets and switches to make sure there is no power. I had purchased coveralls and a dust mask and pinned my hair back and wrapped it in a scarf.

Breaking up old plaster is messy. Cracks can spread to the adjoining walls and ceiling. To prevent that, I need to cut the material with an oscillating tool. After I cut the perimeter of the plaster walls, I then have to cut the wood lath to prevent any cracks from spreading once again. As I cut, I can smell the smoky smell of the original wood used to construct this house. A fine spray of white powdery mist flows from the walls. Plaster. This crushed, chalklike coat covers everything—my clothes, my hands, and my face.

I stop and take a look in the mirror. My reflection is obscured by the painter's plastic. I push it aside and look at my double, covered in white powder, trillions of particles that, if inhaled into my lungs, could pierce into the fine meat of those organs, irritating the airway and initiating coughing, breathing difficulties, or worse.

I look closer, noticing that even my eyelashes are dusted in that delicate pale powder. I am covered in a sheet of white like a ghost.

I hear a soft buzz and look down at the floor, covered in cracked drywall and thin, brittle pieces of lath. I assume it came from the wires, perhaps some last bit of energy remained within them, even after I had cut the circuit. I have not yet removed the electrical wiring from the walls. That job would have to be set aside for an electrician. Instead for now, I allow the wires to dangle there, like the pathetic guts from a victim whose stomach has been sliced open with a knife.

Once again there is that soft buzz, repeating again and again, each time the sound morphing into a metallic ping. I look down at my tan work boots and search around to see if I have kicked anything aside. I have not.

The ping continues, a soft vibration, which now seems to be coming from directly in front of me. I move forward, stepping over the sheet of plaster I had just brought down. It crunches beneath my feet. I peer into the hole in the wall, but it is too dark to see. I grab the flashlight, turn it on, and aim the light inside.

There are stories of items being stored within a home at the time of its construction. In prominent structures, very often something of value was placed in the cornerstone. The cornerstone is generally just a masonry stone set outside in a prominent location. Traditionally it was set in the northeast corner, and an inscription might include the name of the building, the date erected, and perhaps the names of significant individuals. Very often then, a time capsule was placed inside the cornerstone. The time capsule could contain photographs, newspaper clippings, and any other significant material that the people of the past would store to communicate to individuals in the future.

For houses, good luck charms have been known to be sealed into the walls during the build. Shoes stored inside the walls were often found after the home was purchased and remodeling initiated. These were sometimes called concealment shoes and were placed inside the structure to ward off evil spirits while drawing in good luck. Sometimes they were stored around a door or window frame, near the chimney, or at any other point where an evil spirit could enter.

When we think of these things, of superstitious items placed in a home by the original builders, we have to remember that they did these things to protect the ones inside whom they loved.

I don't know much about superstition, but I do know I very much believe in love. I've always dreamt about falling in love, of finding someone who, at the very first moment my eyes meet theirs, there's no question that they are my love and I am theirs, destined to be together. When we were teenagers, Jennie laughed at me when I told her this. She told me that love at first sight didn't exist, and I asked her why not.

"How long, then, do these two people have to hold each other's gaze? Is it for a minute? Longer? A second or less? What is the formula for this length of time, for looking into one another's eyes and spiraling into a deep well of love for each other?"

"I think it's instant," I had said, feeling my cheeks flush red. "The very first time we look into each other's eyes, we'll know."

"You're already assuming you're going to fall in love."

I could not imagine going through life without experiencing love. I had to believe that the person destined for me was out there somewhere. I needed to believe this to be so, because that is what has kept me going, in a sense, swimming through the heartache of my days, all the while believing there exists someone for me, and I for them, and that us together would be the balm to soothe the grief inside me.

"What happens if those two individuals are forcefully pulled apart?" Jennie asked.

"What do you mean? Why would they be pulled apart?"

"What if one is crossing the street and sees the other across the way, and in that instant, they fall in love but are immediately struck by an automobile? What if both of them are killed just moments after first spotting one another, after that love at first sight, that moment their eyes lock on one another, and knowing with their entire being that they have found the love of their lives finally?"

The answer to me was simple.

"Then even in death they would love each other. Two ghosts, eternally devoted to the other, because love is formless and timeless. Defined by nothing and no one."

I return to the wall. I don't expect to find a pair of shoes within this hole. I don't know what to expect, but as I draw closer to the pinging sound, I start to wonder about what Jennie had said all of those times, that the house is a living thing, and so for a moment I wonder if I had somehow damaged it. Had I inadvertently operated on the house, as Jennie previously noted? Removing its skin, allowing it to bleed all over the floor as I hacked away at its form? Was the pinging sound I heard now my home moaning in pain, begging me to cease my destruction of its body? I aim the light inside the hole. A beam of glowing dust motes dance in the air.

There, inches from my face, is the source of that sound. I reach inside and grab a bundle that is wrapped in newspaper. It is small and fits inside my palm. I set the object down on the floor and proceed to unwrap the yellowed paper. I unfold the sheet and set it aside. It is the front page of the *Chicago Daily News*, a newspaper I have never heard of, but then again, many newspapers had shuttered over the years. It is dated July 26, 1915, which makes no sense, given that the house was built in 1911. How and why, then, four years after constructing the house, would someone want to stuff something into its walls?

I am not really sure what this is I am turning over in my hands now. It is a piece of polished metal. That is clear. Flat and round. The object doesn't tell me anything. There is no clue as to what it is. I turn back to the newspaper it was wrapped in; maybe the headline or whatever piece of an article I could read can offer me some insight into the item. I hope it can provide me with an answer as to what this metal piece was for.

I smell fire.

I turn to the doorway and there is Jennie, holding the sheet of newspaper in one hand and a lit match in the other. By the time I stand up, she is holding fire to paper, and the yellow, red, and gold flames sweep across the material, licking away each printed letter, the paper curling black.

Before the fire touches Jennie's flesh, she drops the smoldering mass of ashes. I stamp it out with my boot, the heat melting into the plastic sheeting that covers the floor but not penetrating the foam beneath that protects the tile.

"What's wrong with you?" I demand.

She shoots me a scorched look. "Just like dandelions that sprout across the graves of those who died in Dunning, these things too should be plucked out and destroyed!" She points to the metal disk in my hand and then turns away and leaves me there, unsure of what has happened and why.

I follow her into the hallway, and she stops, turns, and points to me. "You're trailing dust all through our house!"

"Jennie, you could have set this entire house on fire!"

She laughs. "I would never hurt this house. Everything I do is to protect this house." She inhales deeply and looks up to the ceiling. "I am here because no one loves me, except for you and this house." She lowers her head and looks me in the eye, and I see a sadness I know all too well. "No one has ever loved me, or will ever love me, but you and this house, and that is my curse."

Before I can say anything, she turns away from me. "I'm going for my walk."

She's moving down the stairs now.

"Please, I'm begging you, it's not safe . . . and . . ."

"And what?"

"And you're all I have in this world, and if I lose you too, I just don't know how I can continue."

"Each day we continue, regardless of the fears and the threats, because if we stop, then time will swallow us up, a great whale ingesting all of the little creatures it can consume in a single drink of ocean water. If we stop, then we'll never know. If we stop, then we'll never see. If we stop, then we remain as stagnant as filthy pond water. We have to keep going, because we don't know what we will find out there. Maybe some of it will spark something in us—hope or envy, maybe regret. But we can't stop. We can't pause. We continue in one form or another."

I hear the door slam shut, and I'm standing at the top of the stairs, covered in construction dust, with the sting from the burnt newspaper still vibrating in my nostrils, and all I can think is that there's a murderer outside and my sister may very well run into them.

Chapter 8

First there is an email.

Dear Anna -

I wanted to email you to tell you how much I enjoy your podcast. It's what I look forward to every Monday morning. Monday mornings are difficult enough, getting ready for work and cramming onto the Blue Line train, but I like listening to your ghost stories, and it's changed my life. Is that strange to say to a stranger? That your ghost stories changed my life?

I was thinking recently about the story you told about Emma and Clara Pontius. How tragic of those two sisters who died by suicide together, in a place so beautiful. Then again, Lincoln Park is beautiful today. The area probably was not beautiful way back when it was a graveyard.

I guess I just want to say that I appreciate you. I like listening to you. It makes me feel like I'm not so alone all of the time, and sometimes in this city, it can feel lonely. It's funny how even on a packed train or bus we can feel so alone in this city. I hope you don't take any of this the wrong way. I hope I don't sound weird. I guess saying I hope I don't sound weird sounds weird. Anyways, I don't want to do that.

Thanks again for what you do. Your stories entertain me. Even though they're about really awful things happening, there's something about the way you present it all, like you're trying to find hope in something so sad. Just know your voice brings a lot of joy.

Again, I hope you do not take this the wrong way, I just want to say I enjoy your show. I enjoy listening to you.

Best,
Peter

I don't respond to Peter's email. I don't ever respond to messages from listeners. It's difficult to really know who is on the other side of the screen. Their words could be typed out with the purest energy of deception, each letter by letter, a thread in the rope that will eventually hang me.

I never know who I can trust. Everyone I've trusted, each and every one, has deceived me. It weighs on you, a parade of heartbreaks, until you realize one day that perhaps to be loved by someone else is not meant for you.

How could anyone love me, with the scars I carry, and with my sister whom I care for who each day unravels a little, seam by seam. Maybe I haven't found love because I can't love myself, because all I can feel is this cold lump in my throat, and all I can sense when I take a pause from the cleaning or the house repairs are tears stinging behind my eyes.

This waterfall of torment doesn't stop. I just look away from it at times; otherwise I'd drown.

I long to just . . . talk to someone. To just laugh with someone. To just have someone nearby. Someone in my presence who cares, deeply and truly, who cares about me, not like a sister or a parent or a grandparent. I want something more. I want something deep, something indescribable that can only be felt. Maybe that's the treachery of fairy tales. They tempt us with the possibility of love at first sight, but I've never known it, and with each passing day, I come to believe in it less and less, the possibility of true human connection. The possibility of a true, pure, and golden love.

It's difficult to know what people's true intentions are. Jennie believes that anyone who came close to us did so because they wanted the house. A jewel worth millions. Maybe she was right. Jennie knows more than most people. She has the ability, the intuition, to read people. That makes her both valuable and dangerous.

Jennie once said that most people are wolves in sheep's clothing, donning another animal's skin, still slick with its blood. Wolves will adopt mannerisms and ways of communication to align themselves with their prey. They embed themselves into your environment, your life, and your brain. We are all so easily manipulated, and a wolf can smell the weak points, the places that shake and bend and crack easily. And it's these areas that the wolf will carefully poke and prod. Then when these beasts sink their fangs into your flesh, you're too tired and too broken from the exhaustion of all they made you endure that you are unable to fight back.

Wolves are cunning and wolves are cruel, but humans are even more so.

I sit at the kitchen counter sipping my tea and rereading the email, again and again. There is a tinge of sadness to it that I can identify with. This desperate need to reach out to someone in the hope that the other person can understand you, in the hope that the other person can spot a glimpse of you that no one else can see. We're all looking for someone to bring us joy and comfort, and sometimes that comfort lies in spotting something in someone that we can identify with. We're all trying to find reflections of ourselves in others to soothe our loneliness to not just say that we're not alone but that this person understands us and we understand them. That's divine connection.

Jennie has not come out of her room for days, except for her walks to the river. I leave her meals outside her door on a wooden tray. Later in the day, I retrieve the tray. Her food has been eaten, so I don't worry much. Yesterday I tapped lightly on her door after dinner and let her know it would be a bright, warm day and we should have lunch outside by the river. She declined, saying that she did not feel like going outside because the warm air only ushered in sadness.

I stand. I can't reread the email another time, because each time I read Peter's words, it's as if I hear his voice reading to me . . . and I've never heard his voice before, so how can that even be possible? Each sentence pulls me in, and it's as if he's here with me. But again, I've never seen or heard him before. Still, here are his words, and here is my name and his name on the glowing screen before me, and for a moment, I wish that this person I have never met in real life was here with me, just so I wouldn't feel so absolutely miserable and lost in this house.

There's something about his words that give me comfort. There's even something about him . . . his name pulsates with a hint of familiarity. I don't believe in past lives. I don't believe in coincidences, but there is something there, a feeling I cannot shake. A knowing. A longing. An *almost* moment.

I move into the hallway and find myself once again standing in front of Jennie's room. Her television is blaring.

The news provides another update on Joshua Martin. It's a non-update in a way, how he remains missing and area detectives are investigating. I think about Joshua Martin. I wonder what path he walked home, the types of people he encountered along the way, what they may have looked like or said, and I wonder, of course, where he is. Someone knows where Joshua Martin is, and each day that passes, I worry if there will be another. Four men found in the river in a matter of weeks is worrisome.

I worry about my sister. I worry about the river outside our home. And I worry about the great city that we live in, pulsating with something awful. I accept that there's beauty here, but I also accept that something very grim operates here as well.

"Jennie, I'm going to sit outside for a bit. It's gorgeous. You should join me. I know . . ." I pause. The faint memory of blistering terror spreads across my body.

The only thing that answers is the television. The news report continues. Joshua's father is being interviewed. It's a microburst of a sound bite, encapsulating enough grief and entertainment in mere seconds. Then, once the segment ends, the news moves on to the weather. There is no easy transition from dread to despair to the day's temperature. There is just the constant churning of information, with very little time allotted to process suffering.

"You shouldn't occupy your mind with such awful things," I say.

She responds, "I will luxuriate in this fear if I choose."

I ask her once again if she will join me outside, telling her that the air will be good for her, but she doesn't answer. "I'll be outside, then.

If you hear the doorbell, please come and let me know. The electrician will be here shortly to wire the bathroom."

"He already came," Jennie says, smooth and steady.

"What do you mean he already came? I didn't hear anyone."

The door opens, less than an inch, and I can see one of her eyes burrowing into me. "Of course you didn't hear anything. You were recording your podcast . . ."

"How can that be? Doesn't it take hours to do that job?" I pause, thinking. "Jennie, did I leave the front door unlocked?" She does not respond to my question but continues speaking.

"You were occupied for hours. This is a small bathroom. There isn't much wiring. But it doesn't matter. It's all done. You just need to hang up the new drywall, paint, and decorate. I will help you with that," she says, and then proceeds to close the door. I thank her, surprised that she would even agree to help with any portion of updating the house, but then she says, "The house aches, as if it's got an open wound, and I will do anything to heal it. I will do anything for this house. You and this house are all that I have that love me and ground me to this place. I wish someone else would love me. I long for someone else to love me, and I ache knowing that may never be for me, love that's rich and true. All I long for is someone to love me, to look at me each and every time as if they have seen the stars for the first time. I want to feel their energy intensify in my presence, excited for my existence. I want to be needed, admired, adored. I want a man who loves me to caress my face, to kiss my lips gently. To whisper to me that they love me as I drift away to sleep and, when I awake in the morning, to feel their hand in mine, and to hear them tell me 'I am here.'"

I lean my back against the door and wish, for once, that my sister could be a real older sister, someone whom I could confide in, someone who is eager to spend time with me, who could talk to me. Our relationship is built on holding each other up, preventing the other from sinking, as we try to keep our heads above water. We both exist in a constant panic to survive. To remain afloat. Sometimes I wonder if this is enduring. We remain in a steady stillness. I hate to admit it to myself, but perhaps my sister and I are truly unhappy.

Jennie's voice is more distant now. I can imagine her lying on her bed, staring up at the ceiling. "You should be worried about all of the changes you are influencing around here, Anna."

Outside, I sit on the small bench in front of the fairy garden I have not tended to in quite some time. I don't know why I didn't just sweep away the dirt and debris and dead leaves. I don't know why I didn't fix the cracked roof of the little house. Perhaps it's because I find beauty in the faded colors of the marbles, hairpins, buttons, and ribbons. I find the little red-and-blue house beautiful in its sadness. It is a replica of our house, but unlike ours, the front door of this little home is always open. I reach down to pick up a marble, but when I bring it to my face, I notice it isn't a marble at all but the eyeball of a doll. I can't recall ever plucking out any of my dolls' eyes, so I assume that Jennie did this long ago. I place the eyeball back down in the garden, fearful that somehow this wandering eye will tell on me that I have disturbed it.

I look out over the water and think of the length of the river and how it runs through the city, the only river in the world that flows backward, using a series of canal locks and an increased flow from Lake Michigan. I realize this is why the bodies are found throughout the city and not the lake, as the water flows through the neighborhoods. It is very possible, then, that one day I can be sitting out here and spot a bloated, putrid male corpse floating along. Maybe that's what I've been waiting for, and I just can't remember. I know Jennie tells me not to worry, but how can I not? She's all that I have.

Jennie will leave the house again for her walks, and I will know that there is another person out there who is missing. The news only tells us when people disappear and when their bodies are recovered. We are not told anything more, but I suspect there is a lot more happening above the surface.

Inside, I return to my computer, and there, again, are Peter's words staring at me from the screen. It's difficult to explain my stunning solitude. If it weren't for Clover and Thistle, I don't think I would ever have any quality interaction with any living being. Jennie's moods seem to now consume her, intensifying and slowly swallowing up who she once was. And so, all I have are my dogs, my podcast, this house, and solitude. This home is a monastery in a way, and the quiet that we live are prayers to past parts of ourselves. I, like Jennie, long for someone who exists outside these walls to make me feel something.

I turn to Clover, who is whimpering at my feet. "I know I shouldn't, but I'm going to do it," I whisper.

The little puppy lies on its belly, pawing my foot. "I know. I'm sorry. It's not that I don't love you. It's just that . . . I need something more."

The dog growls a playful growl.

I sigh. "A human, I mean. I would like a human to talk to. I do appreciate you and your sister, but having a person like me whom I could speak with would be nice. I just don't want to feel like I exist alone in the ether anymore."

The little gray paw smacks my foot.

"I know. What if he responds?" I study Clover's deep amber eyes. "If he responds, that would be very nice. Then I will respond right back."

I write. I delete. I write again, and then I hate each and every word and how I string them together. How can I summarize my gratitude in a few lines without sounding so . . . sad? There is no point in being perfect here, because perfection is an illusion.

I proceed to type:

Dear Peter,

Thank you so much for listening. I appreciate your
message very much so. Sometimes I do forget that
people are actually out there listening to me. There
isn't much interaction I have, besides the comments
that I read on Monday morn . . .

I stop.

I reread the sentences I have typed and know they have come out
all jumbled and wrong. My heart beats with such an intensity now that
my entire body sways.

"This is ridiculous," I say. Clover yawns, and then Thistle stands,
walks over to me, and wags her tail. I kiss the top of Thistle's head. "I
do appreciate the encouragement. Let me try again."

Dear Peter,

Thank you so much. I appreciate your message very
much so. It provides me great joy that even though
what I do talk about is gruesome and grim that it
somehow provides comfort to those that are living,
to you especially, and that I've given space to the
dead to be remembered.

Thank you again for listening.
-Anna

I hit "Send" before any pangs of regret can swell within me. The
message now exists in the air and no longer in my brain. It sits somewhere in a space between time, existing in his account, and I hope he
will read it, and I hope he will respond.

I leave my office once again, and as I walk past Jennie's door, I realize that many days have gone by without her receiving a package.

I knock. "Jennie, have you been receiving any deliveries? I haven't received any on your behalf."

There is no response.

I knock again and then press my ear against the door and listen. I turn the doorknob and push. She is not here. What I do find, however, is a stack of boxes in a corner. It appears she has been receiving packages, after all, and her work desk is cluttered with old parts from turntables, record players, and other antique audio machines. This is her skill: pulling together pieces of old sound technology so that it can once again sing. Jennie says this is a process of healing, refurbishing something that was once loved. Sometimes one found healing in the forgetting, but at least for these machines, Jennie believes that fixing them soothes her condition and quells her moods.

I feel a nudge against my foot, and my gaze shifts down to Clover pawing at me.

"She probably stepped out back to look for me," I say. At least, that's where I hope she went, and that she did not go searching for other things. The only thing that is tangible is this very second and this very moment and all of our feelings we feel in the present.

I look toward the stairs, expecting Jennie to appear, ready to scold me and to tell me how dare I enter her bedroom without her permission. Jennie is very particular about her privacy—our privacy, really. I know she would be horrified to discover that I had messaged a listener.

The weight as a caretaker is steadily increasing. I had promised Grandmother, and then Mother and Father, that I would care for Jennie and this house, but in all of my promises about the house and Jennie, I never thought about myself.

I wonder, Had Grandmother thought of who would care for me? Because once she died and then Mother and Father, there was no one here to take an interest in me and my needs. Before the dogs, if Jennie was in one of her moods, I would go days without hearing my own voice. Now that I had the podcast, I took great joy in listening to myself and knowing that there were people out there living vibrant lives, and that I was with them, in a sense, in some of those moments. Even if no one was here to offer me comfort, it brought me a little happiness knowing that I was with others, like Peter.

Still, was this all really caring for myself?

In many ways I feel like the Little Mermaid, the youngest sister who wanted to break away from the life her family expected her to live. The Little Mermaid longed for a life out there, because in that strange land where people walked upright on legs, she knew she could live and that she could love and be loved. No matter the marvelous trees and flowers that grew around her palace, or the spectacular walls made of coral and mussel shells—the Little Mermaid's home still felt like a dungeon to her.

Why must I continue to sacrifice my happiness for Jennie? How many more months and years did I have? How many have I wasted in standing by this order to remain loyal to my sister? To remain loyal to a house that torments me? I love her. She is my sister and I need her, but I am bound to her in a way that prevents me from moving on.

I close Jennie's door and turn toward the stairs, and there, right before the first step is . . . a marble. I pick it up, but no, it isn't a marble. It is the very worn plastic doll eye that was outside in my fairy garden. I roll the object between my thumb and forefinger and call out to my sister. "Jennie, are you here?"

I hear the french doors leading to the river open and shut. I race down the stairs and stare out the window but see nothing. I open the door and walk down the path.

"Jennie?"

All I find is soft birdsong, a gentle breeze, and the fishy algae and wildflower smells from the river below.

Back inside, the sound of the leak returns, the repetitive drip behind some wall I must discover before it destroys this house or destroys me, or both.

I call again. "Jennie?"

I now hear the sound of water gushing and spraying.

Both of the dogs are at the top of the stairs, their tails wagging. They are bouncing on their back heels.

I rush up the stairs. I slip at the top step and fly forward, falling onto my knees. I hear water splashing onto the tile in the bathroom.

"Jennie!" I scream.

The bathroom door is open. It's dark inside, but the light in the hallway illuminates the full bathtub and the form floating inside the white porcelain claw-foot tub. Water is pouring out along its sides, spilling onto the tile.

I turn on the lights, and Jennie's eyes are closed. Her black silk nightgown ballooning around her body.

I push my hands into the ice-cold water and pull her up by her shoulders, lifting her until she's sitting up straight. Her eyes open and are fixed on me.

"Jennie!" I reach over to the faucet and turn off the water.

Jennie curls her fingers along the edges of the tub, leans her head back, and closes her eyes.

"What are you doing?" I demand to know.

"I'm trying to feel something."

"What you're feeling is utter madness, Jennie. Get out of there. It's freezing."

She smiles and opens her eyes. "I know what you're trying to do. There's no ignoring it. There's no assuming that the past will change. This is all that we have."

She grabs my hand, squeezing until I can feel the small bones in my palm crush into one another.

I shout at her to release her hold, and she does so with a laugh. I pull a towel down from the rack and lay it on the floor to soak up some of the water. "Get out of there," I plead until she stands up, still laughing.

The cold water cascades down all around her and splashes onto me. Her nightgown clings to her body. Her hair is pressed to the sides of her face and down her back.

"You messaged someone, didn't you?"

I look up, shocked. "Were you in my office?"

"Don't lie to me. Did you message someone?"

I am drying off her arms with the towel, furious that she's been looking through my things. "I thought you refused to enter my office."

"I do."

"How do you know, then?" I hold the towel back.

"The house told me," she says, her eyes darting from side to side.

I want to cry. I want to scream, but there's nothing I can do but tend to her as she comes undone. I fear she'll take me with her, also pulling me apart. I wonder for a moment if there's someone I can reach out to, but I know because of the situation we are in that no one can tend to Jennie's moods, because no one will ever understand the full weight she carries. Jennie has already endured enough, and there is no point in putting her, or myself, through any more unnecessary torment.

Jennie steps out of the tub, water continuing to drip all along the floor. No matter how quickly I pat her body dry, it feels like more water falls around me.

She stands in front of the sink and looks at her reflection in the mirror.

"There's so much that starts and stops without our consent," she says to her reflection. "We are pushed along by a great tide at all hours. The morning sun reminds us of all that's possible, but yet light brings with it the piercing pain that recalls what has been erased, denied, and stolen. There's some tragedy to that, isn't there? In a beginning that's possible only because of an end."

My clothes are wet. I am cold. I am tired. And I cannot comprehend the meaning of any of Jennie's words. I want to cry. I'm so exhausted, and I feel like in this moment of feeling so dejected, of having to pull my sister out from a full bathtub of freezing water, all I want and all I wish I had was someone to tell me I am going to be all right.

But there is no one here.

There has never been anyone, and I choke back bitter tears because of the anguish, because of the belief that there may never really and truly ever be anyone for me.

Jennie looks down at me, sitting on the bathroom floor. I've given up and allow the tears to consume me, because in this moment I believe I deserve to feel the intensity of my loneliness, to allow it to engulf me, like a tsunami.

"Oh, my poor, beautiful Anna." Jennie kneels and presses her palms against my cheeks. "My lovely sister. I do love you. I love you with all of my heart. My love for you is larger than a lake, larger than this river. My love for you is all of the oceans on this planet. My love for you is every raindrop that has ever touched the earth."

I sob, covering my face with the cold, wet towel.

Jennie throws her arms around me and hums that melody in my ear as she rocks me from side to side. That faraway melody I remember our grandmother singing so long ago.

"My dear, beautiful Anna. I'm so sorry. I'm so very, very sorry. I don't think I can stop it. I don't think it can stop," Jennie says.

Chapter 9

We have four dead. One unidentified body at the medical examiner's office and another young man who has just gone missing, Joshua Martin.

Our killer is operating with complete confidence.

I don't care what Sergeant Flanagan says—we've surpassed the suspicion point of a serial killer. They don't want to raise the alarm or notify the feds, and I don't care. I have a case to close.

I'm driving, and Rodriguez is flipping through some images we printed back at the office.

We have confirmed a spray-painted diamond at three recovery locations.

"What else you find in your research?" I ask.

"Not a lot of lucky people around the Great Lakes. Just last year there were over a hundred and five drownings, and forty-five of those were in Lake Michigan. The past year there were fifteen in Chicago waterways, mostly men."

"Ages?"

"Early twenties and thirties. Many also coming home from bars late at night."

My heart's pounding, and the last thing I need to do is give myself a heart attack before Mer and I get to retirement.

"How the hell did you all miss this?" Rodriguez asks.

I shake my head. "I got no clue. Martin and I were whipped up in some pretty bad cases there for a while. A guy gunning down his girlfriend because she tried to leave him. Another guy so high on meth, he carjacked three people in one night, killing two of them, driving one of their cars up to Grand Rapids. Another guy was so upset over what he was quoted for some drugs, he stabbed his dealer in the neck and dismembered the body in the apartment. A landlord goes missing and her neighbors call it in, and we find her body in a freezer. That doesn't even cover the gang assassinations we were on. It's been a hot few years in this city."

Still, I had heard about these cases from time to time. Someone being found in a waterway. We were told over and over: accidental drowning. That meant the investigation was closed, and so we didn't ask questions. We just kept moving.

There was always another case to work, and Flanagan kept me away from the Chicago River because of my history with it. Until recently. He figured this case would be quick and easy training for Rodriguez, until the paramedic told us at the bridge this was the fourth body fished out in a number of weeks.

"They're working faster—why? Are they getting desperate? Are they sending a message?" Rodriguez closes the folder on his lap.

Everything comes back to the water. What is so important about the river? That's their tool. It's not a gun or a knife. None of the bodies have any indications of trauma. "They're punishing their victim for something," I say.

"For what?" Rodriguez is now tapping a pen against his knee.

I've got a migraine, and I'm driving, and I don't trust Rodriguez to drive, so I just need to deal with it.

The answer, I think, is much simpler than either he or I think. "Existing. They're being punished for existing. Now that I think about it," I say, "our killer does take joy in this torture. They want their victims to feel desperate, to feel alone, to know that no help is coming."

We have a ticking clock. The killer is working toward something.

Maybe the city doesn't want to alarm the public or inspire any copy-cats. Fine, I get that. But calling these deaths "accidental drownings" is reckless. This city has an intimate relationship with serial murderers, so the likelihood that another one is operating here is not impossible.

Rodriguez is looking out the window. "We know they're at a club. How do we not know that their drinks have been drugged?"

I merge onto the 90, heading downtown. "There is no easy way to know. Not unless we get video footage to all of these bars and clubs and get a uniform to sit there and sift through all of those hours. GHB is only traceable in the urine twelve hours after being ingested. Up to seventy-two hours in the blood. Our killer knows water washes evidence away."

They always leave alone. They're never seen again. It's like they're completely disappearing right after they step out of whatever bar or club they're at. How is that possible? How is no one seeing them walk home?

"We haven't talked the 'M' word yet."

"Look at you," I say, "moving this case along all by yourself."

"Is that sarcasm?" Rodriguez asks.

"Little bit."

Motive. Lots of movies and cop shows tell us serial killers are often motivated by sex, but their killings are not always sexually based. They often kill because of thrill, financial gain, attention seeking, or simply anger.

"Our killer is mad about something. Don't know what it is. But they're mad as hell about something."

My phone rings and I answer. The speaker takes over. "Kowalski. We're on our way."

"I know that," Flanagan booms. "But we got a call from someone that was at a bar last night at River North insisting on talking to you two. Guy's got an interesting story. Check it out, and then meet me at the morgue."

"Got it."

We find Carl Keene standing outside Celeste. He doesn't notice our approach, as he's scrolling through his phone.

"Thank goodness," he says. His gaze flicks upward when we stop right in front of him. "It's freezing out here."

Again with the cold, like it's my fault or something.

I bite my tongue because I don't want this guy walking, so I play nice. "Detective Kowalski. This is Detective Rodriguez."

"Well, you and your partner took long enough."

I feel my face twist up as he says that, but it doesn't sound right to say Rodriguez isn't my partner. He's my trainee. I'm a rare one. I've had only one partner my whole career, and I'd like to keep it that way.

"Said you had some information?"

Carl's eyes widen, and he extends his hands. "I don't know why everybody isn't screaming about this. Why isn't this on the news?"

I pump my hand downward. We need him calm. "We'll make sure this information gets to the right people, and we'll investigate."

Rodriguez already has pen to pad in his hand, and I notice him eyeing the guy up and down, because you never know. You never know who you can trust, who's screwing with you.

"Last night, I get out of Celeste and I'm walking home alone and a van pulls up and a window rolls down and someone inside asked me if I wanted a ride."

I notice Rodriguez stops writing, looks to me and then back to Carl.

"This has now happened to me twice in the last six weeks. The first time was about three thirty in the morning when I was walking home from Gilt."

"Guilt?"

"Gilt. G. I. L. T."

"Yeah, ain't that something," I mutter.

"I don't drink . . ."

Both Rodriguez and I say "You don't drink?" at the same time and then look to one another. Look at us, slowly thinking the same. It'll never be like Martin and me. We were in sync with everything. It was like we had built this psychic connection over time.

Carl shoves his hands in his jacket pocket. "I don't drink . . ."

"Yeah, we got that," I say, and Carl continues.

"But I was walking home, and a van with a woman rolled up and was like, 'Hey, do you need a ride home?' And I was like, 'No, I'm good.' Like it was a beat-up white van. People are getting kidnapped. People are going missing. And it just happened to me again last night at quarter to ten in River North. I'm walking down Ohio Street, and it's well lit. I'm on the phone and a car crosses two lanes of traffic and I hear a woman ask me if I need a ride. People out here need to know not to get in cars with people you do not know. People need to not take free rides from strangers. I think this is some kinda connection to what's happening. They're probably just waiting for people who are drunk and it's an easy target. Like, we need people to stay safe out here."

Rodriguez and I stare at each other.

"Did you get any pictures of the vehicle?"

"No, I was freaking terrified."

I nod and ask him to repeat the streets he was walking down. We can check if there are any street cameras in the area that can help us identify the van.

"Did you get a look at the woman?" Rodriguez asks. "What she look like?"

He's shaking his head. His mouth is open, and the guy looks like he's in shock. "It was dark. I didn't really see her, but I heard her, and I was like, 'This is not okay right now.'"

"Was it the same vehicle, same woman each time?"

"Yes, both times, it was the same van. I feel like it was the same woman. I'm just going by her voice. I didn't even want to look inside the van. It felt wrong."

"Was the woman inside the vehicle by herself?"

"I couldn't tell. The windows were tinted, and I just didn't like anything about it. I didn't even like looking at it. The vibe. It felt off as hell."

Carl gives us his number, and we say we'll call if we need anything else. Back in the car, Rodriguez is rubbing the back of his head.

"I believe him."

I take a deep breath. "Yeah, I believe him too, but it's not illegal to offer someone a ride."

"It is illegal to dump someone in the river."

That was very true.

"Let's get to this autopsy, and next we gotta find this van."

Chapter 10

Of course, Peter replied.

He asked me questions about my podcast and Chicago history and where my love of ghost stories came from. Our emails were brief at first, but sweet with a touch of eagerness. Each time after I hit "Send," I'd worry that this would be the last time I would hear from him again. But each and every time there would be a reply waiting for me in my inbox, another message from Peter, with another question to me to keep the conversation moving and expanding. The lovely seeds of two people intently getting to know one another.

Our brief email exchanges soon morph into long, detailed accounts of our lives and interests. Soon thereafter we exchange phone numbers, and the messages move into blue-and-white bubbles on my phone.

Peter: Good morning. Are you still in bed?

Anna: Morning! Yes, it's seven am!

Peter: Did I wake you?

Anna: Yes, but that's OK. I need to take the dogs out.

Peter: My mother taught me that when I first wake up, before I do anything else, I should say 'Today is going to be a great day.' I think you should say that too.

Anna: Right now?

Peter: Yes, say it aloud to yourself and believe it, because it's true.

Anna: I just did! Now what?

Peter: Now, today is going to be a great day for both of us.

He told me about his work at the Aon Center, and of financial securities. He said I was more than welcome to meet him for coffee downtown during lunch hours, but I didn't yet feel comfortable leaving Jennie alone for longer than an hour.

Jennie paced the house and listened to the news on full volume, and when she wasn't watching it or repairing devices, she was playing music so loud that the notes vibrated within my very being. Sometimes I wondered if the music was coming from inside her. It was the nights that worried me the most. Those evenings when I would check Jennie's room and not find her there. She would return sometimes in the earliest hours of the morning, when the birds would begin their wake-up calls rousing the city from its bed. And there Jennie would be, standing just outside on our front porch, clutching more folded-up sheets of paper she had gathered on her walks and looking out over the neighborhood. Her face, so pale and consumed with a grief she refused to discuss, but I understood her pain. I worried for Jennie deeply—she was like a wounded bird who fell from a treetop, frightened and frustrated, yet always in danger of being further harmed, or destroyed by everything else around her.

Each time I'd tell her that she could talk to me and tell me what she was feeling, she'd turn to me, collapse in my arms, her face pressed into my shoulder. Her sobs uncontrollable. I understood that well of pain, because I too woke each morning searching for something.

I didn't know how much longer we could continue like this. Jennie slipping away into the night and early morning on her walks, returning home, and bringing greater grief with her, and both of us so miserable in this house. I didn't know if this was a way to live. She never seemed harmed or hurt.

After she'd wake, I'd ask her where she had been, and all she would tell me was that she was wandering our city and thinking about love, or a lack thereof.

"Did you know, dear sister," she told me this morning when she returned, "that a mermaid has no tears, and therefore she suffers so much more."

Every day I feared that Jennie would never return home, that she too would become like one of the people who had slipped between space and time, never to be seen again. When I warned her of the very real dangers of her walks, all she did was laugh and say, "Chicago cannot hurt me more than it already has."

There was nothing I could say to counter that. This was very true. Chicago represented the roots that fanned beneath the surface. We were not like the trees aboveground, our branches extending into the sky. Jennie and I were more like the soft lullaby of the waves of Lake Michigan crashing into the soft white sand, or like beautiful flowers that grew and bloomed underwater beside pliant stalks and leaves in the majestic sea.

Yet there is no separating us from our home or Chicago. We are tethered here in this place. We are eternally connected to this Second City.

These past few days I have been revitalized by communicating with a stranger. Even if his words are disingenuous, even if he is just messaging me because he feels pity for me—a silly, lonely girl—I do not care, because I need him. Maybe we are both using each other, and perhaps I am accepting of that. At this point in my existence, I sadly do not care why he is reaching out. I just need someone to reach out, someone to check in on me, someone to feign care, so that I can remember to take another inhale, so that I can remember to wake up in the morning. I need purpose, and I fear that without Peter to look forward to, I will follow Jennie's state, consumed by moods that could carry me through dark, deep currents.

I told Peter about Clover and Thistle and Jennie, but I kept the details about Jennie brief. Soon we became more comfortable with one another and began to have phone calls.

"The dogs, they're the sweetest little bundles. They are my little shadows, following me along wherever I go," I had told him over the phone.

"And Jennie . . . how is she? You said she isn't feeling well."

I took pause, because I didn't know yet how to describe Jennie to Peter. All I could say was, "She's getting better each day, but she's still not ready for company."

"Well, I'd love to meet her someday. She's important to you, and whatever is important to you is important to me."

I told him about Grandmother, the house, and my few interests: the podcast, antiques, the renovation work. I told him how I had become fairly proficient in removing old plaster and installing new drywall. I told him how I had painted the kitchen cabinets and installed new fixtures. I had just completed the update to the bathroom on the first floor and painted it. I also hung up a few prints throughout the house, I told him, photographs of the river, because the river was ultimately a part of me and therefore my greatest interest.

I finally told him about Mother and Father, and when I did, he said, "I'm so very, very sorry."

I told him that I didn't blame the river. I loved the river still, even though it had ripped my heart from me. The river still lived within me as I lived in it, and I would never blame it for my torment.

He asked why I hadn't spoken about them before, and all I said was that "sometimes we don't want to talk about our open wounds."

He went silent for some time, and I assumed he didn't want to speak with me any further. No one should be forced to look at our scars, but he texted me that evening.

We should go to the Chicago River Museum!

I . . . I start the message but then set my phone aside and rush to Jennie's room, because I need my sister right now.

I push open the door to her bedroom, and there she is at her work desk, plucking away at tiny metal parts, with a piercing desk lamp overhead. She steadily holds a small tool in her hand as she twists and adjusts delicate pieces with a soft clattering.

"I don't feel well," I moan, and for a moment my eyes, nostrils, and throat sting, as if I had accidentally swallowed chlorine water in a large swimming pool.

Jennie doesn't look up. She continues working. "Then you can lie on my bed," she says calmly.

I move over to her bed and lie down, staring up at the ceiling, hoping for the thoughts to slow, for the ache in my burning eyes, nose, and throat to dissipate. I listen to the steady clicking of pieces in Jennie's hands, and then it stops.

"You're getting too close to him. You don't know him. He doesn't know you. Neither of you owes the other anything."

"This is what I want."

Jennie laughs. "You want to fall in love. You want someone to love you. You believe that will heal you?"

"Isn't that what you want?" I shoot back.

"It's what I've always wanted, but . . . no one will ever love me the way I need to be loved, and that is the torture I live with every day, in knowing that the only thing I ever wanted is impossible. I exist knowing my loneliness is eternal."

I hear the snapping and clicking of pieces in her hands.

"What else is wrong with you?" Jennie asks. "Is it another one of your flickers?"

I sit up in the bed and stare at her. "What do you mean another one of my flickers? I never have any . . . flickers. What are those?"

Jennie huffs, raises her eyebrows, and then continues on with her work. Her focus remains on the tool in her hand and the device before her. "We each have attacks. In our own ways. We experience very different outcomes during a single event, but still, there's a residue there that remains. It's like that fine powder that sprang from the plaster walls as you were cutting away at the house. It sprays everywhere and coats everything, and no matter how hard and how long you clean, no matter how diligent and with all of the care in the world, there will still be fragments that remain. That is what seems to be happening with you right now. We both experience these fits, displaced and disjointed."

I am angry at her for making up such lies. "I don't believe you. I don't have any of these . . . flickers, as you call them, or fits."

She looks up from her work. A smile across her lips. "You don't? Then what upset you, and why are you in my room? Think about that carefully. We are tethered to the past. We are attached to that cord, and we can't step back from it, not completely. Certainly not you, my dear sister. Sometimes if you're not careful, if you lose your hold on the present, you'll slip back to that time. Be careful with your flickers, peering into that reality that upsets you so."

I open my mouth to say something, but I don't know what to say. I am confused as to what she speaks of.

Jennie waves a hand in the air, as if to dismiss me. "Don't worry. Your attacks are more infrequent than mine. You'll soon forget. You'll recover, and it will just be another day." She looks up and smiles a sad but pretty smile. "It will just be another day, of you and I in our house on the river."

I ignore her. This must be some sort of confusion, because I know I do not have the same affliction as my sister. I know I am not like her in that regard. I don't go wandering the city alone at night or in the early-morning hours, searching—always searching—for something she and I know does not exist for her out there. I don't lay in a bathtub of cold water. I don't do or say any of the peculiar things that Jennie does. I love my sister, and yes, we are similar in many, many ways, but my mind is not a crumbling haunted house like hers.

"What is it that you're fixing?" I ask.

"This is the nickel arm that supports the lid to an antique Pathe Freres oak wind-up record player. It was originally manufactured in 1915. The client needed this repair, which is fairly easy work for me. She sent me photographs of the cabinet. It's beautiful. Mahogany wood. It's in near-perfect condition. It's an honor to work on these machines."

Jennie brushes a strand of hair from her face. "What has your new friend told you?" she asks, but I know I can't tell her the truth. It would just upset her again. Since walking into her room, everything has gotten jumbled. I came here for help, and instead things just feel flipped and turned, but I suppose my worries have minimized—faded, actually. Now thinking about it, I can't even recall what it was that threw me into a state of worry and brought me here to Jennie's room. What had made me so fearful?

"He's told me about his job," I say, keeping it general, knowing that giving Jennie too much detail is never a good thing.

She glares at me. "Are you going to see him?"

I am not going to allow her to take this away from me, and she should at least start accepting it now, that I deserve my own happiness, even if it doesn't include her.

"I was thinking about it. Maybe not yet, but soon. I'd like to meet him for coffee. Downtown."

"Downtown?" She sounds utterly shocked. "You remember what happened downtown, don't you?"

"Of course, Jennie. You never allow me to forget, and maybe we should. Because when we forget, don't we feel much better? Don't we feel much more like ourselves? Isn't that what the point of life is? To feel good? To wake up in the morning and to be overcome with such a pure bright and intense joy that it illuminates our entire day?"

"The brighter one shines, the more shadows they cast," Jennie says. "And that's just the truth of that."

"We can't allow the claws of what happened to us to clamp down and pull us back in. What good does that do?"

She nods and returns to her tools. "Be careful what you tell your friend. You don't want to bring him into this."

Jennie continues tinkering, the light glistening off the metal in her hands as she delicately proceeds to polish it with a white cloth. "Not everyone is aware of the seriousness of their injuries," she says, "which I know it's surprising to say and believe. We move about the world, experiencing so much, absorbing all of this sensory input, but at the same time, are we really aware of what all of this living does to us? No, we have mechanisms within us, tiny little parts like these pieces I hold and polish in my hand that work at soothing our hearts, at clouding our minds, and shielding our bodies. Each day we move about the world and interact with our reality, we are at risk of being harmed. It can happen to us on an evening drive, or in the early hours standing on a bridge."

I sit up, stunned. "What are you talking about?"

"Nothing, my sweet sister. I'm just telling you that sometimes we cannot fully process the spectrum of pain, no matter the time. No matter the number of years. Be careful with your friend. Be cautious of what you tell him. Not everyone should live as you and I live, covered in a black veil of mourning."

"We shouldn't live like this," I say, but Jennie remains silent because there's no disagreeing with that point, and while we both agree that we should not live like this, we both know we have no choice but to be in this house, enveloped in agonizing loneliness.

I get up. "I feel better now," I say as I move for the door.

"Anna, I mean it," Jennie says, her eyebrows lifting. "Not everyone remembers, and forcing some people to remember will only tear a fabric into people's realities, and not everyone is prepared for that."

I return to my office, and I close the door. I didn't tell Jennie what I was researching for my next episode. I know it would upset her. I think it is best to no longer share with her any of the topics I have planned.

The research is overwhelming. The details are all heartbreaking, and I know that anything could send Jennie into a state from which she may never return, and I need her to hold on to this, to hold on to me.

What I also could not tell her about is all the research I am compiling about the river. So much more was happening there than we knew and believed.

What do you think? Peter texts again. **It's a small museum. Maybe we can meet there during lunch one day. I think you might enjoy it considering you love exploring Chicago history.**

The museum is housed in a five-story bridge house. While it seems like something I would enjoy, there is something within me that prefers another location for my first meeting with Peter. It is too soon to meet on the bridge and on the water. I would be too preoccupied with my own investigation, so I need something else.

I have another idea, I respond, to which he agrees. We would meet in a few days, finally, face-to-face.

I squeal with an intense delight. I have never known this feeling. Never known this joyous excitement. It feels so sweet and so kind. I have made a connection with someone.

The somber sounds quickly snatch away my excitement. I open the door to my office and look down the hallway, where Jennie is standing outside her room, with the door open.

A funeral song plays.

"He would have to love you more than his own mother and his own father and promise that love to you for eternity. That's the only way this will ever work. I know the tragedy of it all too well, and if he lies or if he loves another, then you will die. Maybe that's your story. Or maybe it's mine? Maybe we mirror one another in ways, and the only way to see this through is for us to make it to the end of this tale."

Jennie enters her room and slams the door shut.

I am awake early today. While I am still in bed, my phone alerts me to a new message with a ping.

It is from Peter.

I'm looking forward to our outing at the Union Stock Yard.

I am looking forward to it too, especially given that I've never been there. I have always been curious about the location and its history. It is one of those parts of the city I have always wanted to see but never dedicated time to visiting. It's also a portion of this town that's been torn down and forgotten. That's one sad thing about Chicago—it's a city that prides itself so much on its history but very often silently tears it down. I feel guilty, in a way. I pride myself in knowing and sharing the complex history of our city but have yet to tell my listeners about the stockyards. Thousands of people, all immigrants, toiled there, in the frigid winters, in the steaming summers, and all covered in blood, overwhelmed by the stench of rot and decay.

What are you doing this morning? Peter asks.

Research, I respond.

When he asks if it is research for an upcoming podcast, I look at my notes about the missing men in the river. Four had gone missing. Three had been found. I respond to Peter with a lie. **Yes, I'm researching my next original episode.**

What I am really researching is the movements of a killer who moves about our city.

Chapter 11

I set about walking the dogs and cleaning the house, and then I sit down at the counter with my tea and laptop. I listen, expecting to hear Jennie stir upstairs, but there is nothing. No noise. Not even any familiar moans and groans of the house settling or that mysterious drip that has plagued me for so long.

Turning to my computer, I begin my search. A single river, strewn with tragedy. In any given year, there are, on average, sixty to seventy drownings in all of the bodies of water in the city, but this also includes indoor cases. Most people drown because they cannot swim. In thinking of the people who have recently been pulled out of the river, I imagine there's the possibility that some intentionally jumped into the water. I could even believe that maybe some fell in accidentally, but for most, I imagine someone else was involved. A push, a struggle, something more?

The news has told us so little—someone went missing, and then they were found in the water. Not much else is known about the missing people. I'm afraid. I fear living on the river, I fear my sister being outside walking along the riverfront late at night and sometimes in the morning. Something is happening out there, and I fear she could walk right into it.

Four dead men, and now another one missing. Joshua Martin. I think about Joshua's family, how they must be plagued with the torture of not knowing where he is. I imagine he had parents and siblings, and all of them probably walked the same path he walked last, called all of his friends, scoured his home for clues, and then repeated their steps. I wonder if any of them thought of the river, and how other men had been located there. I wonder if any of them approached any of those bridges, peered over the side, and looked at the water, both desperate and reluctant to find him floating there.

I love the river, yet I know what it can take. I know the very real threat it poses, especially to my Jennie. Yes, Jennie knows how to swim, but not well. I remember our very first day of swim lessons when we were little girls. Jennie refused to enter the pool. Grandmother approached and asked her what was the matter, and Jennie said she was scared of getting in the water.

"But why?" Grandmother asked. "The temperature of the water is comfortable. The water is clean, plus I am here, as is your instructor. You will be safe."

Jennie shouted at Grandmother, and that was the first and only time she'd ever done so. She asked, "How do you know? How can anyone know? What if I go into the water and get sucked down deep? What if no matter how hard I swim or how hard everyone tries, I will not be able to be saved?"

What very little I have been able to piece together from the news is that none of the bodies showed signs of struggle or injury. I wonder, however, how accurate this is. I know very well that the water washes so much away, making things that once were full and whole and beautiful, with all the promise of a new moon, devastatingly unrecognizable.

I think of the victims, those people who existed now in old news-clips and faded missing persons posters or positioned front and center on side tables in gilded picture frames in the homes of those who once loved them. What exists beyond a picture, a few words, and the hurt in the hearts of those who experienced that loss? The dead died, yes, but it's the living who will suffer their loss after their death. It's a long and prolonged anguish to exist knowing that not only are our loved ones dead but that their last moments were those of terror, and sometimes all alone.

It all makes me wonder, Is someone else involved? Is that person then pushing these people into the water? It is nearly impossible for me to place my mind in the position of why someone would do this, because I could never imagine harming someone. It is grueling, then, to think that there are people in the world who obtain joy from not only inflicting cruelty but serving death.

I do not believe these drownings are accidental. I have no evidence, of course, but I live on the river, and I know how people move along it. I've never known this many deaths to happen in the water within such a short time.

I fear that these people knew exactly what was happening to them as they tumbled from the street level above, that they knew they were going to die. What's even more strange is that so many people do know how to swim, and yet not a single victim was known to have swum to the edges of the water, lifting themselves up onto the banks or hoisting themselves up above a concrete barrier to safety. The river is murky and foul in parts, but still, were they just overwhelmed with shock that they weren't able to paddle, float, or call for help?

These aren't accidents. There is a murderer lurking in our city along the river. I continue searching and clicking, and it doesn't take long before I also learn that there is a great misconception, the belief that only men have drowned in the river recently under strange conditions. I find that last year the bodies of three drowned women were found. One was found near North Riverside Plaza, another near the West Loop, and the third at South Eleanor in Bridgeport. The news article ends with:

This is a developing story and will be updated when more information becomes available.

I search again and again for "Chicago drownings," and the tragic headlines seem endless.

> Two drowned in Chicago River identified
>
> Body of 23-year-old who vanished after night out found in Chicago River
>
> Bodies have been washing up on Lake Michigan and river shores
>
> 4th body pulled from Chicago waters in less than a week
>
> Missing man's body recovered from Monroe Harbor
>
> Missing Lake View man found in Chicago River died from drowning

How was I unaware of all this for such a long time? I wonder. I take a deep breath and exhale, knowing that the only reason I care, the only reason I notice now, is because of all that the river has taken away from me.

I check today's date on my phone and remember it's time to check in with the detectives to see if they've heard anything new.

The news blares from Jennie's room down the hall. The alert of a breaking report.

"They've found another body!" Jennie shouts. "Another man floating in the river!"

"What?" I stand. Is this Joshua Martin? I wonder.

The house begins to moan. Floorboards above me creak and scratch against one another. I hear the thud of heavy footsteps moving from room to room. The beams of the house squeal under its shifting weight. I imagine them swaying, like the great limbs of the Giant in "Jack and the Beanstalk." What very few people realize is that the giant actually had a name, Blunderbore, which appears in the eighteenth-century version of the story, "Jack and the Giant Killer." I always wondered, then, why his name was excluded from the popular text and film versions of the children's stories. Was there fear that if people knew his name and thought it or said it aloud that they could give this tale power? That uttering his name could make him materialize in the physical world, playing out his story among mortals?

I run out of my office and down the hall, searching for Jennie. I peer into her room, but she is not there. I run down the stairs. The sun is setting, casting an orange glow over the sofa and chairs, dining table, and the island in the kitchen.

"Jennie!" I shout, above all of the noise, the shrieking and groaning and screams, the sounds of hundreds of people in pain, all coming from inside this house.

Clover and Thistle find me in the kitchen, their tails wagging, their little heads darting here and there, searching for the source of the commotion, but it is everywhere and yet nowhere. I scoop them up as I hear crashing overhead. I rush to my room and lock the door and set the dogs on the floor. They shove their snouts at the space beneath the floor and the door and yip and whine and bark.

I hear Jennie scream, just beyond the door. I try to open it, but it does not budge.

"Jennie!" I shout again, twisting and turning the doorknob, but it does not move. Her screams and cries grow louder. I pound at the door with my fists, cursing the specters of a past that torment me.

"Jennie! What's happening?" We hear voices now, and they sound as if they are coming from all directions—the living room

115

and kitchen, the stairway and the other sealed-off room upstairs. I pull at the door, but it's locked. I collapse and cry at the floor. I beg for Jennie to please be all right. I beg for her to just come to me, to hold me, to tell me that she loves me and that this all is a misunderstanding, that we aren't really experiencing a haunted house. This must all be a cosmic misunderstanding from the fates and the stars. My chest tightens, and I miss my mother and I miss my father, and I miss Jennie so devastatingly much. Even though she is just outside, I need her to find me.

I beg for someone, anyone, to help me navigate this great tide of grief and how far off course I have found myself in life.

I hear an eruption of sparkling laughter, of two little girls, and then I hear their feet running across the hall and stomping down the stairs. Their laughs are like fireflies, cheery points of light in the darkness that prove to us that magic is real.

I look to the window, and the golden setting sun has shifted to twilight, all in an instant.

The walls shake, as if we ourselves are being lifted up by that Giant from that children's story whose name has been largely erased by history. We forget things, and in the forgetting we believe that we will be healed, but we're not. The wound only continues to ache, and soon the infection spreads and soon the pain is a great storm, and it becomes difficult to know what is here and what is now.

I hear the framed picture of the house taken from the Sears catalog slip off the wall. I hear the sound of glass shattering and scattering across the floor.

There is nothing I can do. I am trapped. I rush to my bed and pull the covers over me. The dogs follow, shoving themselves beneath the blankets and resting at my feet. I close my eyes as laughter from those phantom little girls roars all around us.

The door creaks open and immediately slams shut.

"Anna!" Jennie joins me in bed, finding sanctuary under the covers with me. She presses her cheek to mine. It's cold as ice. Her face is wet with tears. Her entire body is shaking.

"It's all growing so intense," she says as her teeth chatter. "I feel like the house wants to consume us, Anna!" she cries into my arm. Or maybe it just wants me? Maybe it just wants to swallow me up.

We fall asleep that way, in a state of trembling, cheeks wet with tears and unsure if this will ever cease. Snippets of a dream come to me in that exhaustion, and even stitched together the sequences don't make sense.

Our city skyline—black, silver, and gray towers sewn across a red sky. The next dream sequence finds me outside a giant sandcastle with a large garden and fire-red and dark-blue trees, where fruit glimmers gold on their branches and flowers pulsate like flames, with their petals swaying. There is a flash, then, at the next dream scene: an eruption of bubbling mud in a land where no gardens grow. Water swirls around like roaring windmills, sucking down anything in its way, fragments of seaweed, grains of sand, and little tiny fish that strain to flap their fins to escape the vortex, but it is too late. They draw too near. The next flash is a house beyond a strange forest, surrounded by plants that look like snakes that stretch and squirm. These monstrous polyps have heads and eyes, and lips that are turned down in a grim frown. The final flash of my nightmare introduces me to her: a tall woman with long red hair that falls down her back in waves. Her eyes are wide and wild. Her expressionless face is severe with all of its angles, and on each one of her shoulders squirms and slithers a great snake with a beige-and-green pattern. She extends a hand to me, and in her palm is a toad. She raises her other hand, and in it she holds a knife.

"I know what you want," she says, and her voice is a siren's song.

Chapter 12

In the morning I wake, and Jennie is gone.

The dogs are at the door, wagging their tails, happy to see me. I kneel and kiss Clover and Thistle on top of their heads. I look into their eyes and tell them each how much I love them.

I inspect the house, and nothing is disturbed or moved out of place except for the framed picture of our house. Jennie had replaced it with a new frame. I find the old frame and the broken glass in the trash. There's something curious about the wall where the framed picture of our home hangs; beside it there's a nail and a sun-faded square, where another picture presumably once hung, but I can't recall anything ever being there other than this print from the Sears catalog of our house's original design. I place my finger on the wall, running it along those four lines, those impressions of something that was once there that I do not remember. Another picture? Of what? Of whom? Something forgotten.

I visit the river, as I'm always searching and hoping. Clover and Thistle follow closely. I pause and peer at the water carefully, hoping, wondering, and waiting.

At my fairy garden I stop myself from making a wish, from wishing I knew all of the depths of Jennie's thoughts and actions. Perhaps I will do that another day. I want to do all that I can to keep her from being afraid, but I'm not sure how long I can hold this back. For now, I will continue to keep those truths bottled up, bobbing along the great ocean of her agony.

In the house, I dust, sweep, mop, wash the windows, and polish the wood, covering every spot from kitchen to living room to bathrooms and bedrooms until the house is left glistening and smelling of sweet and delicate lavender and sharp and bright lemon. I shower and dress, and then I take the dogs down to the river once more for a quick walk before lunch. I stand at the river's edge, feeling silly and hopeless, but still, I speak to the water.

"Help me find her . . . them."

I close my eyes and listen, hoping to hear the whispers of my fairy carried along the midwestern wind, but I only hear the rise and fall of sirens in the distance.

Inside the house, I find Jennie standing in the living room.

"Where have you been?" I demand to know.

"The house is alive," Jennie says. Her eyes are colorless and distant, as if peering into a black lagoon. "And I realize now that I am alive because of it."

I know my sister is deteriorating, and I worry there isn't much I can do other than to keep her safe from the outside.

"Did you just get home?" I look down at her feet, and she's barefoot. Wet footprints are stamped into the floor from the entrance to where she stands.

Before I can say anything, she says, "It was raining."

"No it wasn't," I say, annoyed. "Why are you lying to me?" I walk right over to the front door, open it, and am frozen. A light drizzle falls from the heavens. Just moments ago it was a sunny spring day.

My head begins to ache.

Jennie smiles. "As Grandmother used to say, all that we can do is ignore the noises the house makes. These voices, they cannot hurt us.

"There was a woman today, standing at the boat landing at Clark Park. She was very peculiar looking, peculiar in that way extremely beautiful women look, as if they've just stepped out of a painting or a story. She had on a green dress with silver buttons. She was watching the geese float along, and when I approached her, she turned to me and her eyes were a stunning aquamarine. When she spoke, her voice was like a balm on my heart, but her words . . . were spiked with menace. She told me an awful thing and laughed when I walked away. She said she knew I'd return, and I did not like that. I did not like that at all."

The walk to Clark Park one way was easily an hour. Jennie must be tired, and I beg for her to go upstairs and get some rest. I fear she is confused and not sure of what she is speaking.

"I assure you," Jennie shouts, "there was a woman with red hair dressed in green out on the river who told me she liked to visit during the early-morning hours to see if she could spot the bodies of dead men."

I feel the blood rush from my cheeks. "I do not feel comfortable with you outside so early, especially speaking with strangers. You can't trust these people. We don't know what's happening out there. What if the woman in green is the murderer?"

"Why do you suspect there even is a murderer? What if these are just accidents? Men losing their footing across the bridge."

The frequency with which men went missing in this city and turned up drowned in the river was not indicative of accidents.

"Do not go back to Clark Park," I say firmly.

Jennie laughs to herself. "You don't have to worry about me, my sister. You never have to worry about me or my safety. I will always remain unharmed, and I will always return home to our house on the river. This is our sea castle, and I will never leave it, or you."

There is a *thlunk* sound.

Thlunk. Thlunk. Thlunk.

The dripping has returned.

Some days living in this house feels as if I am on a long free dive, a diver who stays underwater for an extended period of time. Scuba divers are trained to never hold their breath underwater because of the risk of lung overexpansion. Free divers, however, hold their breath on the entire dive, not dependent on any equipment, including a wetsuit or fins. What distinguishes the free diver from the scuba diver is that free divers push themselves to mental, emotional, and physical limits—all in an effort to explore the underwater world, connecting with marine animals and the ocean.

Here I am, holding my breath, surrounded by a great blue world, unsure how much more time I have before I am forced to come up for air.

Jennie wrings her hands. "I'm afraid we will not be able to ignore it for long. The activity is growing constant. The mornings. The afternoons. The evenings and late nights. The times of day are all awash. A watercolor. They awaken me at all hours. I hear them whisper sweet and horrific things in my ear about how everything is going to be changed."

"I'm worried about you. I'm worried about us," I say. It feels like the delicate line of our private world is slowing being sealed off. Jennie lives her reality, and I live mine, and it is as if neither of us can fully see the other, as if a layer of dreamy sheer chiffon exists between the two of us.

"Everything in me just feels as if it's burning so bright, but yet it's so dark, my Anna. All I want to do is take a deep breath, but I can't. So then I walk, and I think of all the precious things that float and sink, of bodies and bones, and of the silent dead, of charms and clocks, chambers and wells, and I think, in all of these jumbled thoughts, all that I want is to feel a real lover's kiss. All I want is to wake and emerge and wash off this tragedy, and the only thing that can grant me that relief is a love, of which I do not have."

I choke back tears because I feel as if my own sister is evaporating before me. "What are you talking about? I love you! I have always loved you. After Grandmother's death, I had you. After Mother's and Father's deaths, all I had was you. You are my world. You are the reason I can awake in the morning and feel as though I'm fully formed. My everyday thoughts drift to you: How is my sister doing? Is she thinking of me? Does she miss me as much as I miss her? All I hope and pray is for you to feel my love so that you can come home to me."

I step forward to take her hand, but she pulls back. "Then tell me, please, what is wrong. How can I help you?" I ask.

Jennie closes her eyes and shakes her head slowly. "The woman at the river, she's dangerous. She's wicked and cruel."

"What do you mean?"

My mind screams at me that this woman knows something. She must. Why did she say such awful things to my sister? I make a note that Jennie said the woman likes to visit Clark Park in the early-morning hours. I decide then that I must go to the park and observe this stranger. What is she doing? What is she waiting for? She must know something, especially if she is at the river each and every morning.

Jennie opens her eyes and waves me off.

"Please," I beg her, "in order to heal you, I must first know what makes you suffer."

The television turns on by itself, and it's on the news again: a recap of what played out recently.

A dead man in the water.

Jennie steps forward. "Do you know . . ."

She looks so pale today, my beautiful sister. The cold spring rain did not do her well. I just want to hold her, but all she'll do is turn away from me.

She continues: "No one lives forever. Drowned men from shipwrecks arrive as dead men to the Sea King's castle."

I don't understand what she means. It's another riddle. Another fable. Another children's story. Another lullaby. Another warning about the water.

Some days I feel as though I'm losing my grasp on her, and today it is a foghorn blasting through the pitch-black expanse. Sometimes at night, when I'm working late in my office and she's pacing the hallway and walks past my door, there are moments when I catch a glimpse of her face, and she looks like a stranger to me.

Jennie's eyes flash to the screen. "It's sad, isn't it? How many people die by drowning in this city? I wonder if they had just made the right choice, stayed home, turned down another street, or uttered the right words, would they still be alive? Everything is chance. A choice. Isn't it? A single decision can change the course of your history."

I reach for the remote control and lower the volume and turn to Jennie.

It was as if my sister's words activated some energy within the walls. In all of my time in this house, we always interpreted these settlings— the noises and knocks, the rumbles and footsteps—as a ghost, but after last night, I was starting to believe that perhaps it was something else.

A poltergeist is believed to be energy that a living person unknowingly controls. A poltergeist often makes itself known by objects in a home being moved, spun, thrown, or influenced somehow. A ghost can be seen, while a poltergeist cannot. A ghost is a person linked to the world of the living, while a poltergeist is often thought of as a manifestation of negative energy, building up over time, not necessarily linked to a place or any location, really, but to a person or persons. It's just energy in a boiling pot, rising to the rim, ready to spill over and scald someone if they're too near.

"Last night when you said they had found a body floating in the river, that's when all of the activity stirred in the house," I say, but Jennie ignores me.

I ask another question that has been plaguing me, hoping she will answer. "Are you . . . happy they died?"

Her eyes set ablaze. "No! Of course not!" She turns her face back to the screen. "I just wish . . . it all had turned out differently. A different hope. A different life. We were waiting for the wrong ship, standing at the wrong port."

We turn back to the television screen and watch as the reporters say very little. Once again, offering only that the police are "investigating." In some ways, I know that wounded word too well, investigating, and all of the anxieties it carries, like launching a paper boat into a pond—you know it's in movement, but only for so long.

"Did they provide the cause of death?" I ask, but I already know the answer.

"Isn't that obvious? Still, if there were outside forces—a strike, a drug, something else—being submerged in water for days and days makes it difficult to tell the true cause of death. The water flushes away evidence, unless of course there's excessive trauma to the body, deep gashes, cuts, bruises, or missing limbs. The killer enjoys them drowning for so many reasons, but mainly because the water carries away so many secrets."

I hear whispers just outside the front door.

"Jennie . . . the doorknob is turning."

"I guess it's as you said, Anna. We have to learn to live with it. We have to learn to ignore it, to pay it no mind. It's a house that lives, and we must accept that this is what we are destined to feel and experience."

We are both quiet.

She takes my hand in hers, and we hear the front door open and close and what sounds like a single set of footsteps walk up the stairs.

I hear a great wailing from the second floor, a deep ravine of hurt and loss—an unending, low, and enveloping cry as if all joy has been drained of this world.

Neither of us acknowledges these movements. As Jennie says, and as I tragically realize, there is no stopping this.

Jennie turns to me, her eyes—two points of a beautiful oblivion reading me, knowing me—really knowing everything about me, my wants and desires. She points to the umbrella stand beside the door.

"If you're leaving to meet with him, you should take the umbrella with you, and be prepared for all that you will welcome into this house. It's going to rain."

Chapter 13

"I hear this is where the tour starts," Peter says.

His eyes look like they're made of electrifying green uranium glass, and his hair looks like it was touched by the Iroquois Theatre fire. He reaches out his hand, as do I. We both must equally feel the gesture weak, because when our hands touch, a quiet passes over us, not as if time has slowed but as if time just knows.

When I looked into his eyes, it was as I had told Jennie so long ago when we were younger. It didn't take a minute or more. It didn't take a second or less. All it took was a single look into his eyes, and I knew I loved him, and I felt that he could love me too.

I'm glad I found him so quickly. I had rushed out of the house in such a haze of nerves that I left my phone behind.

"I'm sorry if you tried messaging or calling. I forgot my phone."

"You said you'd be here, and I believed you, and so I'm here."

I know him. He knows me. Yes, our bond grows with each letter and sentence appearing on a screen and in our phone calls, but we have grown to know each other so well in such a short time. I know that beautiful face that makes me blush. I know that soothing voice that makes my entire being vibrate. When I look into his eyes, hypnotized by the rich color of moss that grows in the shade, I feel a calm I have never known. And when he finally wraps his arms around me, I breathe in deep and close my eyes. I just want to linger here, in his embrace, and dissolve into a million pieces with him.

This isn't déjà vu. I have never been in Peter's presence before, but I feel as if I know him with my entire being. This also isn't jamais vu, the phenomenon of knowing the person, situation, or thing and yet it seeming unfamiliar, because I believe he would have mentioned it.

If it isn't déjà vu and it isn't jamais vu, perhaps instead our meeting brushes on presque vu. Presque vu is that overwhelming feeling we have when we know that we know something but just can't grasp it. That thing hangs there in the air floating alongside all of those wonderful molecules that help us breathe. Yet we struggle with that tip-of-the-tongue feeling, knowing that the revelation is within reach, but just not quite.

We both know.

We had to.

A raindrop falls on my cheek. I peer up to the dreary sheet of gray stretching above us. Thanks to Jennie and her obsession with following the news, she warned me that it was going to rain, and so I brought my umbrella.

"Don't say it," he says.

My face feels hot. "Don't say what?"

"Don't say it's going to rain. Just say like we've said before, 'It's going to be a good day.' If you say it's going to be a good day, then it will be and we'll go on. Say it."

I laugh, feeling silly, and then I'm embarrassed because I laughed, but I say it anyway. "It's going to be a good day."

He smiles. "And so you have your wish, Anna. Is this all right with you?" He motions to my elbow, and I nod as he hooks his arm with mine and we walk toward the historic marker together. It is the first time any man has ever walked with me like this, and for a moment I feel sad that it has taken so long for us to find each other.

The rain is more a fine mist, not enough to soak us through, but enough to notice. "We can share mine," I say, referring to the umbrella. I hand it to him, and he opens it and holds it above our heads with his free hand.

I can tell he's fighting back a smile, as am I. "Thank you very much for your kindness, Anna."

And there he says my name again. I can listen to his voice all day. I can listen to his voice forever.

We approach and stand quiet at the entrance of the former meat-packing hub that made Chicago the hog butcher of the world. Today, all that remains are the limestone gates, a reminder of all the people who once worked here and the industry served.

All of the structures that once made up the 320 acres of the Union Stock Yard were demolished long ago. Directly above in the center of the gate is the bust of Sherman, a prize-winning steer, who welcomes us to step into a world that no longer exists.

It is difficult to imagine that the land before us was once occupied by hundreds of people prepping, slaughtering, and processing animals. Millions of livestock were butchered at the stockyards each year during the height of its operation—cattle, hogs, sheep, and more. At one point, nearly all of the meat consumed in the country was processed here in Chicago, and at this very spot.

The Union Stock Yard was a city within a city, spanning nearly four hundred acres. Hundreds and hundreds of livestock pens housed animals that would then be slaughtered, cleaned, and cut into pieces for consumption. In addition to the actual stockyards, entire businesses and industries had sprung up around the stockyards to support its employees, including hotels, brothels, restaurants, saloons, and various merchants.

When immigrants came to Chicago, many found work in the Union Stock Yard. It wasn't glamorous work. It was dangerous, blood-stained employment.

Today, only this small patch of land remains to tell the living about the industry and death that once happened here.

"Peak production was around the 1920s," I say, "and yes, this really was the meat-processing plant of the world, with Chicago processing more meat than any other place on the planet for a short period of time. It was all done here, from right in the city center. It was a part of this city's history, and like much of Chicago's past, this is forgotten."

"Are the Union Stock Yards the reason you've taken a break from your podcast?" Peter asks.

"No, I'm researching another tragic event in the city's history that's associated with a lot of hauntings—hauntings in houses, hauntings in public spaces—but I will cover the Union Stock Yard soon," I say.

It's quiet here tonight, but decades and decades ago, the sounds must have been deafening. A great cacophony of chopping, slicing, cutting—all punctuated by the shrieks of animals being wrangled and killed.

Peter points to the inscription across the gate that reads:

UNION STOCK YARD CHARTERED 1865

He says, "I didn't think the act of processing and packaging meat could be so important to this town."

"Right, it sounds silly to say, but it was a part of this city's culture for a long time. Immigrants from all over the world came to live and work in Chicago, and many of them started their lives in America right here. The stockyards opened Christmas Day in 1865 and closed in 1971. The meat industry decentralized with advances in technology."

Peter scans the area before turning back to me. A smile crosses his lips. He lowers his voice. "Is it true, then?"

I nod, because I know that while people sometimes like to hear the history of these purported haunted places—the types of places you drive out to, pay a few dollars for a walking tour of—what people really want to know is: Do ghosts exist?

People want to hear accounts of the grim and unbearable things that happened that would later go on to become urban legend and lore, the awful, creeping things that adults whispered about and warned their children to avoid. Yes, many of us are guilty of wanting to know all of the gory details. For centuries, audiences have gathered at the gallows to view people's misery and destruction, and our obsession with pain, misery, and death today is no different. People often bask in the suffering of others, knowing that this suffering is not their own. Even something as commonplace as a funeral—yes, people will show up, pay their condolences, and leave, but how often do they check in with those living whose lives have been forever altered by their great loss? Rarely.

"It's true," I say. "Many people claim to hear the squealing of pigs or cows, goats or chickens, being slaughtered to this day, coming from this area. It's been described as utterly piercing. There are rumors that emergency services have been called for wellness checks in the area, searching for any sounds that may lead to anyone who may be housing a number of animals in less-than-ideal conditions." What's funny is that in Chicago, people can legally own sheep, cows, donkeys, pigs, and goats, and also house horses. The only animals that require registration are working horses, bees, and dogs. I suppose being able to own livestock comes back to this, our history here with the stockyards.

I look around the now-empty lot, imagining it bustling with thousands of workers, stations for processing, and the sights and smells of animals. And how Chicago's meatpackers worked all along the South Branch, with their own workers purchasing animals at the stockyards and bringing them back to their plants. The development of refrigeration did away with some of the area's character, but still, some grisly elements of this part of Chicago's history remained.

The rain stops almost as soon as it started, and Peter closes the umbrella.

"That's completely awful," Peter says, and then raises an eyebrow. "Maybe we can try to see if we hear them."

"What?" I laugh to myself, a nervous laugh, and Peter reaches out his hand.

I look at his hand and then give him mine.

"Trust me?"

Of course, I trust him. I trusted him from the moment I read his very first email to me. I felt his energy in those words.

I nod, and Peter takes my other hand in his and we stand there, eyes closed and listening, trying to find something paranormal, otherworldly perhaps, within the layers of a regular Sunday afternoon in the city, but all I can hear is the steady drone of the living—the sounds of cars driving past, police sirens, music blaring from nearby apartments, and people speaking into cell phones as they walk by.

"I don't hear anything," I say as I open my eyes.

Peter's eyes remain closed. "I hear something." His face lights up.

"You do?" I strain to listen but hear nothing beyond the normal city noises. "What is it?"

He opens his eyes. "I won't tell you. At least not yet."

We continue our walk around the small square, and I tell him more about the history and the people that worked here. After a few minutes, he calls a car to take us two miles to the next location of our tour. We don't speak much during the drive, as it feels strange to talk to Peter about ghosts and this haunted city with a stranger so near. Plus, the quiet gives me some time to gather my thoughts as we approach an infamous former dumping ground—the river of blood, as it has been called in the past.

When we arrive at an industrial intersection, the driver stops the car, looks out the window, and says, "This is such an eerie place." Then he looks in the rearview mirror, his gaze darting from Peter to me, and then says, "Be careful. There's been a lot of strange things happening around the river."

It is as I imagined the South Fork of the South Branch of the Chicago River to look.

It is a miserable little creek.

"This is where they dumped the bodies," I say. "It was quite a noxious place for a long time. Whatever parts of the butchered animals from the Union Stock Yard that could not be sold for use or consumption, all manner of fur, bones, beaks, and entrails, were dumped here. This section overflowed with so much blood and guts that the offal converted to methane and would—"

"Bubble," Peter says as he shoves his hands in his jacket pockets. "It's really quite sad, isn't it?"

"It is, and there you have it, Bubbly Creek, and why this area of the river acquired that illustrious name. It was the decomposition of the bodies of millions of animal remains over time that would contribute to the bubbling of the river here, and the horrid and fetid stench."

I think at this moment that this is probably the only time someone has uttered the phrase "horrid and fetid" on a date.

"You need the living to erase the suffering of the dead," Peter says, and I agree.

We speak of decomposition, of waste, and of the poor immigrants who once lived along this part of the city, and how it was not just them but a vast portion of Chicago that could not escape the smell of death and decomposition. The stench of rotting meat blanketed this town. It traveled along the river, fanning out throughout the greater Chicagoland area. After the stockyards closed and all dumping ceased, and even after the city had tried to revitalize the water, incorporating all manner of cleaning and filtration systems, the environmental damage that had been caused was too prolonged and too great and too deep for time to erase what had been done.

Before we leave, we stand there for a moment, looking over the river. I imagine what Peter sees is a still, dark-green liquid, with miserable-looking shrubs and dead trees with their gnarled and knobbly twisting branches stretched along the banks.

What I see is more gruesome: a chunky soup of butchered and mashed animal parts. White rib cages with glistening strips of cartilage still attached. Emaciated feral dogs, with bloody snouts and tangled hair, who gnaw on large leg bones. Pigeons that peck into the sockets of cow skulls. In the water, large eyeballs float, still attached to stringy, meaty parts. It is indeed a river of blood, layered in stretches of honey-comb beef stomach linings, strips of torn green-and-black rotting flesh, and severed hooves.

I feel a tug within me. I want to dip into that vat of wasted and rotting things, dead fish, and hacked-up cattle, lamb, and goat parts. I want to lay my head back, open my mouth, and allow the clumps of fat and tough pieces of tissue, teeth, and hair to fill my mouth. I want to taste it all, chew, and choke it back.

Peter reaches for my hand, and I'm back. Transported here.

A raindrop falls on the tip of my nose.

Dark clouds are blowing in from the west. "I suppose we should walk back now," Peter says.

"You're right. It's getting late."

We stand there, unmoving.

Peter's voice is steady. "Are you not afraid of meeting with a stranger, especially along the river, considering so many people have gone missing lately? Or"—he looks back out toward the water—"have been found in the river?"

It's funny how I never considered my own safety. Up until this moment, I had only really worried about Jennie.

"Why, are you the River Killer?"

Peter laughs. "Is that what they're saying? There is definitely a killer and they're calling them the River Killer?"

"One of the family members who was interviewed on the news said it must be a killer, the River Killer, because everyone who has been found in the river went missing around it, not exactly in the very location where they went missing. I assume they went in the water at one place and the river carried them elsewhere, as it does. It's been so many people, we can only assume there is a killer."

Peter takes a step forward. He is inches from me, and I can feel him. There is heat radiating between us. I feel his energy blanketing me, and I like it. I want him closer still.

"Do you think I'm a killer?" he asks.

"Do you think I'm the River Killer?" I counter.

He smiles and looks away. "Interesting, I suppose it is mostly men disappearing and being in the water. I didn't consider my own safety."

I answer his question. "No, I don't think you're the River Killer. I don't think you could ever hurt anyone, Mr. Peter Boyle."

"I'm glad you believe I'm gentle and kind, Anna. I feel the same about you. I don't think you could ever hurt anyone."

We walk back the nearly two miles to where Peter parked his car. He tells me he lives here alone. His job transferred him from Ireland to Chicago after he put in the request. He wanted to live in America and experience it. He says it's a beautiful city but that he feels dreadfully alone in this town of millions, and he fills that loneliness with reading.

When I ask him what he's reading, his answer doesn't quite surprise me, considering his interest in history. He had gone straight to all of the Chicago greats: *The Jungle* by Upton Sinclair, *Native Son* by Richard Wright, *Twenty Years at Hull House* by Jane Addams, *The Death of the Detective* by Mark Smith, *Chicago: City on the Make* by Nelson Algren, and more. Peter was reading through every Chicago classic that praised this city's grittiness and beauty.

"Can we hang out again tomorrow?" he asks.

Before I can consider the logistics and, of course, Jennie, I agree. I cannot allow myself to sink any further into Jennie's dark hole. I had found a glint of happiness in a life that had known very little, and I want to hold on to it, foster it, so that hopefully it could remain steady—something to look forward to in my somber days, and maybe this joy could be something that grew ever more so.

He looks to the sky and then into my eyes and says, "But there's one problem."

"What's that?"

"I feel like if I see you again the next day, I'm going to want to see you the next and the next."

I laugh. I want to say, "And that's a problem?" Because this is exactly how I want him to feel, because it's the way I feel about him.

"I mean it," he says as he tucks a lock of hair behind my ear. "I want to keep seeing you. Do you want to keep seeing me?"

My breath catches in my throat, and I don't know what to say. I believe him. I believe in us and the possibility of an us that is eternal. I know that no matter what he tells me next, no matter the conditions, I will forever believe him, that I will forever need him, and that I will forever love him.

I say yes, even though I know that Jennie will be furious, even though I know this will fracture something within her core. Jennie doesn't fear the rumblings in the house. What Jennie fears most is allowing someone from the outside to get too close, and I don't know why, and right now I don't care.

I can hear her now—as soon as I tell her I am going to see Peter again tomorrow—warning me how when the Little Mermaid finally left her home and fell in love, all it produced was a series of events that ended with the sisters separated and the Little Mermaid alone.

But I wonder if the Little Mermaid regretted it all. She went to the Sea Witch, after all, once she encountered her love. The Sea Witch warned her that pain would come, as well as a great transformation, but still, the Little Mermaid agreed, she agreed to accept the possibility of destruction for the chance to be loved.

I don't know a Sea Witch, but I have my fairy and this river. I know the river has yet to grant me what I was begging for, but it has answered many of my requests, including quelling my most recent bout of loneliness. I hope then that my fairy, and this river, can make it so that I can be with Peter forever.

Chapter 14

"I was worried." Jennie is standing in front of the door as soon as I arrive.

"I was out with my friend, Peter."

She narrows her eyes. "You seem to always be out with Peter now. When was the last time you slept in your own bed?"

"I'm not discussing this with you right now," I say.

She steps aside to let me in, then follows me inside. "You know what's going to happen, and you're allowing it. Why?"

"Jennie, please move aside. I need to walk the dogs."

"No." Her eyes are watering. Her voice cracks. "You need to tell me. Why are you doing this? Are you looking for validation? There's nothing that can save us, Anna. This is our fate. This house. This river. Anything else will lead to that painful metamorphosis that guarantees only pity and pain."

"Jennie!" I place my hand on her shoulders, and she collapses into tears.

"Please, Anna, don't leave me." She covers her face, crying. "You're all I have."

I walk her over to the sofa and sit her down. "I'm not going anywhere. Please don't be afraid."

Her face is streaked with tears. "The house knows when you leave. It tells me. It's angry with me because it says I've allowed you to leave, and little by little you're tasting water and you see how different it is out there, and so I fear you will want to leave me and never return."

"Jennie . . ." I want to tell her that haunted houses are not real, that they are the thing of ghost stories, like the ghost stories I talk about on my podcast. They're just stories. They are not real, but I hesitate, because even I know not to speak ill of our home. I cannot deny that the lights will flicker, and the doors and cabinets will slowly creak open, and the footsteps will appear, and the water will run in the tub. And then that ghastly leak, that incessant drip, will begin again.

Are ghosts and haunted houses real? I do not really know what to believe, but I know what it is I live with, this haunting in my heart.

I hear a tapping just behind me, on the window, but I know not to look. I know this is the house sensing my contempt of it in this very moment. I feel each tap as if there is someone's finger pressing into the back of my neck. Then I wonder, Is that what the house wants? Does it want Jennie and me to lose who we are so that we do not know where the one starts and the other stops because we are just extensions of this house?

What I wanted to tell her before the house ruined it was that love was real and that I believed I finally had that, after so long. I love Peter. I love him with my entire being. I love him with a love so deep that it shines light on depths that had been dark for too long. I'd go to bed at night thinking of him. I'd wake in the morning thinking about him again, and that is how I knew. I knew I loved him when I'd linger on an image of him on my phone before I fell asleep and would drift off to my dreams, manifesting a life together with him.

"I love him," I tell Jennie. "I love him with a love I've never known."

Jennie's bottom lip trembles. "What about me?"

"What about you? Of course I love you! You're my sister. I'm here. I'm here for you, but . . ."

"You're selfish!"

I cry. How can I be selfish after all that I have endured? "I suffer here in silence every day because of you, because of Mother . . . because of Father. I'm not selfish. I'm alone."

"I'm alone too. I'm reaching my arms out, and there is no one there to catch me. You want to break free and swim to the surface and find love, but what about me?"

"He makes me happy," I say, and my voice feels so small. I regret coming home, and all I want is him. I want to relish in the sound and the comfort of his voice. I can hear it now, right beside my ear. Oh, how I take delight and am washed over with a warm feeling that courses through my body when I think of his voice, and when I think of him. I am overcome with an intensity in that memory of his eyes and breath on me. I grow desperate even now thinking of him, because I don't want to just think about him. I want him here. I want him to hold me. I want him to tell me we are alive and that he loves me, and that everything is going to be all right, and that I will never be alone again.

He talks to me. He listens to me. There is a great tug I feel toward him, the pull of a magnetic compass steering a ship on a fixed course. That is who and what we are when we are together.

Jennie's shoulders shake. Her entire body trembles. "I do not want you to jump. We were raised to feel it, to live it, to breathe it, to taste it, and if you leave this house, then you will have no choice but to jump too. Those are the rules. You have to feel the urgency. You have to raise the anchor from your mind before we're banished back—"

"Jennie!" I shout. This is all so confusing. I feel dizzy, our house is spinning, and then an object comes crashing through the sliding-door window, landing inches from our feet. A massive river rock has crashed through the glass, punching a large hole in it. The glass is tough and so does not completely shatter, but still, the house is injured.

"You see what you've done!" I walk over to the kitchen and retrieve the broom and dustbin. I sweep up the broken glass and whisper under my breath, "Not another word. We have already gone too far and spoken aloud too much of the strange happenings in the house, and that makes me uncomfortable."

I fear that speaking of these unusual occurrences will only give them power, generating more and more activity.

My sister stands from the sofa and watches me as I clean the mess she caused.

She closes her eyes, hums her song, and I tell her to stop. She sways her head back and forth, I'm sure still playing that song in her head when she says, "You can only see me in the mist, and I will coat your skin and I will cling to your hair. Fresh water. Sea water. Salt water."

"What does it matter? You and me, we are our Grandmother's pearls, and this house is our sanctuary. Our oyster in this ocean that is this marvelous city. That's what she said. That's what Mother and Father said, and I have to believe that to be true, even though . . ." My voice trails off, and I don't want to think of it again.

Jennie's voice cracks. "It hasn't always been so marvelous to the both of us."

"I know that, and I accept it, but I love this city all the same, and no matter what you or I say or do, we'll always be a part of its story."

Jennie takes a deep breath and runs her fingers through her long hair. "A detective called today."

"How do you know that?"

She nods over to the side table. "You left your phone here."

I pause brushing the broken bits of glass into the dustbin. I stomp over to the table, upset that she violated my privacy. "How dare you."

"I didn't listen to the message. I just noticed the name on the screen said Detective Kowalski."

I take the phone in my hand and scroll over to my messages and hit "Play."

"Anna, it's Detective Kowalski. There've been some missing persons cases associated with the Chicago River. My partner and I are hoping we can ask you a few questions. We spotted something in one of the crime scene photos that was taken near your house we'd like to check out a bit further. Give me a call as soon as you can."

I think of the scraps of paper my sister has been collecting on her walks. I stare at Jennie, unsure of what to say. I then turn back to the window and look through the hole in the glass out to my fairy garden. I remember that day, the boats and the flashing lights. The person floating in the water had probably been submerged for days, and so when they broke through the surface that uncharacteristically warm day in December, the person appeared as a large, pale, gelatinous thing. More fish than human. The person's arms and legs, neck and face, were ballooned and bulging. Tragedy in not just their death, but in their disfigurement.

I remember at first being hopeful and then horrified when I got a clear look. I ducked from the window and closed the curtains and shouted for Jennie that there were people—police and medical personnel—in our part of the river on boats taking photographs and retrieving a cadaver.

I found Jennie standing at her window, pinching the curtain back in her room a few inches so she too could view the scene.

She spoke softly, as if there was even a possibility that the people outside and below could hear us. "He swims with the little fish. They brush against his hair and skin, and the algae wraps around his wrists, holding him there, pinning him there." Jennie looked up at me, a glare from the flashlight below reflecting onto our house and illuminating her face in a soft glow.

"How do you know it's a man from up here?"

Jennie brushed her hand against my cheek. "I just know."

My thoughts leave the past and return to the present and that gaping hole in our sliding door and the tiny bits of broken glass on our polished wood floor. I sweep carefully, making sure each shard is found. "I don't think I'll be able to repair this myself. We'll need someone to come into the house."

A breeze wafts through the hole in the door, and I turn to my sister. "Do you think they will call again?"

"Of course they will."

"Whatever happened out there in the river that night, whatever continues happening in the river, none of that has anything to do with us. You understand, right, Jennie?" I nod my head, hoping she'll nod in agreement.

"What about your new friend, Peter? Don't you worry about meeting new people with the River Killer out there? Or does the idea of being with a killer excite you because maybe they can end your suffering?"

I ignore her cruelty and return to the mess she caused.

"You know you can't trust him, Anna. What next? He'll want to come to the house. He'll ask questions."

"And so what?" I shout. "So what if he asks questions? Then I'll tell him the truth. I'll tell him how our parents crashed through the barrier at Clark Street Bridge and their car tumbled down into the river and that's where they drowned, frantically trying to unclip their seat belts and open the doors, but they didn't have any time as the water rushed in. And so here I am, living with the horror each and every day that their last moments were utterly horrific and painful, and they knew they were dying together."

"And it was all the fault of the police . . ." Jennie says.

I sigh. "Yes, it was the police's fault." I pause, feeling so mentally and physically exhausted. "For a long time, I didn't know how to move on, but . . . there's something about him that makes moving on finally seem possible."

She lowers her voice and speaks each word softly and slowly, almost like a song. "You can't trust him, Anna."

"Jennie, please stop," I say, trying to ignore her above the brush, brush, brush of the bristles.

"What is it about him that you like so much? Is he enchanting? Is he alluring? Does he do the things to you you've always wanted someone to do?"

I want to just scream, and so I do. "He's real, Jennie! That's the point! He's flesh and blood, and he's funny and he lives out there in the world that we are too afraid to exist in, and he does so freely and happily, and I envy that about him. I envy every ounce of freedom that he has. And he loves me, Jennie. You should see the way he looks at me, like I am the sea, this awesome and powerful force of nature. He looks at me like he can't possibly take all of me in with a single glance."

"It must be nice to have someone look at you that way. How I wish someone would look at me that way, if even for a second. I beg and I long to be looked at that way, but no one, absolutely no one, will look at me with love, and I hate that." Jennie's eyes are cold. "You think you know Peter, but you don't. He's like all of them, all of those men out there wandering without purpose. All you need to do is stop them for a moment on the street and gaze into their eyes, and you'll see their deceit. None of them are real. None of them know how to look upon us with love."

"No," I snap. "Peter does love me, and I love him."

Jennie places her palms against her ears, refusing to hear me, but I shout, forcing her to listen.

"I feel like you're dragging me into these depths with you sometimes, and I want to swim to the surface but you're just holding me down there with you, and I just wish, Jennie, I just wish you would let me go to live a life. If you loved me, you'd help me move on."

My sister is standing inches from me now. I can hear her quickened heartbeat. Or was it the house's heart? Jennie is so beautiful in all of her rage.

"I do love you," she says, "and that is why I keep you here and keep us safe. This house, this river, is the only thing that will ever keep us safe. And if you loved me, if you really loved me, you would let Peter go. This isn't going to end well. There will be destruction and there will be loss and there will be nothing to save either of you if you continue this love affair."

Even if what Jennie said were true, which I knew it could not be, I would rather swim toward my misfortune just to be happy, if even for a moment, than sink into her madness.

"Did you know," Jennie starts and then bites her bottom lip, "that it's very unlucky to do something unkind to a mermaid?"

I feel a great weight on my chest. "We're not mermaids."

Jennie nods slowly. "On many an evening, the older sisters would rise to the surface, arm in arm, all five in a row. They had beautiful voices, more charming than those of any mortal beings. When a storm was brewing and they anticipated a shipwreck, they would swim before the ship and sing most seductively of how beautiful it was at the bottom of the ocean, trying to overcome the prejudice that the sailors had against coming down to them. But people could not understand their song and mistook it for the voice of the storm. Nor was it for them to see the glories of the deep. When their ship went down, they were drowned, and it was as dead men that they reached the Sea King's palace."

My hands and feet begin tingling, growing numb as if my limbs are all falling asleep. "I don't understand what you're trying to tell me in reciting this part from the story."

"What I'm trying to tell you is that you and Peter together are a great ship approaching a rocky shore during a great storm. It will end poorly."

Outside we hear a great splash in the river. Neither of us acknowledges it; we just continue with our motions.

"I'm tired," Jennie says. "I think I will go to my room, and when I wake I will work and will fix beautiful boxes that made beautiful sound once, and I will help those devices play music once again." She hums her favorite tune as she walks to the stairs, and once there, she calls to me.

"The membranes that form our human lungs and the thin, delicate filaments that make up the gills of fish, both of these things allow the other being to breathe. We both breathe, humans and fish. We pull oxygen directly into our lungs as we're surrounded by it, but with fish, they're magical. Fish breathe in the water, and within their gills they pull out the molecules of oxygen. The amount of oxygen in our air is greater than what's in rivers, ponds, and oceans, but those creatures under the sea breathe oxygen, just like the two of us sisters standing here."

I listen as she retreats to her room, her humming echoing along the hallway. It stops, and from the top of the stairs, she says, "You seem flustered."

I scoff. "Really? I'm cleaning broken glass, and I have no idea when this window can get repaired, and you're telling me I seem flustered? Of course I'm flustered."

"Have you been experiencing your flickers, Anna?"

I feel a cold pinch in my chest. "I need to finish cleaning," I say, ignoring her.

Once I hear her bedroom door slam, I sit and push the dust broom away and cry. There is no one who can prevent my sister's descent.

Chapter 15

Rivers are often connected to the supernatural.

It's believed that fairies and sprites live in rivers and tributaries. They're often benign—helpful, even—but they've been thought to generate listlessness in people, depression, and it's usually among young men.

This is what my research tells me.

These winding bodies of water are regularly tied to the divine feminine, with many being named after goddesses, such as the Osun River in Nigeria, named after a Yoruba goddess; Ireland's River Shannon, named after Sionann, the granddaughter of the Irish sea god Lir; France's Seine named after the goddess Sequana, and more. The Chicago River is named after the city for which it runs through. The city then takes its name from the Indigenous Miami-Illinois word *shikaakwa*, which was the name of the fragrant leeks that grew all along the lake, streams, and river.

Water is fluid, transformative. It's nurturing. Rivers provide a means of travel, food, and, of course, drinking water. A river is powerful. It is not stagnant or still like a pond or lake. A river is active. It is always moving and alive.

Running water has long been venerated, and the flowing water offers a protective boundary. It is thought that crossing a watercourse ensures one's safety from supernatural forces. The protective power of running water has long been thought to keep strange mythical creatures, vampires, and more at bay. Folklorists believe that evil spirits cannot cross running water.

What's interesting, however, is that the Chicago River flow was changed in the 1800s. Where the water used to naturally flow east, through the city and emptying into Lake Michigan, it was reversed to flow west and eventually south to the Gulf of Mexico. While that water flow contributed to the cleanliness of the river and helped the city grow, something about human beings directly manipulating the flow of what is natural to unnatural felt, well, supernatural in a way.

Chicago started out as a small frontier settlement centered on the Chicago River and was later established as a port. The river served as an important factor for fur traders in the area, and later lumber and meatpacking, as I noted to Peter at the remains of the Union Stock Yard.

I've found little folklore about the Chicago River, perhaps because so much has been lost to time. Still, I did find that when the first French explorers came to this area, they were warned by the Indigenous people to avoid proceeding to the mouth of the river. Also, no Indigenous people lived along the banks of the Chicago River year-round, like many Chicagoans do today, including Jennie and me.

I wonder, then, if it is true: If rivers are really inhabited by fairies, does the reversal of our river confuse the fairies that occupy that underwater world? Does this switch anger the fairies? Does changing the flow disrupt the spiritual realm somehow, and have we been paying the price with all of these drownings? How long has this been going on until more people began noticing?

I stare at my computer screen, knowing that none of this can or will help me. What am I supposed to tell the detectives when they come calling, because they *will* come calling. I had summoned them, after all, with my questions and concerns. They were moving slowly. They had generated few to no answers. What were they doing? Enough time had passed, and I needed to know so that I could move on.

I think of Jennie and all of the torment she has encountered. Caring for her has become difficult since I met Peter. It is as if the more time I spend with him, the more her dark moods increase. My meeting with Peter triggered something in her that I fear I can't turn off. She cries in her room all night until her cries muffle and she drifts off to sleep.

My stomach churns at the thought of my sister waking in the morning, brushing her teeth, washing her face, combing her hair, and then making her way downstairs to where she would then put on her ballerina flats and slip out the front door, onward to one of her walks down by the river. What if she returns to Clark Park and encounters the woman with the red hair and green dress again? How does she know that that woman is not the killer who pushes men into the water with glee and then makes her way along the path, where she enjoys the company of birds and other small creatures who live along the river?

Now that I think about it, this is certainly something I should present to the detectives, the existence of this strange woman who knows too much about the missing people and their deaths. Perhaps she is a link—a clue, even—or perhaps she is something more?

I thought about the folklore I had found, of fairies and sprites, and the divine feminine all surrounding rivers. I thought about men walking at night to another bar, or simply on their way home. I wondered who or what would make them stop and take pause along a bridge. Had they paused to tie their shoes? Had they paused because they thought they heard something and they looked around their surroundings? Had they paused because someone stopped them, maybe to ask a question? Or was there something else? What would make a grown man slow down long enough on a bridge so that he would then find himself in the water? It was a quick drop from street level into the water, and at its deepest, the river is just over twenty feet deep.

I decide to walk to the closest bridge over the Chicago River in the morning, right over on Addison Avenue. I knew the bridge had a railing and a life preserver, but what else? Was there anywhere along that bridge

I could conceivably lose my footing and fall into the water below? Or would someone have to push me over the railing?

I had a very busy morning planned now. After Riverview Bridge, I would visit Clark Park to talk with this woman with the red hair and green dress Jennie had spoken of.

None of this is making any sense. Never had so many people been found dead in the very water that runs behind my home. It is still a great puzzle to be solved, and it feels as if the pieces aren't even on the table. It feels as if the missing pieces are across the room, or in a locked room altogether.

Then suddenly, I feel a dull pressure in my chest and I think of Peter.

I send him a message:

Anna: I'm up late working and I started worrying about you.

Peter: I'm fine. I'm right here thinking of you. How is your research coming along?

Anna: There's so much to the river and then there isn't enough. All of these disappearances are strange. We know so much yet we know so little. I'm worried.

Peter: Worried about what?

Anna: Worried about you. Worried about Jennie.

Peter: You already know that you do not need to worry about me. I will be safe and I will be fine.

Anna: Then what about Jennie?

Peter: I'm sure she will be fine as well. Is there anything I can do to help? Maybe when I meet her, I can tell her about how worried you are when she ventures out to the river.

Anna: I don't think that will be a very good idea.

Peter: What? About telling her that you're worried about her getting too close to the river?

Anna: No, you meeting her. I just don't think it's a good idea. Just not yet.

Peter: I understand. I am ready to meet her whenever you are ready for me to meet her.

Anna: Thank you for being so kind to me.

Peter: Thank you for missing me.

I smile and want to just call him and tell him to come over and we can crawl into my bed, and hold one another beneath the covers, and talk and laugh until we fall away to sleep. Instead, I just tell him . . .

Anna: Goodnight, Peter. I miss you.

Peter: Goodnight, my Anna. I miss you always.

In bed I dream of hundreds of shapes floating beneath the surface of dark water. The black water swirling and churning these objects in great, mesmerizing spirals. Dresses billowing, black jackets and hats floating across the surface, and hair, long streaks of hair, swimming slowly back and forth. As I step closer to the river's edge, all of the objects freeze in place, and hundreds of faces all at once break through the surface, water pouring down eyes, ears, noses, and foreheads, and all of them staring at me. Their blue mouths open in silent screams. In that second, something takes hold of my ankle, and I am pulled under the water. It is too late to take in any air to hold my breath. I am already sucking in water. It's flowing through my nostrils, clogging my ears, and as I open my mouth to scream, to cry, to call out for help, it is as if gallons of slimy river water are forced down my throat so forcefully that the pressure snaps my neck.

My eyes open, and I sit up straight in bed, reaching for my throat. My heart is pounding in my chest. I am in my room. I am dry. The river is moving, flowing just outside.

It is still night outside my window. I look over to check on Clover and Thistle, and they are cuddled together in a deep slumber, their little bellies rising and falling gently, undisturbed by the figure that paces my room.

A woman in a white silk gown walks toward me and then turns on her heel to the bedroom door. Once she reaches the door, she again turns around, walking back and forth, her pace quickening. Her slick arms swing with each step. Her face is a single sheet of skin, without eyes or slits for a nose or mouth. A single layer of skin for a face is shining with moisture. With each footstep, her bare feet hit the floorboards with the sound of a wet slap.

Her white dress is soaked through, clinging to and exposing all of her skin, all the parts of her—showing off her round breasts and small pink nipples and the curves of her hips. Her body is the body of a siren, and the desire of any and all. But her face is an undiscovered sea creature, a nightmare we don't know we're living. Her long black hair is plastered to the sides of her face, down her back to her waist. It looks like Jennie, but it is not Jennie. This woman, this leviathan, has emerged from a great body of water, or had been caught in a torrential downpour and had found herself somehow trapped in my house. Or is she a nymph that had clawed out of the water clinging to sea rocks? I don't care what it is. It belongs in her world and not mine, and I want it out of here, and I never want to look at this ghastly thing again.

My room feels cold, like a Chicago night in November. I can sense mist and smell the saltwater air. The woman has brought with her a dreary rain that hangs above us. Water now trickles down her head, arms, shoulders, and nightdress. There is heavy rain, or a waterfall, in my bedroom, but still she walks, stomps, her feet slapping against the floor, each step leaving behind another wet, slimy footprint. She is undisturbed by the rumbling of thunder that surrounds us.

The dogs remain asleep, unable to hear any of the chaos engulfing our room.

Her pace quickens, back and forth. Back and forth. Practically running now.

The floorboards shake with each of her movements. My bed vibrates. The house sways and I sway with it. It is as if we are on a vessel in rough waters, and I have to hold on to the sides of my bed to keep from tipping over. Each of her footsteps produces more rain. The water accumulates, rising on the floor, soaking the dogs. I try to get off the bed, but it tosses and turns, and with each jagged movement, I scream from how my body thrashes around.

I will my eyes to close, but they cannot. I am forced to see the terror unfolding before me. I reach out to get off the bed. I need to swim toward the dogs. The water has reached up to the height of the bed, but I am thrust down onto my back by a blast of wind.

I am forced to listen to the lightning and thunder, a great storm surrounding us. The water continues to rise, soaking my bed, my bedsheets, and then me. I look back at the woman who continues to pace, the water above her knees. Then in one quick motion she dives into the water. A great green, gold, and blue fish tail behind her, where her legs had been, smacks the water as she swims to my bedroom door. The door opens and then she is gone.

The water is gone.

It is silent.

It is dry.

Clover and Thistle spring from their bed, bewildered. I rush to my door, open it, and look into the black hallway. I close it and then turn the lock, knowing that this alone will never help keep it out.

Chapter 16

Jennie sleeps in that morning. I hear her shower, get dressed, and walk aimlessly about the house as if searching for something.

When she comes down to the kitchen for tea, I ask her how she slept, and she simply says, "Our nightmares never allow us to fully rest."

"What is it that you are looking for?" I ask as she opens the drawers in the kitchen island.

"My scraps of paper. From my walks. They're gone. Did you take them from my room?"

I take another sip from my teacup and set it aside. "No. I haven't been in your room, and even if I had, I wouldn't remove anything from there."

She groans. "They were all on my workstation, folded up so neatly, and now they're gone. Disappeared." She places her hands on her hips and looks to the ceiling. "Maybe the house took them from me. The house doesn't want me to have anything to hold on to. To remember them by."

"To remember who by?"

She doesn't respond, and I just assume it's her again, fading away. I move to stand up. "I'll help you look."

"No, it's no bother." She waves me away. "They'll turn up. They always turn up. In a day or a week. When the weather shifts. They always appear. That's the single constant. Those little scraps of paper printed with black ink and pasted to fences and poles. They look so sad out there, and that's why I bring them here, so that they can keep me company."

I want to tell her about my nightmare last night and the waking terror I experienced. I suppose they were both nightmares, seeing those faces in the river and the siren in my room, who seemed so real.

I can't shake the sound of its feet, and even now, I can't brush away that smell, that salty sea air mixed with something else. The sharp bodily odors of someone who has been outside in the sun too long on a summer's day. It is the smell of that woman, that creature, that nymph. Whatever it was, I still see that faceless form when I close my eyes, and I fear I'll encounter her again tonight.

Each of us is terrorized by our own unique ghosts. Jennie has hers, and I have mine, and that is how we live, being haunted by things we cannot explain, that we cannot understand, but yet we accept it, because we have nowhere else to go. Grandmother specified that Jennie and I were to live and maintain this house. Mother and Father later emphasized that.

There was no selling it, just as there was no option for either of us to leave and make a life without the other. But as the days stretched on, I grew to resent Jennie. Truly, I grew to fear her episodes, those moods, frightened of what she would say next that would sting my heart, or worse. What was Jennie capable of during one of these fits where she was consumed and confused by the trauma that defined her life? I surely did not want to know.

Peter messages me good morning, and we then speak on the phone for an hour as he readies for work. His voice soothes me in that short time from the horror that had slithered in this house and crawled over me in the night. He asks if I want him to come over after work, but I decline, thinking that would only upset Jennie, making things worse. She is not yet ready to meet him, or for him to meet her.

I try to distract Jennie from her missing scraps of paper. I try to see if we can create some brightness in this dark spot. "Maybe we should spend some time together here in the living room, reading. We can read to each other, or even just read to ourselves. I know how much it comforted you when Grandmother sat here with us and a book. Maybe that will do us each a bit of good, considering . . ."

A smirk crosses Jennie's face. "Considering all that has happened, is happening, and will continue to happen. You feel it too. Rain is approaching, the lightning and the thunderstorms, and what can we do? Will we allow it to toss and turn our lives around once again?"

"Maybe there's another way," I say, already regretting my words.

Jennie's eyes widen. "You see what that man is doing to you? He's making you believe that you have the option to escape. It's very sad too. He came here with such great intentions: to work, to establish himself, and look at what happened to him. Adventure that will end in ruin because of you."

"That's enough now." I stand up from the island and walk my tea-cup to the sink. I gently wash it and place it on the drying rack, ignoring Jennie's silence, but I know she is only just calculating each word, poring over how to emphasize her next statement to ensure it reaches my core and pierces me there. But Jennie doesn't say anything. Instead, I find her standing beside the sliding door looking out over the river, inspecting the tape over the hole in the glass.

"This hurts," Jennie says. "It's a festering wound oozing with thick pus that is never going to heal quite the same. The house felt it and cried. I heard its cries. It was most miserable. That's why it sent you her."

"What are you talking about?" I demand that Jennie explain. "What do you mean 'her'?"

"You had a nightmare . . . so I just assumed you dreamed of her."

That I did. I dreamt of her.

Jennie throws her arms around me and places a kiss on my cheek. "I love you, Anna. You're the best sister, and thank you for what you did for me . . . before, and thank you for being here, even when I'm not."

It is one of those now-rare moments of lucidity, when I have my Jennie. My kind older sister, who is gentle and so childlike. I wish I could capture her in this exact moment, keeping her like this, but I know there is no way to keep any good moment static. Everything changes, even when we beg the universe to please not move the dial away from our joyous moments, for fear we may never have another.

I think more of our bedtime stories when we were girls and how before bed Grandmother would fill our heads with wonder instead of tragedy. When we were younger, she read to us every single night, from every single tale of fancy she could find. She read us stories written by Aesop, Charles Perrault, Marie-Catherine d'Aulnoy, Joseph Jacobs, Andrew Lang, Gabrielle-Suzanne Barbot de Villeneuve, Antoine Galland, Ludwig Bechstein, Jacob and Wilhelm Grimm, Hans Christian Andersen, and more.

I can remember how we would beg her to read to us. When Grandmother read, it was as if my ears became unclogged. The world looked clear again. And that sun, the sun that hung in that hard blue sky, seemed to sparkle with such magic that it was as if I could easily pluck it out from the heavens and plant it in my heart, where it would rest like a tiny star.

The written words of fairy tale masters spoken by Grandmother became almost a conjuring. For us, Grandmother presented hope, healing, and peace, and each night as she read, that is what she delivered to Jennie and me—hope, healing, and peace.

And without another word, without any hesitation, we would sit beside Grandmother, and she would dive into one of the stories from one of the fantastic books that lined her shelves.

"Far out in the ocean the water is as blue as the petals of the loveliest cornflower, and as clear as the purest glass . . ."

Jennie and I would sit silently, her head on my shoulder and her hand in mine. We would grip each other so tight for fear the other would slip away.

We were close, Jennie and I, for a time. After Grandmother's passing, our relationship became strained. Mother and Father said Jennie grew distant because she was sad. When someone you love dies, they aren't really gone; they remain a part of you. The impact that they made on you and your life is part of the tapestry that makes us. Still, there's that yearning for more time, more moments, new memories, and all that we have are those feelings they made us feel while they were here that we reach out and tap into. Tapping into those moments feels both loving and painful, because we know that no more new moments will be had.

Mother and Father tried as best as they could to support Jennie and me after Grandmother died. They were both busy with work, always working, and we had babysitters until we didn't need a babysitter anymore. Even when we did have babysitters, they never really cared for us. What did care for us were Grandmother's books, that magical library devoted to fairy tales.

Mother tried reading to us from those books, as did Father, but it was never the same. I suppose Grandmother's voice was enchanted somehow, offering us comfort and a path to dreams. Sometimes I wondered if the tonic to heal Jennie's melancholy was Grandmother's soothing voice, reading one of our favorite fairy tales. If so, it was a cure that no longer existed, and I would have to care for my sister as best I could, as she devolved further into a place from where I could not save her.

Jennie's demons delighted in reminding her about the water outside, how it was both our salvation and our curse, that river cutting through this city. Jennie welcomed the grief into her heart and allowed those strands of algae to grow and spread across her soul.

She gave into it at times. But I did what I could to hold her together.

I tried once before, like Grandmother used to, to read aloud to Jennie in the hope that the story of "The Little Mermaid" could somehow ease the heaviness within her.

One night, I sat at the foot of Jennie's bed and read:

"The sun rose up from the waters. The rays fell warmly and gently upon the deadly cold sea foam, and the Little Mermaid did not feel death."

A sly smile crossed Jennie's lips. "We both know that the mermaid in this story is gifted with neglect, then loneliness, and finally death. There is no happy ending to our story. All because she was stupid enough to love someone and to believe that they could love her in return."

Jennie then reached up and snatched the book out of my hands and threw it across the room. She reached forward and grabbed my wrist, squeezing it tight. "There is a theory," she gritted through her teeth, her eyes blazing, "that we emerge finer and stronger after our suffering . . . and to advance in this world, in any world, we must endure trials by fire. Wait?" She pressed a finger to her lips. "Or is it a trial by water?"

"Let me go! Please, you're hurting me."

"Return that book to Grandmother's room. Lock the door and drape it in black mourning cloth. Neither of us is ever to enter there. There is no salvation for us written in those books. We exist to know fear and loneliness and drink deeply our distress."

I finish my tea.

Jennie left the house on one of her walks. She looked bright and cheerful, and for a moment, I did not fear for her safety. She needs the air. She needs to be away from the house, because the longer we are outside, the less time the house can claw and scrape at our insides.

I am lying on the sofa preparing for a nap when the phone rings. I answer, expecting the repair service for the window, but no. It is what I set into motion.

"Hello, it's Detective Kowalski. Anna . . ."

The man's voice goes muffled for a moment. I hear him speaking with another man on the other end.

"I'm sorry . . . I . . ."

It is as if my balance teeters off a few degrees, as if I am losing my center, or maybe I never knew where my center was.

"My partner, Detective John Rodriguez and I, we'd like to ask you a few questions. We're on our way there, and we are hoping instead of a phone call we can speak with you in person for a few minutes."

I sit up. Feeling a stabbing pain behind my left eye. "This isn't a good time. My sister . . ."

"I didn't know you had anoth—"

Clover and Thistle bark. Both are at my feet, whining, begging for their walk to the garden.

"It's time I walk the dogs," I say.

"We'll be quick. Look at how fast that was. We're parking right now. Nice bungalow. My wife and I live in a ranch house. We bought it forever ago thinking we'd upgrade to a bungalow, but you know, the ranch suited us just fine. We're moving to Florida after I retire. I'm not good with the heat, but her niece and nephew live there and she wants to be close to family, so I guess I lost that fight."

I want to cut this call short and attend to my dogs. "Now isn't a good time," I say.

"But you called us. You asked for an update."

I don't want to talk about any of this, not here, not in the house. The house could become upset, and in turn Jennie would become upset, and I do not want to lose grasp of what little progress we have made in this world. I just want it all to pause for a moment so that I can think clearly and not be surrounded with the memory of those flashing lights and that scream, that scream that wasn't mine, but maybe it was.

"There's a drip, a leak, in the house I need to attend to, and if I don't, then it may turn into a larger problem," I say.

The steady thunk, thunk, thunk of the drip returned.

"I'm not the best plumber, but I can take a quick look at the sink if you want."

"No, that won't be necessary."

I remember the old detective stories that Grandmother loved written by Sir Arthur Conan Doyle, and his protagonist, Sherlock Holmes. I never told Grandmother, but often when she was done with her detective novels, I would scoop them up and read them late into the night. I adored all of the stories in which our perceptive detective appeared, from the first tale, *A Study in Scarlet*, to the short story "The Final Problem," in which he meets his archnemesis Professor Moriarty and where the saga ends with Sherlock Holmes's death. I can only assume it was too great a pain to kill something he loved so much that Sir Arthur Conan Doyle would later go on to resurrect the character of Sherlock Holmes. I believe in many ways we, and the things that we love, cannot die if there is someone alive in the present thinking about us.

I remember now the very quote in one of Doyle's books that has stayed with me:

"There's the scarlet thread of murder running through the colorless skein of life, and our duty is to unravel it, and isolate it, and expose every inch of it."

Indeed, there is a scarlet thread of murder running through our city, and I feel it is my responsibility to unravel it, isolate it, and expose it for the devastation it has caused.

It isn't just the fact that so many men have gone missing and that they were later found dead and drowned. What has also plagued me long into the night is that someone must have heard that crash. Someone must have heard those cries and pleas for help, and someone merely stood by as they heard the splashes and gasps, voices stricken with thick panic and fear, and all they did was listen, observe, and walk away.

It is as if my story and Jennie's story, our life of calm and quiet, has been disrupted by the deaths occurring out there in the river, and neither of us can move on unless we have answers, a solution.

"Look at that . . ." I hear the other voice on the call. It must be Rodriguez. "That sure looks like a diamond to me."

I feel my jaw tighten. My voice is trapped in my throat, and there is nothing I can do. They are already outside of my house, of our house.

"Look, we're right here," Kowalski says into the phone. "Five minutes and we'll be outta here."

I peer out the front window and see two men standing outside, one older and one much younger. The older one is in a suit, and the younger one is in jeans and a hoodie. They look like complete opposites, nothing like I'd imagine a detective duo would look like from my grandmother's novels.

"We can talk outside, inside. Whatever you like. We don't have much of an update for you as to what happened, but we did want to ask you about the diamond on your roof and one we spotted while reviewing some evidence."

They didn't have an update for me as to what? What are they talking about?

"Do you mean . . . my parents?"

"No, not your parents. Your . . ."

I stop him. "I don't want to talk about this. Not right here. Not right now. Not in this house."

Everything in the past is blowing into the present.

"We're looking into the missing persons case of Joshua Martin . . ."

I don't want to speak with them, because I don't trust them. I don't trust them to do their jobs right. I don't trust them to care. I also don't trust what they would do if they had more information. Law enforce-ment and emergency medical professionals are disorganized, negligent, and reckless. I suffer because of their disregard. They could have moved faster, but they didn't. My family was obliterated, and what could I do? Ask questions over and over.

"What now?"

"What are you doing?"

"Do you have any more information?"

They care now because the case is recent, but would they care in a few months? A year or two from now? The only reason homicide detectives are even assigned to investigate is because the connection to water and the location where my family crashed their car is the same site a body was discovered months before.

"Yes," I say, knowing very well that the river does things that it should not do. "I know what you're looking into. I heard about it on the news, but I can't help you."

"Maybe you can," he says, and then there is a knock on the door.

I open it, hoping that a quick discussion will assuage them enough that they will leave and let me be.

Each has a puzzled look on their face when I appear, confused and almost speechless. I look down at my dress, wondering if it is stained, but no. It is perfectly clean. A simple blue silk housedress with a black ribbon cinched at the waist. It is an older style, admittedly, but I am becoming fond of these simple and clean looks. They help me feel con-nected, to what I don't know, but being tied to a port in the past makes me feel a little less alone.

"I'm sorry it's been so long," Kowalski says. "This is Rodriguez. He'll be working with me for a bit." Kowalski lowers his head. "We saw each other last under difficult circumstances."

I laugh. The insult. "Difficult circumstances?"

"I'm sorry. I really am."

Officers were in pursuit of a suspect, ignored traffic lights, and slammed into my parents' car. They lost control of the vehicle, crashed through a railing, and there they died.

"We're very sorry for your loss," Rodriguez says.

Another insult. "What do you know about loss? Did you all catch your suspect? What were they doing? Oh, that's right. They were in pursuit of someone who ran a red light, of which you all later determined they were speeding to get to Lurie Children's Hospital, which was just a few blocks away, because they had a child who was experiencing anaphylactic shock. I'm happy to have heard that the child made it, but I've never received an apology, and what does it matter? Here I wither alone . . ."

"I thought you said your sister—"

"I don't want to talk about her when she is not here."

"Great," Kowalski says. "Then we'll come back later to talk to your sister."

"She's not been well. I don't know when it'll be a good time for another visit."

"Then we'll call," Rodriguez insists.

"I don't think that will be a good idea either."

The detectives exchange a look.

Rodriguez crosses his arms over his chest, and he's swaying side to side. "Then we'll talk about that another time. Let's just focus on why we're here today."

"This is about that night you reported a person in the river behind your house," Kowalski says, shielding his face from the sun.

"What about that night?" I snap. "It was terrifying. No one expects to look out the window and spot something like that, ever, no matter where they live. It looked like a great rotting mass of flesh being pulled from the water. I knew they were someone's sibling, child. People loved that person that had been turned into a clump of waterlogged flesh."

Rodriguez's attention moves to the roof of my house. "So, that a blue diamond?"

"Yes . . ." I say. "It's a decorative detail that was placed there when my grandparents purchased the house."

"Why a diamond?" Kowalski asks.

"Grandmother said it was to honor the family that built this home, to acknowledge their tragedy." I look around the street. There is no one else outside, just a line of darling houses across from me, perhaps filled with lovers and children, grandparents and cousins. Not my home. For some reason, this house longed to bask in tragedy, from the original owners and now to me. In this house we suffer.

Rodriguez now has one foot planted on the bottom step of the stairs. "What year was that?"

"I believe they purchased this house in the late 1960s. They were the second homeowners. The first being the Evenhouses."

Kowalski shoots a look over to Rodriguez, whose attention is still on the diamond. "You all lived here that whole time?"

"Yes, this is our house," I say.

Rodriguez speaks in the direction of his partner, who is still standing on the sidewalk under the great weeping willow tree in our front yard. "Why would they paint a blue diamond on a tree back there?"

"I don't know," Kowalski says.

I know of the tree and the marking they're speaking of. I believe they won't leave me alone until they see it, and so I welcome them to follow me to the backyard.

Out back we walk down the gravel path to the river. They comment on how it feels peaceful here and how it doesn't feel like they are in the city, covered by a canopy of trees. They spot the fairy garden and say it is pretty. Once we reach the end, Kowalski steps right to the edge and cranes his neck to see the dry paint on the tree.

"Yup," he says. "That's it. A blue diamond."

Rodriguez rubs the back of his head and carefully steps to the edge, holding on to the tree to steady himself as he does so. Once he sees it, he steps back to more stable ground, produces a sheet of folded paper from his pocket, looks at it, and then hands it to Kowalski.

Kowalski presses a finger to the paper and says, "Same hand. Look here. I'm not even going to pretend I'm a handwriting expert, but once we get this compared, I guarantee my badge it'll check out."

"Really?" Rodriguez says.

"What?" Kowalski says.

"Guarantee your badge. That's not really comforting. You've been dying to hang it up."

"Not true. I'm getting overtime training you. So it's a win-win."

I speak as forcefully as I can. They are here and they are already invading my space. "Can you explain your interest in our tree?"

Kowalski places his hands on his hips, the sheet of paper still in his grasp, and he tilts his head back. My eyes track upward, searching for the point he is focusing on, and all I see are white puffs of clouds, slowly being pushed along by the wind. The branches around us sway, and mere feet away we can hear the ripples and bubbles rising and bursting along the surface of the river as flathead catfish, trout-perch, longear sunfish, carp, and more move beneath the surface.

"We've seen this same symbol painted on trees and other surfaces at spots where drowning victims were last seen," Rodriguez says.

Kowalski brings the sheet of paper back to his face, then holds it up to me. There's a blue diamond on it. "We've also seen this symbol at places where drowning victims were recovered."

Chapter 17

Jennie's reaction is as explosive as expected.

"You're going to ruin everything," she blurts out, her cheeks red. "Why would you want to do that? Throw everything away? This house is us, and you allowed those people here? How dare you, Anna. You violated our home."

"They didn't come inside. They merely wanted to look at the river and look at the tree to confirm a marking."

"What marking?"

"The blue diamond on the roof and the blue diamond on the tree out back."

"No one knows who placed it there or why," Jennie says. She stands in front of the french doors, looking out into our garden. She then turns her head and looks to the spot where the break in the glass had once been. "You had it replaced, I see." She presses her palm against the glass carefully.

"Yes," I say. "While you were out, the repair service came."

"You've had a very busy day, then, haven't you? Directing detectives to our part of the river. Attending to repair people. What next, Anna? Should we just unlock the door and leave it open? Just let the outside in finally? Is that your intention?"

"No, Jennie. That was never my intention. I want to feel as safe and protected as you do."

Her laugh is like dozens of daggers piercing my spine. "We're safe and protected only because of what floats along the ocean floor."

"This is becoming too much for me to hold."

"No, don't you understand?" She is standing in front of me now, inches from my face. "We are keeping all of this inside, where we're meant to." She points to my chest, right at my heart. "This is where it all belongs. We are this house. We are this city. We cannot strip one from the other without setting everything ablaze."

"Or drowning it all?"

She fights back a smile. "When you want to remember, you do so ever so conveniently, my very clever little sister. You do remember it, then. It was early in the morning. It was a rainy day . . ."

I do not want to remember any of it. I do not want to linger in it any more than I already have. That event and the subsequent ripples are the cause of my accursed transformation. Life was lovely. It was simple and sweet and kind, but then the accident happened, and ever since then, a mist of gloom and meanness has soaked through me.

"Stop it, Jennie. Please."

"They better not come back." She rubs her hands down the sides of her black silk dress, smoothing it out, but as always, there are no wrinkles.

"They won't be back," I say. "That's all they wanted to see."

"Wait." She grabs my shoulder. "What else did they tell you?"

Her eyes study the depths of mine, searching for any spark of deception within. "Don't lie to me, my sister. Any lie will not only crack the foundation we stand on but sink us into oblivion."

I feel a cold pressure of hesitation in the center of my throat. She will not like what I had divulged, but still, I speak. "The diamond, at the peak of the roof and at the great cedar tree in back, are similar to blue diamonds painted at the points where people were last seen and where corpses were fished out of the water."

She releases her hold on me. "What do they plan on doing with that information?"

"I don't know. Maybe it means something. Maybe it all points to someone, the person who has been committing these crimes."

"What about Peter, then?" Jennie leaves my side and proceeds to walk toward the kitchen.

I follow her closely. "What do you mean? What about him?" I demand.

She stops at the counter and places her hands on the white marble surface. "How do you know you can trust him? A random man calls to you, and you fall in love after just a single meeting? Don't you find that strange, Anna?"

It wasn't just a single meeting. It was a series of correspondences across months.

"You're consumed with him. How can you be so sure he's consumed with you for the right reasons?" She raises an eyebrow.

I dined on darkness in this house for every meal. This house guaranteed my constant fear and loneliness, but Peter remained that single point, a lighthouse I could move toward to lessen my suffering, and I had no intention of ever letting him go.

"Because, Jennie," I snap, "I see it in the way he looks at me, how the contours of his face soften. I hear it in his voice, how it drops low and steady, a soothing and hypnotic tone that I feel within every cell of my being. He is innocent and soft-spoken and gentle and sweet and kind. He makes me laugh with his freedom, in which opens up an utter ecstasy for life. When I'm with him, everything is magnetized. I can feel life. I can feel the air, the sun, my breath flowing in through my nostrils and fanning out through all of my parts and radiating within my heart. I love him and he loves me, and a love like ours I would never expect you to know, accept, or understand."

She releases a sob and slowly says, "Oh, how you kill me, my sister. How you've punctured my heart with the totality of those cruel and eternal words."

Jennie and I have been confined to this house for so long. Sometimes I wonder if Grandmother, Mother, and Father knew what would happen to us. The effects of that cold, gray morning seeped into our pores, contaminated us, and since then we have been trying to find our way back. Peter is the only elixir I can drink who makes me feel whole, but when he is gone, I return to this dark cavern, miserable and alone, mocked in my grief.

I speak my words slowly and confidently. "I'm going to start seeing Peter more frequently."

Jennie reaches a hand down and opens the utensil drawer. It flies back with a bang, and the clanging of forks and spoons and knives within hangs in the air.

"I will not allow him to take you away from this house."

I hold my palms up to her, pleading. "Jennie . . ."

My sister digs her hands into the drawer and produces a large knife. "I will not allow you to leave me." The knife shakes in her hands.

Jennie slams her free hand onto the marble top. "I won't allow it. You will lose me. You will lose us, all for what? To tell a story that no one needs to hear? It should remain unknown, forgotten, and ignored, whispered only at holiday dinners among family who live with this ancestral stain."

"The story will play," I say softly, my hands still in the air, pleading for her to put the knife down.

"The story will play, and you will pay. I will pay. All of us." She points to Clover and Thistle, who cower behind me. "This is our house. This is our home, and you're going to allow them to rip it all away from us again."

The temperature in the room drops. The light fixtures all around us hum, growing brighter. The front doorknob rattles. Disembodied voices chatter on the stairs. Unseen feet run up and down the hallway. Doors open and slam. Lights turn off and on. The faucet in the kitchen bursts on. Laughter erupts all around us.

"A ticking clock." Jennie's eyes widen. "Don't you remember Mother's watch and how it ticked that day? Don't you remember the clock tower that loomed over all of us as we screamed for help that morning?"

"Stop it!" I shout, not just to my sister but also to the eruption of noise and movement around us.

She aims the knife at me. "You do remember. You refuse to admit it, but you do remember."

"Jennie, you're not well."

"Oh, I know more than you will ever know. You think you're so smart. You think that you can hide everything from me. You and your lover and your plans to abandon me. You think that you can break free, but the both of you can never break free from this cycle that we were pulled under. When will you realize that I am the one who's been trying to protect you this entire time? But all you do is keep secrets from me. I heard you as you were working on parts of the house, reaching into the walls. I saw you hiding things you found there. What is it that you were finding in the floorboards and behind the cabinets? What did the house gift you?"

"Stop it, Jennie!"

"What are you going to do? Lock me up in Dunning?"

"The Dunning asylum closed decades ago!"

Jennie takes a deep breath and says, "I know . . ."

"I'm never going to leave you. I promised you that. I'll promise you again now and for eternity that I will never leave you. I love you, Jennie. I just want to keep you safe, to keep us safe."

Tears roll down her face, and she wipes her cheek on her shoulder. "Promise me," she says, her voice cracking. "Promise me you will never leave me here, with them." She looks up to the staircase, her eyes open in fright. I follow the direction of her stare, but I do not see what she sees. I do not hear what she hears, and I never exactly experience what Jennie experiences. Yes, there are terrors we share, but most of our demons are specific to us, tormenting us to the brink of madness, or for my sister, holding her head down in it.

I approach her slowly, hoping that she will not hurt me, but yet unsure if the house would entice her toward harm. "I will never leave you," I repeat, and I feel a weighted guilt in the center of my chest, because I know each and every word of that is a lie.

She stares into my eyes, searching for the deceit, until she spots the betrayal. I had always been convinced that Jennie could read my thoughts, that our consciousness was intertwined, that somehow, on some level of reality, we existed as one—two sisters, but like Grandmother called us, two pearls within a single oyster.

"Did you know," I say, aiming for distraction, "that a pearl is a precious gem and that it comes from the sea? All it takes is something to invade the interior of the oyster while it's out at sea. This can simply be a speck of dust or a grain of sand. Once that tiny particle invades the mollusk shell, the animal becomes wary and protects itself from the outsider. The animal will then begin to cover the item in layers and layers of secretion. In time, a natural pearl forms. This is how a real pearl is born, and this, Jennie, this is very much what we are. We came into this house, and this thing that lives in here, it's gone into a defensive mode, and so it torments us with your moods and my flickers and forms that stalk us, the banging of doors and the tapping of windows and the . . ."

Just then, the steady drip begins again, reminding us it is always here.

". . . leak. Did you know that the chances of finding a true quality natural pearl in an oyster is one in a million? Do you know what that means? That pearls, in many ways, are miracles. That we exist in the state that we do because we are miracles."

Jennie releases the knife.

It cuts through the air and dives, the tip of the blade sinking directly into her foot and piercing through the flesh above her middle toe. The knife stands upright, blood squirting from around the blade and oozing down her foot and onto the floor.

"You're going to leave me." Her lips quiver, but she does not at all acknowledge her injury.

"Jennie!" I kneel and wrap my fingers around the handle, inspecting the wound and measuring the damage I would cause if I removed the knife. Deep-red blood continues to flow.

"We will not leave this house. This is our house!" Jennie cries.

"I have to call an ambulance—"

Before I can finish my sentence, Jennie reaches down with her right hand, grasps the handle, and yanks the knife free. Thick, dark blood seeps from the gash, covering her foot completely now.

As she stands there, the knife at her side, she says, "Do you know what happens to a human body when it drowns? How it bloats and putrefies? Do you know about skin slippage? How a once-beautiful and youthful face can be peeled off, down to the bone? It's all just matter. Organic matter that feeds the little fish and the tiny organisms that live in bodies of water."

I reach for the paper towels, unrolling dozens and dozens of white sheets. I bunch them up and gently place them on top of her foot. Red soaking into the white material. I can feel Jennie's eyes beaming down on me as I do this. She does not flinch. She does not moan. She does not seem to register any bit of pain from such a serious injury.

"You'll never leave this place. Remember that. If you leave this place, you'll be like that face I spoke of. You'll peel off right down to the bone too."

I can't take her raving anymore. I put pressure on the wound and shout, "You leave the house! I leave the house too! I go for walks. I go out for tea. I take the train and go downtown. I see Peter now, outside these walls. There is nothing wrong with leaving this house. Perhaps we need to do more of it, because we're allowing this accident to just fester, and we have to move on, Jennie. Please. I'm begging you, we have to move on."

Jennie blinks back tears. I focus back on her foot and the blood-soaked paper towels.

"We should get you to the hospital to look at that . . ."

Jennie closes her eyes and raises her hands to her ears. "You're just a liar, and I'm not going to listen . . ." She falls away into her tune. Humming that melody that comforted her but scared me.

The dogs spring to the french doors and begin to howl.

Jennie opens her eyes. "They sense it too," she says, and spins on her left heel, dragging her injured foot across the tile, blood smearing in long streaks across the floor.

"I'm not leaving this house!" Jennie shouts. "And if you continue to leave this house, you'll find yourself at Dunning too. Or worse . . ."

Jennie shuffles to the stairs.

I plead with her once more. "We need to get you to the hospital. That could get infected."

Jennie holds on to the banister. She takes a deep breath and then gazes up the stairway. "I'm already infected. This house is already infected." She turns to me. "And you, you with your dead and your ghost stories and your fairy tales and your secret gifts the house has handed you and only you, you're infected too." She lowers her voice. "And that's what's saddest about all of this. How you are unwilling to believe that you too are decaying from within. Those detectives and Peter, they all smell the rot on you."

Jennie slowly climbs the stairs, dragging her bleeding foot behind her, leaving a trail of blood across the wooden steps that I would later clean.

The dogs are barking and pawing at the glass. I run over to them, and they cower behind me, their tails dipped between their legs.

"What is it?" I ask, and when I peer out the window for just the briefest of moments, I see something that's not possible in this world or the next. A figure, a faceless woman in a long white dress, floating above the water. When I regard her slick, blank face, she dives feetfirst into the river. The surface ripples outward.

"They're nightmares that taunt us while we're awake," I tell the dogs, and usher them over to the stairs with me.

I sit on the first step and lower my head into my hands.

I listen as Jennie moves about her room. The door opens and slams, and then music plays. The house fills with the sounds of the Heidelberg Quintet:

> By the sea, by the beautiful sea!
> You and me, you and me, oh how happy we'll be!
> When each wave comes a-rolling in
> We will duck or swim

Clover and Thistle rest their heads on the top of my knees. "There's nothing I can do," I say. "I can't force her to go to the hospital." There is, of course, the option to call an ambulance, but I'd imagine it'd go terribly, with Jennie screaming and refusing to leave her room.

"She'll be fine." I rub behind Clover's ears and kiss the top of Thistle's head. "I'm sorry we scared you." I close my eyes and hug both dogs tightly, my loving little ones that I found caught in the river but that saved me and continue to save me each day with their tenderness and concern.

We sit there for some time, listening to the record play and end, play and repeat. The sound of a song recorded so long ago filling the house, as only it could. I move over to the sofa and continue to listen to the music. I close my eyes and dream about people crowded in street-cars, women in white dresses and large hats, their small children clinging to their legs, and smaller children cradled in their arms. The men wearing dark suits and equally dark hats, but all of them are missing eyes. In place of eyes are deep pits, portholes peering into the hull of an empty ship.

I gasp and then awaken on the sofa. Both dogs are huddled at the far end by my feet. Jennie stands over me in her black nightgown, completely drenched. Her eyes are rolled back into her head.

She whispers, "Bow. Starboard. Stern. Port. Bow. Starboard. Stern. Port."

"Jennie," I say, and her eyes stop fluttering and focus on a point behind my head, out the window toward the river.

She clutches her stomach and retches, vomiting dark liquid all over the hardwood floor.

She collapses into the mess. On her hands and knees, she cries and wipes her lips. Jennie raises a shaky hand toward the window. "She waits for you in the water, Anna. We all wait for you in the water."

After I get Jennie cleaned up and back to bed, the wind howls outside my window, and I can feel the house sway gently. I think of it all, including the blessing and curse of a house on the river. We feel everything and feel nothing all the same, all the elementals—earth, air, fire, water, and spirit.

But this is a different type of wind. This is the type of wind that signals the shift that Jennie warned. This is the wind that signals the end is near.

This is the beginning of the end of it all.

Chapter 18

I did all that I could do. I tended to Jennie and helped mend her foot. I changed the bandage and kept the wound clean so it wouldn't get infected, but still, she walked. Each night I would check her room, and each night she would be gone. In the morning I would find her again, outside on our porch, standing there, clutching those strips of paper she would gather along her walks. Folded, always folded, so I could not see what they contained. She stood there staring out over the block we lived on as if expecting someone or something to happen. As if a great answer to all of our worries would come galloping down the street to explain our existence and this house.

Each morning I would ask her where she had been, and she would respond with the various points in the city she had traveled to on foot: Streeterville. Old Town. Wrigleyville. Little Italy. Pilsen. Avondale. Ukrainian Village. Palmer Square. Humboldt Park. And more. Each city neighborhood had its name and its own charm, distinguished by the people who lived there.

"They were all towns once," Jennie said, referring to the neighborhood names.

I nodded, very much knowing this. The Town of Jefferson. City of Lake View. Town of Lake. And so on. But Chicago grew like wildflowers. Less than forty years after it was first incorporated as a town itself in 1833, Chicago expanded to become the fifth largest city and, not too long after that, the second largest city—the Second City.

Chicago became a quick success because of its population growth, merchants, information, technology, industry, arts, and investment. Part of what assisted in Chicago's explosion into a bustling world-class city were its docks, granaries, ships, water houses, and the riverfront. From the very beginning of settlement, the Chicago River defined this city.

Jennie said, "Do you remember Kimball's farm and Rose's Hill? So many things you expect to stay the same forever change, and sometimes you don't change with it, and so I wonder what that makes me. What does that make us? We're stagnant like pond water, standing here growing algae as the world evolves around us. I wonder some nights, What are we even connected to anymore?"

I think of the river and how it is connected to Lakes Michigan, Huron, Erie, and Ontario, even spreading out to the Saint Lawrence River and how that stretches on to the Atlantic Ocean. The depths of the oceans are known in many ways to be a fairy land, where fairies and mermaids live.

Conversations about these creatures didn't begin with Walt Disney. Pliny the Elder, who lived from AD 23–24 to AD 79 mentions the possibility of them based on accounts off the coast of Gaul. It's said that mermaid corpses frequently washed up on the shore there. Witnesses spoke of how their beautiful bodies were covered in gold, greens, blues, and rose-colored iridescent scales. Even the infamous pirate Blackbeard recorded mentions of mermaids in his logbook. He was known to avoid waters where they lived. He called these charted waters enchanted.

Mermaids were sighted by the conquistadors during the conquest of the Americas in 1493, in the Kai Islands by Japanese soldiers in 1943, off Mayne Island in 1967 by tourists, in 1998 by boaters in Hawaii, in 2009 at Kiryat Haim Beach, at a dam in northern Zimbabwe in 2012, and more.

The Chicago River has been important for people for thousands of years. Tribes used the environment for food in the form of beaver, otter, muskrat, and turtles. Deer were also a major source of protein, as were elk, bear, bison, and fish. Nuts from the nearby forest trees were an important staple, and maple groves provided sugar. But no tribes lived around the river year-round.

Maps I located in my research of tribal settlements showed villages uphill overlooking the river at the North Branch, though some did move downhill during dry months. The river was a lifeline for the tribes, but with the introduction of European contact, disruption, warfare, and dislocation became routine. The process of displacement began shortly after the first missionary Father Jacques Marquette and explorer Louis Jolliet.

Chief Black Hawk of the Sauk in Wisconsin refused to recognize the United States and resisted. The Sauk were defeated at the Battle of Bad Axe in Wisconsin, with men, women, and children massacred. This conflict ended Indigenous resistance to European settlement. The Treaty of Chicago signed September 26, 1833, ordered the end of all tribal presence east of the Upper Mississippi. The Potawatomi left shortly thereafter, with the land being in full control by European settlers in 1845. This marked the first time in thousands of years that this place, which is today called Chicago, no longer belonged to its native people.

The Indigenous people of the area knew that the river was not a place that could be trusted to live by year-round, and I just wish I could locate more to speak to that.

It's not unusual that apparitions and unexplainable activity are reported around bodies of water, particularly rivers. For early riverboats, the water was full of dangers that could sink their vessels, and boiler explosions were common. Fridays were thought inauspicious days to launch a boat or to be on a boat. Another superstition said it was unlucky to name a boat with the thirteenth letter in the alphabet, M. One text from 1889, *Gould's History of River Navigation* by E. W.

Gould, said that "all steamboats built and run on the Mississippi River and its tributaries, whose name commenced with the letter M, were either burned, sank, exploded or were unsuccessful as an investment to their owners."

Over 70 percent of the world is covered in water. Humans have only covered less than 10 percent of that with sonar equipment, meaning that much of the world's bodies of water have been unobserved, unmapped, and unexplored. We do not know what lies beneath. We know that the Chicago River connects to the Illinois River and then to the Mississippi River, and then that flows into the Gulf of Mexico, a basin surrounded by Mexico, the southern United States, and Cuba. From here, there is the Caribbean Sea and the vast North Atlantic Ocean. And it is in those two seas, the Caribbean and the North Atlantic, that are full of stories regarding pirates, shipwrecks, and beings that live underwater.

Accounts of mermaids have existed for thousands of years. Of course, it's been suspected that these reports were all an illusion. Or were people mistaking manatees or dolphins for these supernatural beings.

Maybe all this time mermaids were just gods, always existing below the surface of the ocean. The civilization of Babylon existed over four thousand years ago, and it was there that people believed in Dagon, the fish god, who was depicted as having a bearded head with a crown and the body of a man, but waist down, he too like the mermaid had a fishtail. Greek mythology gives us Triton, a merman and messenger of the sea, and more ancient cultures mention these beings, including Syrian mythology, which spoke of the goddess Derceto.

Threats of death at sea often included mention of supernatural beings. There have been warnings of sea nymphs and sirens and mermaids luring people to the water and to their deaths for as long as people traveled by water. Often, they would be compelled by the beautiful sounds of singing or music. Sometimes it was even said that these sea creatures would charm the very winds that blew across the oceans so that those on board vessels could hear their songs. All of this was in the hope that passengers or workers on these ships would peer over the sides of the vessel, be entranced by the beauty of the mermaids, and reach too far over, losing their grip and balance and falling into the waves. Often, also, it's thought that the ship's captain would become gripped with the obsession of locating the origin of those sounds, and the water spirits would entice him to navigate the ship closer and closer until it crashed into rocky coasts. Many shipwrecks were blamed on mermaids.

It is all connected, I think, and I look at Jennie and answer her question as to what we are connected to.

"We are connected. You and I are connected to each other, to this house, to the river, and, like Grandmother and later Mother and Father said, to the sea. We are salty sea air. We are glistening, multicolored, brilliant, and bright river rocks. We are the unexplored depths of the ocean, the deepest part of the Caribbean and North Atlantic . . ."

"The Puerto Rico Trench," Jennie says.

"Yes, the Puerto Rico Trench." I smile that my sister recalls this interesting fact our father told us. Ocean trenches are depressions on the seafloor. These chasms represent some of the deepest parts of the ocean. The Puerto Rico Trench is one of the most complex in the world, where the North American tectonic plate scrapes against the Caribbean tectonic plate. It's also the site of a volcano that sits five miles below the ocean surface that spews mud over the water. Sometimes what's below rises to the top, even if by force.

My days feel longer than they ever have. Jennie's moods have become more and more explosive. While I never fear that she could hurt me or anyone else, I worry that her emotions distort her reality and could accidentally influence her to harm herself. When I am not tending to Jennie, I work on gathering research for the episode that will air in a few weeks, and I spend time with Peter.

In time, Peter began to notice the dark circles that dressed my eyes, and how often my thoughts would slip away, and how I would lose track of time. He soon learned of the hallucinations, or what Jennie calls my "flickers," when he and I were standing on the corner of Canal and Adams, and I feared to cross the street at a stoplight. What he saw was just an empty street. What I saw were horse-drawn carriages, their hooves clomping along the cobblestone road, a trolley car bursting with passengers rushing by, and people exiting and entering Union Station, which looked not like what Union Station appeared to be today, but a large redbrick building with half-moons for windows that wrapped around the structure. I willed the old moving picture to cease, to bring me back into the present, but I made the mistake of making eye contact with a man in a black suit and black hat.

He approached me, his face melting with each step he took, chunks of flesh peeling off in large, sticky strands, and when he stood in front of me and opened his mouth, he was less flesh and more bone. "Hurry now," the skeleton spoke, "or you'll miss the picnic."

It was Peter squeezing my hand and asking me if I was all right that pulled me back in, and when he did so, all I could do was throw my arms around him in relief, because he saved me. He saved me from that awful nightmare, and I believed that more were to come.

Peter asks me questions about my day or past things like where I went to school and what I studied and so forth. Often, I brush aside these conversations and direct the questioning back to him.

Whenever I attempted to speak about my life, my own words would come out clipped or garbled. I assume it is the house, always waiting, always listening, and making sure I will not disobey it. It had its hold on me and wielded its control.

I also didn't want to talk about my life. I didn't want to think about my life before the accident, because I knew I could not return to being that person again. I am slowly trying to heal, to become new, and with Peter I believe I can do that.

I blamed my behavior on all that I could, really—a lack of sleep. At first he believed me, but as my exhaustion grew, he begged me to tell him why I was not sleeping well.

It is the house that keeps me awake, the knowing and the remembering, and my dearest Jennie. How I love her, but also how she brings me such rushing sadness. I begin to worry that I can never break free from her. It is as Grandmother said so long ago: Jennie and I are two pearls, existing on the river, waiting for I don't know what, quite frankly, but I hope this is not all that life has to offer.

Eventually, Peter grew to suspect something more was the matter, and if he pressed me, I don't think I could lie to him. I would have to tell him the truth. All of it. Each painful detail, but I willed that day to not come anytime soon. In the mornings I would go out to my fairy garden and ask my fairy to please allow me another day with Peter, and each day I did this, I had another day with my dearest.

Today, Peter came over after I bandaged Jennie's foot and served her breakfast. She was silent and bitter, knowing that Peter is now a regular visitor, but there is nothing she can do to stop it. I told her that in no reality would she be allowed to deny me this joy.

She stays in her room, sulking, refusing to meet him on any of his visits. It is as if denying his existence in some way will make it so that he is not real, that he just exists in my mind. If Jennie needs to deny Peter being real, then I am not going to trouble myself with that. As long as she does not interfere with my happiness, I do not care.

When I walk downstairs after gathering Jennie's tray from breakfast, I note something curious: a single wet handprint on the glass door. I walk over to it and place my hand on the surface. The glass is dry. The handprint is on the outside. My hand nearly matches the size of the stranger's impression outside.

I think of the faceless woman pacing my room in my waking nightmares. She has returned again several times. Her loose, wet hair. Her drenched white dress that clings to her body. Her bare feet and her skin the color of the full moon, bright and radiating. And how when she dives into the water, her legs fuse together into a single limb covered in thousands of tiny, brilliant, and beautiful scales.

Her presence is an omen, just like the sound of music being heard out at sea by sailors. The nightmare that haunts me in the night is warning me about the end. I want to tell Peter about her—more like *warn* Peter about her—because if she is here for me, then she is surely here for him too, but I am too afraid to mention it for fear he would leave. Deep within, I know I should tell him. I know I should test the waters and prove to Jennie that he really does love me and that he is prepared to face this nightmare with me.

When Peter arrives, he notices that there is something upsetting me. When he asks what's the matter, the only thing I can utter is, "I think our house is haunted."

He laughs at first, thinking it is a joke, but soon he reads the dread in my eyes.

"Why do you think that?" he asks.

"There are noises," I say, and it feels like a great wave of relief to finally tell someone other than Jennie.

"Does Jennie think the house is haunted as well?"

"Yes, she has seen things. She's done things. All because of the house. It compels her to. She has fits and attacks, and then she hears the house whisper to her. Then there's the sounds, they come at all hours. In the day or in the night. The sounds range from footsteps and doorknobs rattling to cabinets opening and closing and the faucets being turned on. Then comes the sounds of water, dripping water, and now we've started hearing the sounds of waves crashing."

His eyes are kind, and I can feel he is not judging anything I'm telling him. "Wait." He places a hand on my shoulder. "Is this why you've been upset?"

I nod. "Yes, I'm afraid of what I'm seeing and what I'm hearing."

His face shows concern. I know he believes me. "And what do you hear the voices say?"

"They talk about the house. The river and water."

Peter goes silent, but I can see by the way his eyes fall distant that his mind is turning. We have tea and then sit out in the garden. We sit there in silence for quite a while, admiring first my fairy garden and then turning our attention to the river. I talk to him about the river superstitions I have come across. When he asks me if it is for one of my upcoming podcasts, I say it is. There was such strange activity occurring that, yes, I believe there was someone involved, but I also believe there is a hint of peculiarity in all of this, in a river that was stolen, manipulated, polluted, and now sentences death. The water is angry at us.

Some days pass, and I continue my research and continue to see Peter. He doesn't ask me about the ghostly activity, nor do I offer to speak about the detectives who continue to call and appear unexpectedly at the house, asking to speak to Jennie, always to Jennie and never me. As always, Jennie refuses to speak with or even see them.

Another day goes by like this, Jennie terribly upset with me and blaring the television, always on the news, speaking of the missing Joshua Martin who had yet to return home. His mother now appeared on television, her face flush with tears, begging for any information to bring her son home, and that's what we all wanted, was just for our loved ones to be home with us. I cried myself as I watched her. I felt her suffering completely.

I later thought of the woman in the green dress and if she knows anything about Joshua Martin and the other drowned men. One afternoon, Peter took me out for a walk along the trail at Clark Park that runs parallel to the river, and I thought I spotted her, a woman with red wavy hair wearing a green dress with silver buttons, but her face was obscured. Blurred somehow. I could make out her form and shape, but not her. When I went to say something about it to Peter, I thought it silly and dismissed the thought. Then we had a picnic at the Humboldt Park Lagoon.

That evening he asked if I would like to join him for dinner in his apartment, and I agreed. He cooked, and then we ate, and then we drank, and then we danced so much and laughed so much I felt like I could explode with joy. I collapsed into him, longing for him to touch me everywhere, and kiss me everywhere. I took the scent of him in, and his lips against my ear, uttering my name, was a shooting star of ecstasy. I clung to him, fearful to let go, worried that each movement, each moment, would be our last together.

In the morning, Peter brings me home and insists that we walk down to the river and sit on the bench for a few moments, because he doesn't want to leave me quite yet. I agree, and I glance at the stairway, dreading to find Jennie's form looming there, but the house is silent except for the little excited barks from Clover and Thistle welcoming me home. The dogs tumble outside, and we join Peter down the path and at the bench in front of the great sassafras tree that shields my fairy garden.

He folds his hands on his lap. "I have to tell you something," he starts, and it feels like a heavy, cold steel door is closing.

I don't like when people prompt what they are going to tell you with a warning. The warning signaled doom.

He takes a deep breath and then his words come out swiftly. "I'm moving. Work is sending me back to Ireland for a major project, and . . ."

I stop listening when he says, "I'm moving." The door closed. I want to sink to the riverbed, because I am a fool for believing that love was real. I had been so fearful that Jennie was the one who was going to tear us apart, but no, it was the ways of the modern world that had wrapped itself around him, ready to pull the only person I loved, wanted, and desired away from me.

I thought he loved me too. What happened? Why was he so coolly and calmly breaking my heart?

I feel like I am submerged under a great cloudy depth, and my vision blurs. The only person that I had made a connection with, not only in recent memory but ever, just told me they were leaving me.

My thoughts turn to bodies floating and bobbing downriver. They are covered in a tangle of branches, smeared with mud and blood, black waste, and animal entrails. I think I hear Grandmother's song and Jennie's song, a song on an endless loop, a song destined to play at my funeral and beyond. A song designed to mark my memory. A triumphant dirge playing across our city.

"So will you . . . ?"

My vision clears, and with its return the music fades. "Will I what?"

Peter is on his knee with a black velvet box opened to present a simple solitaire diamond set on a gold band. Everything about him is like from another time—old-fashioned, simple, sweet, and kind. I both loved and was terrified by that, because it wasn't just his eyes, or face, or even his voice that risked pulling me apart. It was all of him. Yes, Jennie or the house were both very capable of harming me, but it is Peter who is the only thing that could absolutely destroy me, because I love him so much. I beg every stitch of the universe to allow his love for me to be true.

"Marry me?" He smiles at nothing else but me.

All of my nerve endings, from my fingertips to my toes, feel as though they are activated by a soft electric pulse. I feel for the first time so very much alive.

I can feel the house watching, waiting for the response it demands I give. Before I can answer, I turn around, and there is Jennie standing in the window.

"My sister," I say.

Peter stands up and waves toward the house. "Your sister? Where is she?"

"In the window," I speak softly.

Just moments ago, where I felt the bright sun of possibility, I now sense the sting of cold and a pit of darkness because of Jennie's presence.

"You can invite her down if you like."

Peter is so very kind, but he will never understand the gloom that is my sister.

"I don't think she's yet ready to meet you," I say.

"But I'm hoping to meet her soon," Peter says. His words aim for comfort, as always. My beautiful, and thoughtful and loving, Peter. Always reaching for the right thing to say. "Because I'm hoping to be your best friend, your family, and, if you let me, your husband."

I turn back to him, and his eyes plead with me to give him an answer. The lines around his mouth deepen, preparing for a response he does not want to hear, the very response I now hear the house screaming at me so loud it rattles my insides.

I think about all of the forces that want me to say no—this house, Jennie, the river and the ghosts, tragedy, and superstitions that make up each and every drop of that body of water.

I want to scream my answer as loud as I can so that the heavens above, and all of the great bodies on earth, can vibrate with the knowing that this is my answer. So that the house will never be mistaken about my great defiance, of my disruption to the river and everything that lives below. I long to break free of this land that drains me of everything that I could potentially be.

"Take me with you." And my answer is not just a yes, but a plea to be saved from my misery.

When I turn back to search for Jennie, she had slipped away from view.

This evening, I know that things will be bad.

Peter squeezes me so hard I hope I can just melt into him. I turn my face to the sky and silently pray to my fairy that Peter can take me away with him right then, because I dread another day in that house.

"Then yes, you will?" He pulls me away, holds my arms out, and smiles. "I love you so much, Anna. I will love you forever. Neither life nor death will know the limits of my love for you."

And when he says those words, I believe him, knowing that he will have to be committed to the rules of death in order to love me.

Chapter 19

"Now, everyone knows the name RMS *Titanic*. It's taken on a new life as a source of ghost stories and legend and lore. It's like the *Titanic* became greater than the ship and its ill-fated maiden voyage. The passengers, both those that survived and the victims, were catapulted that night to reluctant fame.

"RMS *Titanic* proved to live up to the value of its name by sinking spectacularly over a hundred years ago, dragging hundreds to the far reaches of a watery grave.

"We know the story of the RMS *Titanic*, whether willingly or unwillingly. It's that horror story we can't escape. There are references to it in historical, academic, and pop culture texts. There have been stage productions and films and books written about that vessel. We've seen re-creations and sometimes original pictures of the interiors, from the lush and detailed first-class guest rooms, the luxury cabin sitting rooms, the quaint second-class sleeper cabins, and, of course, the iconic Grand Staircase, the opulent centerpiece to first-class passengers.

"The ornate Grand Staircase boasted intricate wood carvings and one of the most famous clocks in the world that would be forever defined as a deeply romantic symbol. The clock, named Honour and Glory Crowning Time, was designed in the neoclassical eclectic style and was set at the top of the first central landing. In the central pane of the ornamental oak wood paneling was a column, adorned with laurels, and on either side of that stood two female figures. The figure on the left, holding a tablet, was thought to represent honor. The figure on the right, holding a palm branch, was thought to represent glory.

"Two sisters.

"Honour and Glory, who set sail across the great Atlantic, only to sink to the ocean bottom.

"The entire voyage and disaster of the RMS *Titanic* is a conversation of class. We romanticize it, this beautiful, glorious ship full of rich people dressed in fine clothes and jewelry. Yet we deliberately dismiss the hundreds and hundreds of third-class passengers and how they were doomed from the beginning because of where they came from, how they spoke, what they wore, and the amount of money, or lack thereof, that they had. Yet each of them—first, second, and third class—were on the very same ship, together, riding together towards America with prospects of dreams, a new life, a brilliant hope in a wondrous land. Each of them was traveling together in the same structure, yet each of them was ultimately worlds apart, in life and even today in death, because those third-class passengers continue to be forgotten and ignored.

"Let's step back just a little. The RMS *Titanic* was a luxury steamship that struck an iceberg off the coast of Newfoundland in the North Atlantic Ocean on its maiden voyage in the very early-morning hours of April 15, 1912.

"There were 2,240 people on board. Of that, 1,500 people lost their lives in the bitter, ice-cold waters. Survivors reported that the ship took on water from the gash where it hit the iceberg. Evacuation efforts are the stuff of legend, considering how chaotic they were and how lifeboats were given in preference to first-class passengers, women, and children.

"Laws have changed since the sinking of the RMS *Titanic* in regard to the number of lifeboats stored on a vessel, but what's important to highlight is that by the standards of their day, the RMS *Titanic* did surpass the number of lifeboats it was required to carry. It's macabre to say this, but way back then there were considerations made as to how many lifeboats to include on any ship, ranging from how long it would take for people to get to the lifeboats to a belief that there could be people on board who were already dead so there was no need for space for every living passenger that had boarded. The number on board the *Titanic* was 2,240 passengers. The British government determined that lifeboat space for only 960 passengers was sufficient. The *Titanic* carried lifeboats for 1,178 passengers, surpassing the requirements. But when the *Titanic*'s lifeboats were launched, they were purposefully not filled to capacity. More people could have been saved, but it's believed they were afraid to fill up the lifeboats, as there was worry that too many people on board would capsize the craft.

"There continue to be allegations to this day that many third-class passengers never had a chance to make it to the lifeboats, as they were locked below decks. I guess there's no way to prove that. And even if we did, who is there to prosecute or to hold accountable for how the third-class passengers were treated?

"That's the thing about history: we can look back and see how the vulnerable were used and manipulated, taken advantage of, abused, and downright hurt and harmed. But who is there to tell? Who is there to listen? Who is there to set things right for them in the present?

"There's very often no one.

"There's just those of us researching, reading, or listening to their stories with a hint of curiosity and sometimes sadness that washes over us as we hear the accounts of their tragic ends. But then what do any of us do? There's often very little that we can do to set right the events of the long past. And so, we return to our lives and soak in our distraction. Why? Because maybe it's foolish to think we can set right the past, particularly when we cannot find justice in the present. For terrible things happen, popping up on the news, in an alert on our phones, a chyron on-screen, anything to mark its viral fire.

"Today we have an epidemic of the missing and murdered in our very city. The dismembered body parts of a woman are found folded delicately, stacked atop of a garbage can. A newborn infant is found wrapped in plastic in a dumpster, the knot tight, ensuring it can't cry for help—ever. And young people, who are simply walking home, are plucked from the street, never seen again. Our safety is an illusion.

"We exist on an endless loop of tragedy, unsure of which of these events to pick and choose to hold in our hearts.

"But I choose to be consumed by this, to be consumed by water, for whatever miserable reason.

"More than half of the deaths on the *Titanic* were third-class passengers. Many were stuck in the lower decks and were unable to make it to the lifeboats. The lifeboats were conveniently positioned just outside of the first-class cabins. The lower classes were trapped below the ship, unable to open those supposedly locked gates that were set there originally for the sole intention of separating the various classes of passengers. You may think that sounds horrible, a gate to separate one class from the other, but aren't there separations between the classes today, whether visible or not?"

I hit pause, unable to speak any longer. My throat is raw from recording over and over again. No matter how many times I record, nothing sounds right when I play it back. My voice sounds weak, my words garbled. I sound hesitant and unsure. I lack all confidence to not only tell this story but to emphasize why this story should even be told and why people living today should care.

I thought the podcast would make sense by first telling people about the RMS *Titanic*, an event they had heard about repeatedly throughout their lives, and comparing it with a somewhat similar tragedy, but one they knew nothing about. Interest was often piqued with familiarity, and so I hoped that, making these connections, people would understand, and it would help in what I was trying to convey.

I move to the kitchen and make a cup of chamomile tea. I add lemon and honey and then close my eyes on the sofa. I sense it as Clover and Thistle hop on and curl at my feet.

The front door flies open.

There is the wild sound of metal crashing, bending, and twisting in on itself. It sounds like the wails of a great mechanical beast, but there is nothing except an open front door that looks out to a warm summer day.

The dogs spring up, jump down, and run to the door, barking and growling, their teeth snapping against something I cannot see. I stand on weak legs, feeling very tired and very scared all at the same time.

The outside air rushes in, and with it the sweet scent of rain tucked within it. A light drizzle begins to fall, staining the concrete porch.

"Hello?" I call out, but there is nothing and no one there. I walk down the steps and then look up to the very top of the house and at the decorative blue diamond situated on the peak. It is a symbol I saw the day my life changed, and so it is fitting that it should be placed here on the house, to emphasize that Jennie and I are transformed people who have gone through a great and painful metamorphosis.

Jennie comes rushing down the steps. She looks bewildered. Her face twisted in fear. Her cheeks glistening with tears.

She throws her arms around me and then notes where my eyes are focused. She takes my hand in hers and we both stand there, looking up at that peak of our beautiful house and that blue diamond that will forever define us. That blue diamond that was our warning but that we accept all the same. Her hand is as cold as the Northern Atlantic Ocean and is trembling.

We stand there for a long moment, listening to the rumbles from the heavens above, and the sounds of cars at a distance, and music that seems to come from everywhere and nowhere.

Branches sway and leaves fall to the ground. A storm is approaching.

I look at Jennie, who has silent tears continuing to fall down her face.

"It's begun," she says.

I nod silently, agreeing.

Chapter 20

I return to my office. I can hear Jennie wailing in her room.

We stood outside long enough so that when the sky opened and rain came pouring down over us, a complete baptism of grief, it was too much of a reminder for Jennie.

A cloudy summer day.

The chorus of the city.

The blue diamond.

The rain.

It was all too much.

I walked her inside and led her to her room, where she slammed the door and turned on the news. I listened just outside her door. The search for Joshua Martin had been extended to include all searchable parts of the river, because authorities know the river is always calling.

Rivers are valuable ecosystems that provide drinking water and irrigation, produce electricity through hydroelectric dams, offer leisure activities in the form of swimming, and serve as areas of transportation. Rivers are not supposed to serve as watery graves, but in Chicago this is what our river has become. Our Chicago River was luring people to their deaths.

In winter, the water doesn't completely freeze. There are sections along the North Branch, however, that do freeze totally each year. It doesn't matter if there are frozen sections at the surface, because the river will continue to flow. Water temperatures are warmer at the bottom, and even if there are sheets of ice at the top or a thick layer of snow, activity beneath the river continues. Fish will continue to swim and live even if their activity decreases due to the temperatures. Other small animals may hibernate for the season. When the surface of the main stem of the river freezes in downtown Chicago, the city will launch an icebreaker that will break up the ice, freeing up the waterway for safety purposes.

Seeing the river in winter, with large chunks of ice floating across the surface, is an otherworldly sight. These thick slabs of glistening white ice floating there look like sections of stained glass. People fall in the water during the winter months, and their bodies are discovered in the spring thaw. They fall in during spring when the rains come for new growth, and they fall in during the blistering summer and the cool autumn. The river is always calling; you just have to be careful to listen, and if you hear its song, you must turn the other way.

I look to my computer screen for a moment and to the image I had left up: an artist's rendering of what the great *Titanic* looked like standing on its end, moments before it sank to the bottom of the ocean.

I wonder what the great crash sounded like as it struck an iceberg. How was the interior of the shipped rocked? Were people asleep in their beds, and did they tumble out in their nightclothes? Were babies disturbed in their slumber, and did they burst into tears screaming and crying for their mothers, who spilled out of their own beds to cradle their infants to their chests? Were revelers still awake, dining and dancing, about to toast to luck and love, and just as their glasses were about to clink, with that golden liquid fizzing with bubbles, they slipped from their hands and crashed to the floor.

In an instant, everything can change. In a moment, death comes calling, clawing out from the ocean, and it does so often as a song is playing in the background, the soundtrack of our final moments.

And what is an iceberg anyway but a piece of frozen fate? Waiting there still and watching. A sentinel guarding the path, or more like holding the gate open to the underwater world. An iceberg is a rebel chunk of ice that splits away from a larger glacier and floats away into the open sea, ready to initiate disorder and destroy.

Through my research I learned that it's thought that the iceberg that sank the RMS *Titanic* began its journey around the time of Pharaoh Tutankhamun, more than three thousand years before the ship came into contact with it. That iceberg floated out there in those frigid waters, and it existed as civilizations rose and fell.

The *Titanic* iceberg was one of the few that ever made it as far south as it reached. Only 1 percent of icebergs ever make it to the Atlantic Ocean. The iceberg that was struck by the *Titanic* likely made it five thousand miles south of the Arctic Circle. The water temperature where the *Titanic* sank was about twenty-eight degrees, freezing and lethal for humans but too warm for an iceberg for the long term.

So, after the great ship sank, the iceberg likely floated south into the Atlantic for another year or two until it melted and merged with the rest of the ocean. And so the ship that the gods could not sink was sunk by a statistical anomaly.

Many people who were awakened that night or who were swept up and drowned in the corridors of the RMS *Titanic* didn't even know what had happened, that they had struck an iceberg. Tragedy often unfolds in a burst of chaos and ends quickly. A struck match that fizzles out. Many of those passengers were bathed in darkness as the lights in the lower levels of the ship shut off, and as the cold water rose and the metal tipping back into the ocean roared, many perhaps just thought they were being swallowed into the night.

Maybe the ship was lured to its doom by something otherworldly, something supernatural. A siren song. A mermaid. And how they relished and fed to their satisfaction on the terror of the passengers and on their screams.

Did anyone think as they saw the multi-ton vessel take on water, stand on its end, and then sink into the icy ocean that maybe it was the great and powerful king of the ocean, Poseidon himself, who had pulled the ship down into his watery kingdom so it could be used by Theseus, Triton, Polyphemus, Orion, Belus, Agenor, Neleus, Atlas, Pegasus, Chrysaor, and Cymopolea—all of his children—as a new toy?

There was no way to know how those screams sounded that night, but I can imagine. I've heard screams like that before, and I hear those screams sometimes above Jennie's humming and her music. There is no way to know what those room lights must have looked like shining down on the shocked passengers in lifeboats, but I can almost see their wide eyes and mouths slack. Terror has a certain distant look to it that can only be experienced in the moment. It's the look of defeat.

I've heard screams such as those.

I've seen those faraway looks.

What a pity, their faces.

I wonder, as the ship sank deeper, if the survivors on the lifeboats could hear the screams and pleas for help, for salvation, for anything from those remaining on the boat? I imagine the people in the lifeboats would go on to carry that trauma until their deathbeds.

And as the vessel was finally swallowed up, covered by crashing waves, were all of its lights extinguished? Or did some spook lights reflect from below, dancing from ballrooms and dining halls, as human beings breathed in water and were crushed by the weight of death?

There is no way to know what any of it looked like or sounded like, but from my own history, I have my suspicions of what terror felt like that night.

I think about the people, those terrified people who saw such a frightful, ghastly sight, something that likely will never again happen in history. How does one survive that? How did those who survived it actually *survive*, go on to live their lives? Did they have to run from their rooms? Did they see others fall by the wayside as they rushed past?

Did they see people being struck by falling furniture and chandeliers? Or did they push someone out of their way so that they could make it?

Most of the survivors were wealthy passengers, able to enjoy the comforts on the most modern of luxury ships of the day. As those wealthy people strapped on their life jackets, did they ever once look into the eyes of any of the lower-class passengers that were held back, panicked and afraid of death spread out waiting in the cold sea for them?

I turn away from that picture of the *Titanic* and sit silently in my chair.

Jennie speaks from the doorway.

"You're going to lose your voice," she says.

I am confused by what she means and ask her to explain. She says, "They had more beautiful voices than any human being could have, and before the approach of a storm, and when they expected a ship would be lost, they swam before the vessel and sang sweetly of the delights to be found in the depths of the sea and begged the sailors not to fear if they sank to the bottom. But the sailors could not understand the song; they took it for the howling of the storm. And these things were never to be beautiful for them, for if the ship sank, the men were drowned, and their dead bodies alone reached the palace of the Sea King."

"I . . ." I start, unsure why she is telling me the story right now.

Jennie points to the microphone on my desk, and that makes sense, because I do not hum like her or play music loudly from my room. Music belonged to Jennie and not me. It was her gift and not mine. That was determined long ago. We each come with our own enchantments in life. It is important to discover them, and once we do discover them, we must never ignore them, for if neglected, these powers can then fade to dust, and if that happens, we might as well die.

"It's what I do, Jennie. I tell stories. It's what I'm supposed to do." I wince. A sharp pain runs down my throat. I can taste blood. It feels like I had been screaming and screaming. My throat feels scratched and raw.

Jennie crosses her arms over her chest. "See, my sister. I know you. It's all a part of our great transformation. It is coming, and we should be prepared."

"Jennie, please stop," I say. "I probably caught a cold from being out in the rain."

She raises her eyebrows. "Very well. Don't believe me. What are you telling them now?"

I knew she was going to be upset, but none of it matters any longer, especially according to her.

"I'm recording an introductory episode before I tell them what happened here. I presume they all would have heard of the *Titanic*. I hope that by telling them about the *Titanic* that maybe they'll understand . . ."

I cough. Feeling my voice catch in my throat.

She laughs. "If you're trying to get them to sympathize, then you'll be sorry. They didn't care then, and they will not care now. They'll never care." She pauses and then speaks about what lingers on both of our minds.

"Do you think the detectives who came to visit us will find the missing man?"

"I don't know. I hope so, but they haven't quite helped me."

"Those detectives will come calling again. They are going to come here, and they're going to want to speak with you and me and especially your darling Peter."

I reach over to the teacup beside me and bring it to my lips. "I'm going to ignore you," I say. "I'm going to ignore those detectives as well."

"Tea will not help. It's not the weather. You're losing your voice because you're not supposed to tell. Maybe we can stop it. Maybe there's still time." She brings her hands to her ears, presses down, and closes her eyes. "Some days it's just so loud."

I don't hear anything, but the house speaks differently to her than it does to me.

"Weren't you going to stop that dreadful leaking?"

I didn't know where else the noise could possibly be coming from, but there it was, that drip that echoed throughout the house.

Drip-drip-drip.

I had redone the walls in both the upstairs and downstairs bathrooms. I had refreshed the kitchen. I had repaired and replaced cabinets and floorboards and found many, many curious treasures along the way.

I had followed each and every single place in the house where there were pipes. I even checked in the basement. There was nothing, except what I hadn't told Jennie. That in each place I went in search for that dripping noise I found another little metal piece, each of them different. Some flat and some circular, and some looked like little gears. I assumed if I put them all together they would create something. In fact, they looked like all of the little pieces that Jennie had spread out before her on her work desk. And just yesterday, when I went down to the basement to repair one of those old, creaking stairs, I found that the house had left me a little gift there as well: several pieces of freshly polished wood laid out on one of the steps.

I wonder, then, if I should ask Jennie to inspect all of the presents the house has given me to see if she can understand what it is the house is trying to tell me to construct from it all. I stand up and walk over to the table across from my desk and reach under it and produce a box and take it over to Jennie standing in the doorway.

She accepts the box. "What's this?"

"These are things that the house gave me while I was doing repairs and searching for the leak. I think that you might know what they're for."

Jennie opens the lid and takes a look inside. "Yes. I know what this is, but we're missing the final piece, which is rather large. You'll know it when you find it."

She takes the box to her room and then returns, there again standing in the doorway, wanting to know more about the story I was going to tell. It seemed as though today she was more disappointed than upset. Perhaps she had resigned herself to the fact that this could no longer be prevented. The tide was coming, and we were going to be swept away with it.

I thought of the Little Mermaid and her bargain, to give up her voice in exchange for shedding her mermaid tail for human legs so that she could live above the sea and so that she could be with the man that she loved. I knew that Jennie had warned me about Peter, that falling in love with him meant breaking my bond with her and severing my connection to the house. I knew that when I left, there would be no one here to take care of her. She would be alone and cast away to a dark grotto where I could never reach her. But I was not going to allow that to happen to my sister. I was not going to allow her to be taken from me again.

Jennie contemplates the threshold, and then she does something she has not done in years. She enters the room. As soon as she does, it's as if the temperature drops.

I stand up from my desk, in shock. "Jennie . . ." I do not know what to say. She has refused to ever enter one of these rooms that are dressed in mourning. She said that she could hear them howling in here in pain, and if she stood in here long enough, it was as if those spirits would slip into her body. When I asked her what that felt like, she said it just felt like an endless pit of sorrow and that it was the worst feeling she had ever known.

Jennie falls to her knees at my feet and takes my hand in hers. "I was thinking about you, my dear sister." Her lips change color, turning blue. She is cold to the touch. I wrap my arms around her to keep her warm, as that is all I can do in this sinking moment.

"We can stop all of this, and it can go on as before. Just you and me. You can just forget about your Peter for now. And we can go back to what it was like once upon a time, you and I and the quiet."

201

But there is no quiet. There is the steady dripping. There are Jennie's moods. There are the ghosts and poltergeists that grip us in fear. There are Jennie's long late-night walks, and then there are those detectives with their blasted questions. Motion had already been set. We are already cast out to sea, and there is no changing course. This is what we need to do.

I hear water rushing in the bathroom.

The voices return.

This time it sounds like several women laughing upstairs.

Jennie squeezes my hand tighter. "Don't listen to it. Just listen to me. Stop the story. Stop seeing Peter, and this will end."

I take a deep breath. "But I don't want it to end."

Jennie bows her head and releases my hands. "I don't want to go back . . ."

"I can't live like this anymore, Jennie. Don't you see what's going on? Don't you realize how we live? I am your caretaker. I am your guardian. I am your everything because you are sick."

Jennie inspects my face. Her lips are parted just so. "Do you really believe what it is you are saying?"

We hear water now splashing onto the tile of the bathroom floor.

I throw my head back. "Why do you think I continue to live here? And exist here? This place is like a tomb. A beautiful tomb, but it's a tomb no less. And I'm drowning here, Jennie! Don't you care about me and my happiness? Maybe it's time we leave the house. Maybe you can come live with us until we find you another home. Maybe getting out of this house has always been the answer."

And with that I hear a great metallic bang. The crashing of waves and the piercing screams of hundreds trapped in eternal anguish.

Jennie releases my hand and stands up. She rushes to the door.

"Jennie," I call after her, but she doesn't look back.

"You will regret this." I hear her talking to herself as she rushes down the hallway and down the stairs.

She is muttering to herself now. Repeating a series of words, over and over, and with each syllable she speaks, I feel a great pang in my heart.

"Jennie!" I call out to her, but she ignores me. I'm walking out of my room and moving down the hallway.

She's repeating those same words, over and over.

"Bow. Starboard. Stern. Port. Bow. Starboard. Stern. Port."

Chapter 21

The news is blaring and notes that it has been three weeks since Joshua Martin went missing.

"You can't leave me!" Jennie screams from the bottom of the stairs. She is a ghost seated on the sofa. Dressed in black silk and lace. A mourning dress.

I have been packing in my room, trying to ignore her. She continues to cry, and I open the door and watch her. I stand there for a moment, wanting more to see if there is something that I should say, but I had said it all over the past few weeks. I was miserable living in this house.

Jennie turns her head slowly and faces me. "Can't you finally understand? Can't you finally see it's that this city will not let you leave? You are the steel in the skyscrapers. You are the cobblestones hidden beneath the asphalt-covered streets. You are the Chicago River."

Jennie stands up, her long, black mourning dress cascading around her ankles. She slowly shuffles to the back door. Clover and Thistle, who had never felt safe in her presence, follow her.

They stand there a moment, staring out the window, the sun shining on my sister's face, and for the first time in a long time I can truly see the stark pallor of her skin. I am pained by how pale she is.

"You cannot let this house consume you, Jennie."

"I'll let it consume me as the river consumes me," she says as she sets a black-gloved hand on the french door leading out to the river. "I will let it eat me alive."

"Why don't you come with me? You can meet Peter. He's going to be your brother-in-law."

"I've already met Peter . . ." she whispers. "I've met plenty of men like Peter, with their words dipped in honey and promises coated in chocolate. They're all lies."

"Have you never loved?"

"Once, and I wish I knew his name. I've been searching an eternity for him."

Her voice is soft now. "He really did try to save me. I can see it all unfold. I could see how he locked eyes with me from above. I never believed in that phrase 'love at first sight' until I lived it. It was a beautiful and tragic moment all the same. I can see it so clearly now." She closes her eyes. "How he came for me, and only me. One never forgets that look, that look a man gives you when he first falls in love with you."

"Jennie, you're not making any sense."

She shakes her head slowly. "You could have made this so simple, my dear, darling sister. We could have had a good life here. I thought we were having a good life here, of quiet and of peace. I'm sorry it will end like this for you once again. For me. You can come with me now, or you can wait for them. They are already gathering, waiting to witness our great Chicago story once again."

"I don't know what you're talking about." My voice catches in my throat.

I can feel the house rumble. Jennie steps aside from the door, and then the back door flies open. The front door flies open. A great swirling wind fills the house. All of the cabinets open. Glasses and plates and porcelain fall and shatter on the floor.

The antique candlestick and rotary telephones throughout the house, which have not worked or been connected to landlines in decades, all begin to ring, a great symphony, warning of news to come.

She slips out the back door and walks down toward the river.

"Clover . . . Thistle . . ." I call, but neither dog acknowledges me as they follow my sister along the path.

It is as if a tsunami has torn through it.

I stand in the doorway and look at that framed picture of the house plans and of a picture of my sister and me. I do not remember hanging it back up, and I do not remember Jennie looking this way in this picture.

"I will not die here," I say to myself. "I will not die in this house anchored to a point of loneliness."

I have found someone who wants to be with me, who loves me, and we will go live and love one another. I was finally going to break free of whatever haunting and curse my family had planted for me here on the river.

This was no longer my home.

My husband was now my home.

Chapter 22

I wake.

I walk the dogs. I make tea, and I sit for some time in my office, wondering and waiting.

I look at my list of projects I wish to get to around the house:

- Sweep
- Mop
- Polish the floors
- Dust the antique telephones
- Scrub the bathrooms
- Install a new vanity in the first-floor bathroom

I will get all of this done, and then I will continue with my research, and then I will walk all of Jennie's favorite paths, and I will visit Clark Park, and I will sit there, and I will wait for the woman in the green dress to appear. I will ask her questions about the missing men, and about Jennie, and I know she will answer, because I believe this is how it must be.

I look to my notes, and to the tragedies the river has known: how the original peoples who called this land home were pushed away, displaced, and murdered; how the river would flow with sewage, the putrid mix then folding into the drinking water of the growing city, sickening and killing with disease; how it was common for the surface, oily slick because of all the waste to come ablaze, and how the blue fires were ignored by the fire department and the river burned; how the river flooded and continued to flood, filling and killing, destroying progress in its path; how members of organized crime used this as a place to rid themselves of enemies. So much—there were just so many stories of decay, destruction, and death aligned to this very river, the one that outside my house beamed with life.

There are few things with the staying power of water. The four classical elementals are earth, air, fire, and water. And ancient cultures proposed to explain the complexities of our world in terms of these simple substances. Some cultures also believed that there was a fifth elemental, aether, or spirit. These five were thought to be the elements that everything was made up of. Of course, today modern science doesn't always speak of things in the ways the ancients did. They'll speak of materials in the chemical elements, of their composition, iron or mercury or oxygen, and so on.

Sometimes we have to wonder, What did the ancients really know? Esoteric traditions associate water with the qualities of emotion and intuition, and so maybe we can say, based on those beliefs, that water not only holds memory but that water knows everything.

Earth. Air. Fire. Water.

The elementals.

Each has its place in the folds of the mysteries of the universe, and each holds power, great and all-encompassing power. Not everything is meant to be understood. Not all mysteries are meant to be solved. There is beauty in the unknown. Man has always been obsessed with discovery, with conquering that which already existed, because if it's presently living and breathing, then there is no need to find it. It is so, and disturbing it and its motions, beliefs, and powers can cause great ripples that twist time and cause accidents.

All life requires water. Water calls to us. For some of us, it's with a song. For others, it's with the brilliant reflections on its surface of the sun or the moon or the stars. That reflective surface shimmering at all hours entices us to walk out toward it, to feel the cool water beneath our feet, covering our legs as we're submerged and more, all of us as we're then diving below.

Some of us never break again to the surface, because our home was always the water. And for some of us, we had beings that guided us there.

Is it an end or is it a beginning? Or is it time looking back on itself, repeating a mystical pattern that cannot be explained, just like we cannot explain how and why we exist? We just are. Like air. Like water. We exist.

Water will continue to call to us. It's a great temptress, and I will continue to listen.

You're at a beach. The trillions of grains of sand, the dust, organic matter long deceased spread before you, a great soft blanket leading and welcoming you to liquid reflecting the sky above. Why would you want to deny the gods that gift?

We are so small. We are just a single point, a prick from a sewing needle in the eternal fabric of the universe. And to me, God in that universe has always been like the great Poseidon, god of the sea, who strikes the ground with his powerful trident, shaking the earth and causing shipwrecks.

In turn, I believe that the devil is what appears before us when we awake in the morning, groggy-eyed with dreams still clouding our heads. When you turn on that bathroom light, when you inspect that reflection, know that humans are fallible.

We make terrible and life-destroying mistakes each day, and sometimes our missteps contribute to the deaths of other human beings, and sometimes there is no consequence to that error.

For some unlucky few of the elementals, it's water that taunts us. It's always taunted me. The river outside reminds me that if I leave, I will pay a great price. And I am willing to lose so much, and to suffer greatly, so that I can love Peter and so that in turn he can love me. I throw away ideas of honor and commitment to family. I have my family, and that begins and ends with Peter.

Most parents and grandparents warn their children to stay away from the water, but for my entire life it has been the opposite for me. Grandmother told me never to leave the water's edge, that I must remain by the water, or like the Little Mermaid, I would suffer punishment.

When I pressed Grandmother to tell me why, she said it made the house happier that way. I asked her to explain further, and she said she could not, because thinking of the tragedy that the house experienced felt like pulling her chest apart and allowing her heart, lungs, liver, and intestines to spill out and flop onto the ground like a dying fish.

"They drowned. They drowned most terribly," Grandmother told me.

She never told me who drowned most terribly, but I suppose it didn't matter. I knew what the water could do. I had seen it myself. I did not recognize their bodies. Their faces were scratched and blood-ied, and my mother's pretty dress that she had chosen with such great care to attend the Chicago Symphony Orchestra's La Mer, L. 109 III, "Dialogue of the Wind and the Sea" by Claude Debussy was ripped and torn. My parents were covered in a layer of slick grime. What they can't prepare you for, what no one can prepare you for, is when you have to identify bodies that have been submerged in water for so long and seeing the damage they endure. They were only in the water a few hours, but in that time, their blood settled to the lower parts of their bodies. Their feet were shades of black and purple. Their hands were so wrinkled I could see the skin peeling back from their fingers in rolls of translucent clumps. They were disfigured in such a short snippet of time. It was horrible. All of it horrible, and every time I close my eyes to go to sleep at night, I see what was done to them, and there is no one I can hold accountable for it. There is no one who will take responsibility for it. All I have are grave markers to visit.

That night they drowned, I came home and rushed to Grandmother's room, crying and in pain, seeking the only comfort I could find in this house. Fairy tales. Hans Christian Andersen. "The Little Mermaid." I wondered then, Why was it always "The Little Mermaid," and it became so clear. Andersen was not afraid to end his stories unhappily. He was not afraid to tell us about sadness and cruelty, all the while creating a story a child could comprehend. I turned to the story, over and over again, and then read more about the man who had written the fairy tale that hung over my life. Andersen himself felt like he was an outsider, never fully understood or accepted, especially by those he wanted to love him. And so, he was never able to shake a great cloud of sadness that hung over his life.

Stories of mermaids exist around the world. The *iara* of Brazil, who were said to live in the rivers of the Amazon; *la sirene* from Haiti; *aycayia* of the Caribbean; *hafsfru* of Sweden; Lí Ban of Ireland; *rusalkas* of Eastern Europe; the *naiads* of Greece; the *ningyo* of Japan; Ravana from Cambodia; *njuzu* from Zimbabwe; and more. Many cultures and regions have stories of women who are half fish, who live out on bodies of water.

Accounts across the globe report similarities in their appearances: beautiful women, nude from the waist up, and the waist down, a fish-tail. Half animal. Half human. All legend. In *One Thousand and One Nights*, mermaids were described as having "hair like a woman's, but their hands and feet were in their bellies, and they had tails like fishes."

Many of these legends came with warnings.

Folklore often spoke of mermaids, and very often their appearance was an omen, announcing misfortune and death. Yes, most of the sightings occurred around the sea, but it wasn't difficult for aquatic life to travel along various waterways. All rivers, including the Chicago River, at some point, came into contact with the ocean through a labyrinth of twists and turns down several routes.

Underwater is as foreign, as grand, and as alien to us as the far reaches of the universe. There are over a million different marine species, and we certainly are not aware of all of them. What we know is that we know very little, especially about what lies beneath the crashing waves.

All bodies of water are beautiful and offer life and the possibility of death. Water gives us life. Over half of what we are as human beings is made up of water. Yet pull in just a small amount into your lungs and you will die. What brings us comfort in the shower, in the bath, dipping our toes into the cool lake on a hot summer day at the beach—that very liquid that brings us a sense of joy is our very poison.

Every day people die from drowning. Intentionally and unintentionally, just like my family. Not only did they suffer immensely as they drowned, but so did we, in a way, given that our suffering lingers. It's constant, just as we breathe, it's always there—the knowing that their last few moments were those of anguish. Their voice boxes bursting as they screamed, kicked, and struggled to reach land, but the water didn't allow them.

Our pain doesn't go away. It's constant, because we are reminded each day when we wake up of the agony that our loved ones are not here. That's what happens when people go missing, when they are killed—the living are left to endure, fractured representations of their former selves, moving about and functioning without the motivation to truly exist. Living, then, becomes a series of predetermined movements. We are slotted into the mechanisms spread out for our lives: breakfast, and a walk—for the occasional exercise—cleaning, and work, because one must always work. We must always busy ourselves so as not to think long enough about the horrible things that happen each day and about the gruesome things that taunt us from our pasts.

For those of us who have lost loved ones most tragically, we endure each day in this haze of agony. It's a residue that lingers on every aspect of our lives. We're never fully alone in our thoughts, and our thoughts are never free from the desperate question of why—why did this happen to someone we love? Why in turn did this happen to us? Sometimes the dead are far better off, because it is the living who are left with broken lives.

We are the family of missing and murdered people.

Water is what took my family away, and water is what Grandmother committed us to live with. We were ordered never to leave this house or that river. I was then given the direction to be the caretaker of my older sister. No one cared about my suffering.

I tried; I really did try.

I tried to make a life with my brittle and broken sister, the two of us tortured by the sounds and sights we could not explain. Our world was inside this beautiful house, two dolls in a redbrick Chicago bungalow dollhouse. I made a life for us in this place for as long as I could, but I can no longer honor my grandmother's promise. I can no longer live with my sister's moods, her wailings and shouts and thoughts that seem to twist and wrap around her, like ribbons of seaweed that stretch and tangle into forgotten things under the sea. That was me, the forgotten thing that was being restrained here, but not anymore.

It is as if when Jennie enters these moods, it is the house speaking and not her. That's what the house is—it is an entity, and it is steadily infecting her, polluting her, possessing my sister with each passing day until what she once was will be swallowed whole, into the belly of a whale.

Why would the house be so against our leaving? Why must we remain fixed to this very spot? Unmoving and unchanging. The world shifting and changing, advancing without us as we rot and fade into the fibers of this house.

Each time I step foot outside the house and return, it is always to my sister's explosive screams, followed by her moods or something worse.

I suppose none of it matters. It is almost time for me to leave anyway. I am not going to deny my love of Peter for another moment. I am going to go with him and live with him and love him with my entire being until I wither away to nothing and beyond, because I know that even in death our love will continue.

I wait up for Jennie, but she doesn't return. Hours pass, and each time I look out the window, I expect to find her in her regular state, standing there, arms hugging her shoulders and staring out into the street, humming that song.

I fall asleep on the sofa, Clover and Thistle snuggled beside me. At one point, I wake up in the middle of the night thinking I hear Jennie whispering her sweet melody into my ears, but there is nothing.

Just silence.

Once again, I fall into a deep sleep and dream, like I often do, of water. I see myself beneath the surface, in a white dress, not struggling or in pain, but beautiful, my face serene and my hair flowing out behind me. The sun breaks through the top layer, and I am engulfed in a radiant beam of light, and I look happy there, just swimming, with my eyes open and a smile across my face, small bubbles flowing out from my nose.

The water is a clear and vibrant blue, with layers of shadows flowing in and out gently: turquoise, aquamarine, cornflower, azure blue, royal blue, navy blue, and midnight blue. All of the blues.

I am the observer, looking out at myself, and then I see an object floating just by my bare feet. It is a pair of glasses that continues to rise past me until it is no longer in view. Then comes a pair of little white baby shoes making its direction above, and then a gold open pocket watch, its chain trailing behind. More objects come, dozens of them, hundreds of them: dresses and hats, spoons and books, plates and teddy bears, chairs and baskets. I am engulfed in an underwater storm of forgotten things.

I wake suddenly to the sound of a phone ringing, but it isn't my phone. Clover and Thistle are barking and growling madly, bouncing on their little legs.

"What is the matter?" And when I realize what it is that is ringing, I take pause. It is the black candlestick telephone.

"There's no way," I say, but the ringing surely is coming from that phone that has not been connected to wiring in decades.

I approach the phone with quiet hesitation, wondering if this is all a dream but knowing it isn't by the cold surface of the floor slowly waking me.

I lift the handle and place it to my ear and bring the receiver to my mouth.

"Hello?" My voice sounds thick with dreams.

"Hurry, Anna, or you'll be late to the picnic."

I drop the phone to the floor. Water and then a thick red liquid begin to flow out from the receiver.

"Don't forget your ticket, Anna!"

The light bulb above me flares and then bursts. I am too afraid to make any noise, and it is then that I realize it is already day outside. The light streams in from the large window looking over the river. I rush to the front door, hoping Jennie is out there, waiting for me to let her in, but there is nothing but the sound of early-morning birdsong and wet footprints leading away from the house stamped into the concrete.

I rush back into the house to check the time. That can't be. My heart sinks. Just moments ago, standing on the front porch it smelled like morning dew, and the sparrows and the warblers were singing good morning, and now the clock in the kitchen reads that it is past three in the afternoon. Jennie has never been this late to arrive. I rush to her bedroom, hoping that perhaps I had missed her.

"Jennie!" I call, pushing her door open. It's empty, except her bed is covered with sheets of paper tossed about. I approach and see her scraps of paper, all unfolded and spread across her bed. Missing persons posters. Dozens of them. All of the men who have gone missing around the river. Their faces stare up at me from black-and-white photographs, young men smiling, many of whom were later found dead, and there is Joshua Martin right in the center. Still missing.

My heart begins to race.

"What is this?" I say to myself and back away, legs shaking beneath me.

I step into the hall, looking down the hallway at each of the doors covered in mourning, and I know she would never be in any of those. I check in my office and then stand there in shock as I note the strange object on my desk that had not been there the night before.

It is a large wooden box finished in oak. I open the little doors and peer inside and find all of the little metal pieces that I had gathered throughout my exploration and repairs of the house. Those objects are now inside this box, mounted and fused together and polished by Jennie.

"It's a talking machine," I say to Clover and Thistle, who are sniffing about my feet. "A phonograph. This was made in Chicago by the Chicago Talking Machine Company, but they closed so long ago." I run my finger along the edges, noting that there is no record there. I assume that's what Jennie meant when she said there was still a piece missing. I am sure the house will bring me that too.

"The parts I was finding, they were for this very machine," I say to the dogs. "Jennie wants us to play the song. When we play the music, that's when it'll happen. When the story will commence. I know that now."

I walk down the stairs and note that it is now twilight. The candlestick telephone is back where it belongs on the end table. I find a business card beside the telephone. The name reads Detective John Rodriguez.

Chapter 23

The next morning, I get dressed. I walk the dogs and then we eat. I go through the motions, sweeping and mopping, dusting and scrubbing the first floor and stairs. I note how quiet it is coming from Jennie's room, and I knock on her bedroom door and do not hear anything. I knock again gently, and when I still don't hear anything, I push the door open and find nothing out of place. I finish my chores upstairs and then move back down to the first floor, where I will rest.

The drip starts, that slow and persistent sound that grows in intensity. I walk over to the kitchen sink, and there is nothing there. I look in the first-floor bathroom and again see nothing. I rush down to the basement, searching the laundry room for a drip in the faucet in the sink there, but there is again nothing.

I run upstairs to the second-floor bathroom, doubting I'll find anything there, but there it is. The bathtub is full and overflowing now, water splashing over its sides. This time Jennie is not inside, but there is something within the tub, a large black plastic disc at the very bottom. I reach for the faucet, turn it, and then push my hand into the freezing water and pull out the record.

I walk the record over to my office, drying it on the skirt of my dress. I sit down at my desk and then look at the name of the band and the title of the song, and I feel a great anchor finally being lifted, setting me free.

I place the record down on the phonograph Jennie has constructed from all of those tiny parts the house has gifted and adjust the needle carefully on its surface, and that song, Jennie's song, begins to play.

> By the sea
> By the sea
> By the beautiful sea
> You and me, you and me
> Oh, how happy we'll be

There it finally is, the actual song Jennie had once heard that stuck in her head and that she turned into comfort, humming in times of stress. There is that song playing finally in its entirety.

Once the song ends, I walk downstairs and take pause at what I see. On the side table with one of the black candlestick telephones there is a vase full of fresh white lilies. The flowers of mourning. I'm sure Jennie did not purchase these, and neither did I.

Chapter 24

"Phone's ringing," Rodriguez says as I park the car in front of the familiar bungalow with the blue diamond on the roof. We arrive before any uniforms. Anna called us first, and then we routed the report to the rest of the team, who'd get here soon to take down the formal statement.

Rodriguez and I look at each other. It's one of those looks that doesn't even need words added to say what we are thinking.

I take a deep breath and then say "Look . . ."

Rodriguez finishes my sentence. I'm not liking that this kid is in my head.

"Real weird the sister goes missing," he says.

"We asked to talk to the sister, and she refused and goes missing. Let's talk to the boyfriend and see what happens there."

"My gut?"

"Yeah, Rodriguez, what's your gut telling you."

"She's going to refuse to give us his information."

I push the car door open. "Not gonna happen. We're talking to the boyfriend." I stretch my arms up over my head. My back is screaming at me, it's so stiff.

"Hopefully your back holds on until we can close this case," Rodriguez says.

I laugh. "Look at you, already eager to find quick resolution. Good luck."

We cross the street, and for the first time we notice one of the neighbors. He's standing on his porch a few doors down, sweeping the steps. His mouth falls open in a look of surprise. I raise a hand and say hello, but he just stares silently.

"Nice to see other people have the same reaction to you as I do," Rodriguez says.

"We look like cops," I say, but then pause. "Well, I look like a cop. You look like a bum. You young detectives like to dress down."

"Right, because chasing suspects in a suit and dress shoes is ideal."

I nod. "Good point." I point up and down the freshly mowed lawns. "See, this is what people call a 'nice' neighborhood. To me a neighborhood is a neighborhood. It doesn't matter, but these houses cost double, triple, more than what you'd pay for something in the West or South Sides. These folks, they like cops to patrol their area. Makes them feel safe. Like our presence is keeping out the bad guys, but it doesn't matter what people look like, how much they make, and where they live—anyone can be the bad guy. These people here, see, they like us to be around but keep our distance. The minute we get out of our cars, they panic."

"Why's that?"

I look him dead in the eye, because the answer is obvious. "They worry that us being out of our cars, knocking on doors, asking questions is going to bring down their property values."

I reach up to knock on the front door, but before I can, Anna is already opening it for us.

"Sister didn't come home last night?" I ask. "You called all of her friends?"

Anna tilts her head and opens her mouth as if to say something, but then two little pit bulls dart out, yipping and charging forward.

"Ahhh!" I kneel, feeling my knees protesting, but I need to pet these little two. "I've got a pit bull at home. Named him Wrigley. These two are?"

"Clover and Thistle," Anna says, her hands folded in front of her.

"Got no idea what baseball field those are named after." I laugh, to which Anna remains silent. She seems much more serious today than she has in the past, and that's saying something. Anna has always been quiet, reserved, but today her demeanor is much more stiff, cold, disconnected. She's in her early twenties, but she speaks like she's much, much older. Mer doesn't even talk that way, and she's in her sixties. I don't understand the world that Anna Arbor lives in. I don't even want to understand it, but I have to at least try if we're going to figure out what the hell is going on around here.

Anna invites us inside, and the house is beautiful. Spotless. The woodworking alone is a work of art. Looks like it's all original wood floors. Original wood trim. Original stained-glass windows in the entryway. It looks like a showroom. A museum display, even, of what a house in Chicago might have looked like a long time ago. There are modern things, like the refrigerator and stove. I only know these lines and details because Mer loves all things Frank Lloyd Wright, and this house reminds me of all those pictures from books and catalogs she'd shown me of the homes he built.

Rodriguez looks to me for some type of guidance, but I don't know what signal to give him. He looks weirded out by the place, and I'm just as weirded out by it. This is strange. Anna is strange.

"Nice house," I say, really wanting to ask, "How many millions you think this place is worth?" I'm sure a few at least.

I already know Anna doesn't come from a rich family. If she came from a rich family, she'd live up there over by the North Shore, maybe the Gold Coast or Lincoln Park, even. But she's someone whose family bought in an area a long, long time ago where no one wanted to live, and they just dealt with all the waves of nonsense that would come and go. Back a long time ago, no one wanted to live along the river. The stench was enough to deter you, let alone the rumors or very real reality of bodies being dumped in it. At least now, it's a very nice desirable time to live along the river and to live in Ravenswood.

"You see this?" I point Rodriguez over to a little window over the front door. "That's original. You know how difficult it is to find bungalows with this stained glass? Lots of folks painted, plastered, or drywalled over these things. Damn shame. Mer had me looking for one all over town to hang up in our window. Found a nice one too in a salvage shop, but it was too pricey for me."

"Lisa and I are in a condo right now," Rodriguez says.

"Condo's not good for a kid. You need a yard. Grass and mud so the kid can run around and get dirty. That's good for kids."

"You selling your place before you retire?"

I look him over and think about how nice it might be for my old house to be home to a kid again. "I'll think about it."

"Better sell it to me on discount."

"I'll charge you double what it's worth."

Even though the house is clean, it feels empty. There are no personal effects like picture frames or anything that references the family. I note the print of the Sears catalog hung beside the door, furniture, and books on the bookshelves. I notice a blank space next to the Sears catalog, an impression of something that was up there once.

"What was here?" I ask. "Another picture of the house?"

Anna shakes her head. "No, a picture of my sister and me. It went missing."

This home feels like a shell, without hints about the people who live here.

There's a large green fabric sofa and two chairs. An end and coffee table. The kitchen with wooden cabinets, and a large built-in that takes up much of a wall filled with tons of old books. There are books on Chicago history, biographies of some familiar Chicago names, Daniel Burnham's *Plan of Chicago*, books on the 1893 Chicago World's Fair, the city's architecture and design, and more. This house feels like a tribute to old Chicago.

"I like to read . . ." Anna says, her voice trailing. "About the city, that is. The older books belonged to my grandfather. The newer books belonged to my father. They both shared that in common, an interest and fascination for Chicago history."

"Makes sense. Research for your podcast and all."

"Yes," she says, her eyes fluttering. She looks tired. It's expected. Up late worrying about her sister.

Still, I'd figure she'd be more upset. Anxious, agitated, something. Not so calm. Her sister is missing.

"You talk about your grandparents a lot, Anna. What'd they do?"

At first she looks confused by the question. "Grandfather worked at the Hawthorne Works, and Grandmother stayed home and raised my mother, eventually caring for Jennie and me. And here, Jennie and I remain, and we will remain."

Anna Arbor is a bizarre kid. She's in a long black dress. She sits with her hands folded on her lap. Her legs are crossed at the ankles. Her hands are folded on her lap, and her hair is pinned up in curls.

"You religious, Anna?" Rodriguez asks, and I groan.

She tilts her head and looks around the room, confused. "No, we were not raised in any religion."

"Really?" I mutter to him. Insulting her is not going to help.

Rodriguez raises his eyebrows in that "So what" motion. I ignore him.

"Anna, how old are you again?" I ask.

"Twenty-three."

Another glance from Rodriguez. He's probably not that much older than she is, so he knows how odd this behavior must be.

"And your sister, Jennie?"

"She's older, twenty-six, but I take care of her because of her condition."

"Do you mind?" I point to the sofa.

She shakes her head. "No."

"Got a bad back. Suspect tackled me from behind a few years ago and slammed me down over by Lower Wacker Drive. Haven't been the same since."

"What happened to the suspect?" Rodriguez asks.

"Doing twenty-five to life."

I lean forward as I address Anna. "And what condition is that, the one your sister's got?"

Anna looks from Rodriguez to me and then says, "Her nerves. She has fits. Moods. Since the accident."

"Post-traumatic stress? Anxiety, then?" I ask.

Anna shakes her head. "Perhaps. We don't have a formal diagnosis, but we don't need one."

Rodriguez interrupts. This kid needs to learn the art of tact. "She's missing. I don't think her moods are what's the matter right now."

Anna's bottom lip quivers.

I run my hand down my face and try not to scream. I look back to Anna and apologize for my impatient partner. "Sorry, Anna." I give Rodriguez the side-eye and murmur, "This ain't the time for good cop and bad cop."

Anna's eyebrows knit together. "Good cop? Bad cop?"

"You never heard that phrase?" I ask.

She shakes her head slowly, and I really am confused as to what's going on here. Everyone's heard that figure of speech. It's almost like this is not the same person we met months ago standing outside the Clark Street Bridge. Back then, Anna wore dark eye shadow, a leather jacket, black leggings, and Doc Martens. Today her speech is formal. Her dress is formal. I've known people who had lived through traumatic events themselves or lost loved ones and had completely transformed their lives, but this just made me uncomfortable.

"She was just here," Anna says, fighting through tears, pointing at the door. "I thought she was going to go for one of her walks."

I raise a hand. "One of her walks?"

"Yes, she goes out for walks. Sometimes in the evenings. Sometimes early mornings. She likes to walk along the river walk."

"By herself?" Rodriguez blurts out, sounding shocked. "In this city? With all of these people going missing all of a sudden? That's a little brave. Hell, I don't even think I'd go out for a walk by myself at night with what's been going on."

"Most of the people going missing are men," Anna says. "So my sister doesn't worry." Her eyes widen. A look of realization. "The woman with the green dress and red hair . . ."

I lean forward. "What woman?" Through the corner of my eye, I see Rodriguez jotting down notes in his notepad.

"My sister, she said she encountered a strange woman at the boat landing at Clark Park. The woman spoke of the drowned men."

"We'll check it out," Rodriguez says.

"Anna . . ." I start, knowing that there is no easy way to ask this. "Does your boyfriend Peter—"

"Fiancé . . ."

"Congratulations." Rodriguez claps once. "I love weddings."

I bite the inside of my mouth to keep from saying something not so nice to him.

"Congrats," I tell Anna. "Does your fiancé know that your sister likes to go for these nice long walks at night?"

"What are you trying to imply?"

I hold my hands up, and when I do, that's when I think I hear the faint sound of a drip. Probably that leak she was talking about. I look over to the kitchen, thinking someone is there, and for a moment I think I see something, like the last few seconds of someone before they disappear into a room. "No one else lives here except you and your sister?"

"Just my sister and me, and Clover and Thistle."

It goes quiet for a little, and then Anna says, "You hear it too, don't you. It's because you're close to the water. When one is close to the water, these things tend to merge, stacking on one another. I am close too, not by choice, but it's because it's what the house asks of me."

"What?" I ask, feeling foggy-headed for a moment.

"I didn't say anything," Anna says, adjusting her hands on her lap.

I look to Rodriguez and he mouths, "You okay?"

I nod, but I'm really not. This is all starting to make me feel uneasy. I don't like feeling uneasy. Makes me think of how I felt jumping in the river that day for that training exercise. All I could feel that day was the grief of losing Bobby, and how that feeling never really goes away but comes and goes in waves. It still does, but something about being in the water that day made it all feel close, like the water had a grip on me.

Maybe I'm tired, not having slept well. Maybe pushing to prove this is a serial killer and solving this case is finally going to cause that crack Sergeant Flanagan warned me about. He said that working in homicide, there was always that possibility we'd lose it after a case and not be able to come back from that grief right. There were dams in our brains we could build to hold back some of the things we saw, but there was always another case and another and another. And what was a case? Another victim. This is a career that knows no end. It is perpetual suffering, knowing the range of monstrosity humans are capable of inflicting on one another.

I know there is no bringing the others back, like there is no bringing Bobby back from that water. There is now Joshua Martin and Jennie Arbor. We are gonna find them. We have to.

I look to Anna and feel my heart sink for her. She's encountered lots of tragedy in a short time. Some of us could go much of our lives without losing someone we loved. Anna, however, wasn't so lucky.

I don't even know the kid, but I'm worried about her and her sister living here in this big house alone in the city. I also don't know how I feel about her fiancé. All I know is the guy's avoided my calls and has refused to speak with us.

Anna rubs her temple. "I suppose I don't understand why Peter would be brought up in conversation right here."

"We're just trying to make sure we cover everything." I clasp my hands together. "We want to find your sister just as much as you do. Peter's just another person who's close to the family, and we'd like to talk to him."

Anna looks frightened, and unsure of what it is that is happening. "Anna, your sister's just been gone for a few hours. She could be out with friends. Maybe everything is just fine . . ."

"You don't understand. We . . . I mean, Jennie doesn't have any friends. All Jennie has is me, her work, and this house."

"Everybody's got friends," I say. "I've got Rodriguez . . . Well, I've got my wife, that is."

"Don't think that helps," Rodriguez says.

"We're going to go see Peter and ask him a few questions. Maybe he's seen Jennie. Who knows? Either way, I'm sure she's all right. She'll probably walk in here any moment telling you some great story about her night out. Maybe she met up with some people. Had a nice time. Spent the night with them. That's fine and normal. That's life."

Anna gasps. "Jennie, my Jennie, would never do such a thing. It's . . . improper. Unladylike. People would talk. Jennie is the most proper woman I know."

Rodriguez's mouth hangs open. "You know we're not judging your sister if she did. All that's fine and normal. She's old enough to do what she wants. We just want to make sure she's all right."

This is way stranger than I ever expected it to be.

What Rodriguez and I are holding back from Anna is that Peter fits a pretty good profile. He is young. He is strong enough, and he doesn't have much of a past that we can piece together. Gaining the trust and admiration of a young woman who lives alone in a home valued in the millions in the city is a pretty good idea, if you're not a good person. And if you're not a good person, well, your fiancée co-owning a property with her sister is a bit of a complication. But get rid of the sister and, well, that just opens up your financial prospects, doesn't it. You get rich all by wooing a young, beautiful, and fairly strange woman. I'm not sure if Peter is the River Killer, but he sure did pick a woman to date who lives on the river with a sister who is obsessed with it. Seems odd. Especially since Jennie is known to go on frequent walks along the riverfront, alone. Who's to say that Jennie didn't see anything? Hear anything? She could have easily been walking along the river path and run into Peter. That same day a missing person could have been announced. All it would take would be for a little suspicion to grow and Jennie to say something, and if Peter was the killer, or capable of being a killer, he could have easily waited for her and gotten rid of his problem.

Anna is crying now. I can see she's worried. I wish I could tell her not to worry, but this doesn't look good. With Jennie missing, I'm worried we're going to find someone else in the water in a few days or weeks. The department continues with its line about the drownings being accidental. "Accidental deaths" sure does take the blame off anyone. Plus, that's a lot of people having the same accident, falling into the river. The Chicago River is no San Francisco Golden Gate Bridge. No one wants to take a swan dive into that green, murky water and end their life there, choking back sewage and sludge.

Outside I hear a car park and then that familiar cop banter between partners.

"I don't understand," Anna says, startled, as if emerging from a dream. "Why are you here? Why do you even care? You had said you're retiring soon. In what? Weeks now? Why bother with any of this? With us? You can both move on and live your lives away from this city. No one cared about us then. No one truly cares about us now. We are used to this emptiness. We will be fine and will care for ourselves the way only we can."

I'm really worried about Anna, but there's nothing I can do other than to help find her sister. "Your sister is missing. We just want to help."

She shoots me a sharp look. "How well did your department help my parents?"

I feel a grip on my chest and a stabbing pain in the back of my head. There's nothing I can say to that. "I lost my boy in the river. He was at a party. It let out and spilled into the streets, right by a bridge. Some people started fighting. He got in the way trying to separate folks, and well, alcohol and firearms mix and someone's gonna get hurt, and my kid was shot, fell over the railing. By the time the Marine Unit found him, he was gone. I'm just saying, I know what it's like to lose someone you love in that water."

Rodriguez and I stand up when the two uniformed officers enter to take Anna's formal report. We say our goodbyes, and as we're sitting in the car, and I'm looking up at that house ready to drive away, for a moment I think I see someone looking at me from a second-floor window.

It's a woman in a white dress with long black hair, but she doesn't have a face.

Chapter 25

After the detectives leave, the police arrive. One of the detectives has left their cell phone. I set it on one of the end tables because I know they will return.

I can feel myself clenching my jaw, stressed that there are all of these strangers in my house.

The last time there were so many people in this house . . . well, it was to mark a day of remembrance. Grandmother would be furious if she knew all of these people were here, their energies potentially disturbing the balance of how things should flow.

"Each of us vibrates on a certain frequency," Grandmother would say. "And it's important to note when someone is vibrating at your same frequency, because that's when you know."

"Know what?" I had asked.

"That they are the one you should call towards you."

"Like a telephone call?"

Grandmother smiled, closed her eyes, and nodded. "Exactly. It's as if you're making a telephone call, and you want that person on the other line to answer."

"If they do answer, then what happens?"

"You'll know what to do when they answer you. We all always know what to do when our call is answered."

The police officers make the official report, but there isn't much official about the report other than that they ask me a lot of questions and write down a lot of notes. They ask me for a recent picture of Jennie, which I provide. They snap a picture with their phones. Then they hand me a slip of paper, my copy of the written report, and they tell me that they will be following up. And when they all leave, I am left alone in a furious house demanding to know how I allowed Jennie to leave.

"She left on her own!" I shout at the ceiling, and the response is high-pitched laughter deep within the structure's foundation.

I hear tapping on the glass behind me.

I refuse to turn around and witness the terror that emerges from that river. "I'm no longer scared, because you've taken one of the last things I had to hold on to."

I hate this house, and right now I hate all of me that cannot stop this unbearable motion. I hold in my heart the weak assurance that my sister might be cared for in this house in the event she doesn't come to live with me, and how this home keeps trying to spin me back to a time that's not mine. But there is no guarantee of anything now. There is no knowing if she will come back or if she will be found.

I know what the river did.

All those people in suits and uniforms told me in a cold and pre-scribed way that they would be following up. There was no consider-ation that she was a person with a history and identity who belonged with me. And now, I feel the crushing guilt in my wanting to leave her so that I can be happy. I call Peter, but his phone only rings and rings. I have not spoken to him since before Jennie disappeared, and I too am beginning to grow worried about him.

I stand in the kitchen drinking my cup of tea and peering outside the window. My bedroom is packed, as is most of my office. Now, with Jennie gone, I plan to record one more podcast before I leave. My life is gathered into just a few boxes. Grandmother's things will remain in this house, and when Jennie returns, I believe she will remain in this house. I doubt she will want to come with Peter and me.

I set my cup of tea down and walk slowly up the stairs. I turn back and see Clover and Thistle seated at the bottom of the stairs. Their large eyes plead with me to not disturb the house, but I am already the cause of this disruption.

I walk past Jennie's room, and a great funeral dirge plays: Chopin's "Marche Funèbre." I don't know if it is intended to mock me, but I don't take the somber tones lightly. It feels dismissive and cruel.

In Grandmother's room, it is as it has always been, her bed made with white silk sheets and embroidered flowers, and the four small dolls lined against the wall. On her pillow is the book of fairy tales, as I expected it to be. I open it and find dried lilies tucked in between the pages of "The Little Mermaid."

The bookmarked page reads:

"In the moonlight, when all on board were asleep, except the man at the helm, who was steering, she sat on the deck, gazing down through the clear water. She thought she could distinguish her father's castle, and upon it her aged grandmother, with the silver crown on her head, looking through the rushing tide at the keel of the vessel. Then her sisters came up on the waves, and gazed at her mournfully, wringing their white hands. She beckoned to them, and smiled, and wanted to tell them how happy and well off she was; but the cabin-boy approached, and when her sisters dived down, he thought it was only the foam of the sea which he saw."

I tuck the book beneath my arm. It will be coming with me as well. It is the only piece of my grandmother I am willing to remove from this house, and I'm sure it is the only piece of her the house will allow me to steal away. When I walk down the steps, I think I see her, my grandmother, sitting there on her usual spot on the sofa reading a book.

We are all recordings. We are all voices in some distant past waiting to be heard again, understood, and loved.

It is as if my mind is playing back a memory, and for an instant Grandmother is, indeed, there sitting on the sofa, patting the space beside her with her hand.

I am taken back so many, many years ago . . .

"The river threads through the city like a great artery. Over one hundred and fifty miles of water that pumps life into this city."

My eyes scan the room. It is our house, Jennie's and mine, but it is different, all the same. I am different too. I am not me.

"Are you listening?" Grandmother asks.

"Yes, Grandmother." Now I remember. Back then, there was nothing to do in this house for entertainment but speak, read, and listen to music. There was no television set. There was no radio. The world was once so different, and I wonder why it is we are in a hurry to forget. Is it because it pains us too much to hold on to the way things once were? Maybe that's been the key this entire time, and I'm the one who is reluctant to let go. Maybe I should have let go as soon as the tides of time signaled the end. I wanted to believe in many ways that the past, present, and future existed simultaneously, and that every single possibility for us plays out in parallel.

In one reality, you could be on your deathbed; in another reality, you could be slipping on your shoes to head out of your house on your wedding day; in another reality, you could be asleep on the sofa of your new home with your little dogs snuggled next to you; and in another reality, you could finally be reunited with the love—not just of your life—but with the love of your entire existence.

Because when we die, we do not end.

The Little Mermaid knew this, and that is why she wanted to strike a bargain in order to gain a human soul, because even *she* knew that human souls were eternal, and so is love.

"All that matters is history and memory, but what about . . ."

I want to ask her something about the present and its importance, but I am slipping, shifting between then and now, her and me, unsure where I start and where I stop.

I nod. "Yes, Grandmother."

"Who was one of the earliest settlers on the Chicago River?"

I answer. "Jean Baptiste Point du Sable."

"Correct, our city's founder, Jean Baptiste Point du Sable. He left his home in the Caribbean, in Haiti, and made his way north here, to this cold outpost. What drew him to this area, I can only imagine, was the magnetic pull of this very land. He too also settled on the Chicago River, over on what is Michigan Avenue and Pioneer Court today. There he married a Potawatomi woman, and there they had two children.

"Chicago's frontier settlement centered on the Chicago River, but what the explosive population growth failed to tackle for a time was their neglect of the natural habitat surrounding the city, including the river. There was poor drainage, and thus flooding. Diseases like cholera killed thousands. The river was neglected and foul, as residents dumped horse and other animal carcasses and waste from sewers, breweries, and packing houses into the water. There, that awful mix of human and industrial waste turned the dark, inky river from green to red to black. The river flow dangerously impacted the city's drinking water and the health of its people."

Grandmother closes the book on her lap. "What year was the flow of the river completed then to improve the city's drinking water?"

I close my eyes, begging for the answer to appear somewhere within the shadows of my mind. "Eighteen . . . eighty . . ."

"No!" Grandmother claps her hands together. "The flow of the river was completed in 1900!" Her face is now inches from mine. "Don't you ever forget that. Don't you ever forget that what was done out there was called the Civil Engineering Monument of the Millennium. The flow of the river was reversed away from the city so that waste did not settle about here and stagnate."

I shake my head, and hot tears drip down my chin. Grandmother reminds me again of her urgent plea. "Don't you ever let any of them forget what we lost out there. We lost them all out there."

The ghost of my grandmother retreats up the stairs back to her bedroom.

I burst into tears in the dimly lit house, because that is all I can do here in Grandmother's house.

Read, write, eat, sleep, and cry.

This is a most miserable house.

Outside, I find another apparition, and this time it is of me, really me, but when I was a little girl. I am skipping down the path in a white dress with two long braids wrapped in ribbons on either side of my head. I hum a familiar song, but I cannot remember right now where I had heard it before. I have a pad of paper tucked under my arm, and there I go, singing to myself on a bright summer day, joyful and full of hope for a future destined with beautiful things.

I sit down beside the tree that holds the odds and ends of the little fairy garden I am constructing. I watch my little self pick up a blue crayon, coloring along the sides of the little replica of our house. There are marbles and buttons, drawings and little hairpins, tiny little seashells and coins all gathered around. I pull out a sheet of paper. My present self stands behind my past self and reads over my shoulder at the letter I am writing.

> Hello, how are you?
> My name is Anna Arbor.
> What is your name?
> Love,
> Anna

I remember those letters from when I was a little girl. How I wrote and wrote each day, multiple times a day sometimes. Tirelessly wishing and hoping for a friend. I had been wishing and hoping for someone to love me for a very, very long time. It did not matter that I didn't get a response. I continued to write because, in my loneliness as a girl, it was all that I could do.

It is a new day, and my past self is in a new dress. A powdered blue dress with white socks and black Mary Jane shoes. I write another letter.

> Good day, Fairy.
> This is Anna again, how are you today?
> Do you like to read, Fairy? I sure do love to read. My favorite story is "The Little Mermaid." It's a sad story, but it's ever so magical. It helps me believe that when we die we continue on. Here, I will read you a portion. I hope you can hear me.
> Love,
> Anna

My little self then sits up straight and reaches over for the book beside her, thumbs through the pages, and falls on a spot that has been bookmarked. I look up in the direction of the river. Take a deep breath, exhale, and then begin to read to the river, to my fairy.

"She grew more and more fond of human beings and wished more and more to be able to wander about with those whose world seemed to be so much larger than her own. They could fly over the sea in ships and mount the high hills which were far above the clouds; and the lands they possessed, their woods and their fields, stretched far away beyond the reach of her sight. There was so much that she wished to know, and her sisters were unable to answer all of her questions. Then she applied to her old grandmother, who knew all about the upper world, which she very rightly called the lands above the sea."

I watch as little me morphs to adolescent me, from a child to a teenager, still writing to my fairy and still reading to my fairy sections of my favorite fairy tale.

Dear Fairy,
I'm sad today.
    I will read you this sad little portion then from our favorite story.

"If human beings are not drowned," asked the little mermaid, "can they live forever? do they live forever as we do here in the sea?"

    I wonder what it means to live forever. Does that mean we will live forever in the very bodies we occupy now? Or do we continue on in the ether somehow? What is forever, and is it worth being around forever if we are alone and there is no one with whom we can speak to?
    I suppose that's all I have today, my dearest fairy. I hope you are happy there, under the water. Do you ever feel cold?
    Love your friend forever,
    Anna

Another day appears, of me watching my past self write to my fairy.

Fairy,
I was thinking the other day, are you a fairy, or are you a mermaid, because don't mermaids live in the water? Do you travel along the river and all of the great waterways, to the large and majestic oceans and back? Is that why sometimes I cannot sense you for great

periods of time because you are out on your adventures following these wondrous ships? Do the people on board ever see you? Do you ever wave to them?

Do mermaids live forever? I would very much like to live forever, as we spoke about, but I wonder if that would hurt somehow, because the passing of time brings with it the fading of those we once loved. I read this part in my story again, and would like to read it to you now:

"Why have not we an immortal soul?" asked the little mermaid mournfully; "I would give gladly all of the hundreds of years that I have to live, to be a human being only for one day, and to have the hope of knowing the happiness of that glorious world above the stars."

If I were to live forever, I hope that those whom I love most dearly will never leave me. I hope you never leave me, Fairy.

I do hope to see you soon. We are the bestest friends.

I love you so much,

Anna

Then one day, I ask the fairy what I had been meaning to ask since the first day I wrote to them.

Dear Fairy,

I hate it here.

Will you take me away to live with you, under the sea?

Love,

Anna

The scene changes, and it is an early morning now, and younger me has discovered a letter set at the base of my fairy garden. Shiny pebbles, little stones, and an empty oyster are placed on top of it to weigh it down so it won't blow away with the wind.

My hands tremble as I lift the folded sheet of paper, and there written in a delicate script are the words I had been dreaming to find me:

> Dear child,
> I am not a fairy. I am a mermaid. I live in the ocean,
> but travel along the river at times. Don't you fret. One
> day, I will be sure to take you with me.
> -M

My younger self never mentioned these exchanges to my Grandmother or Jennie or Mother or Father. I continued to write letters to the mermaid and continued to toss them into the river, but no more replies came. I had assumed that my mermaid was on a wondrous voyage, across great oceans. Some days and nights my younger self sat outside beneath the dark sky and stared at the water for what seemed like hours, focusing on each ripple, each bubble or leaf carried along the water's surface. I did this day and night, night and day, and one day I saw myself at the very same age I am now, standing there, and something floated along the water.

It was a bag. Within that bag was a bag and within that bag was a book.

The bag contained a book of ghost stories about Chicago, and I thought this must have been a gift from my fairy . . . mermaid.

I ran into the house and read the stories, memorizing each one and reciting it to Grandmother before I moved on to the next.

Of course, she asked me where these tales came from, and I told her about the book and how it came along on the water. She said it must have been a gift, and I smiled to myself because I knew it was a gift from my mermaid.

Grandmother told me I was a natural storyteller with the perfect voice to captivate the listener. I liked the sound of that.

Jennie, however, grew upset with the stories and refused to listen to any of them, especially the ones dealing with the river. She would scream and cry and fight and demand that I stop. Grandmother would shush her to sleep.

When I asked Grandmother why Jennie was so upset, all Grandmother would say was that "some don't adjust so well to the changes."

And I never understood what that meant, but I imagined that I would learn one day.

In the book I learned that Chicago had all sorts of ghost stories. There were the ghosts of early immigrants who died, ill prepared for the neglect they would experience in this new land. There were specters of children who wasted away from tuberculosis, flu, polio, and other illnesses. There were ghostly screams of men and women, many of whom were not mad but were committed anyway to the Dunning Asylum, who died alone in cold, musty corridors, unattended and alone, surrounded by their own waste.

There were ghosts of the mob, and the rip roars of tommy guns from Al Capone's days of North Side and South Side gangs that could be heard along the route of the Saint Valentine's Day Massacre.

There were ghosts that floated between tombstones at Rosehill, Graceland, and Mount Olive Cemeteries and more. There were the panicked cries of ghostly children in Alley of Death who died escaping the raging inferno of the Iroquois Theatre fire.

Chicago was a city of death, a phoenix that emerged from the ashes of the Great Fire but that continued to be knocked down and built back up with each new tragedy, whether on land or in . . . the water.

And there were many, many stories about deaths and drownings along the river. Especially that one.

I showed Grandmother a page with a grainy black-and-white image of a ship rolled over on its side in the river.

Another image showed bent metal, and men in long jackets and hats looking on as four men in police uniforms lifted a woman from the water. One of them was raising the skirt of her long white dress so gingerly so as not to get her already soaked attire even wetter.

Grandmother stared at the image for a long moment, took the book in her hands, and said, "The family who built this house, who lived here first, they all drowned in that ship that day."

I take a deep breath and scream out over the water, releasing all of the anger I hold within me. I stare down into that green water.

"You are going to bring her back to me," I demand of the river. I turn around and then head back to the house, and as I walk up the path, I hear a loud splash behind me, as if a great fish has leaped out of the water and then dived back in.

Chapter 26

"Why this park?" Rodriguez asks.

Seems a little obvious to me. It's an oasis. A patch of green in the city. It's not a big park that's got all that heavy foot traffic, like Humboldt, Garfield, Jackson, Lincoln, or Millennium Park.

"It's a good spot for the killer to visit." In the city, no one is going to notice you, not really. Chicago isn't like New York. New York is like static electricity; it snaps back at you. Chicago's got this soft glow to it. Makes you want to touch it, but if you do, you can get burned. In Chicago, people aren't going to notice you, what you look like, what you're doing. New York is similar, yes, but most people in Chicago just don't care about fancy things or social status. Chicagoans are prairie people, midwesterners. Yes, Chicagoans did what they could with what they had—sometimes meaning they made things work if they needed to, but ultimately, in Chicago, people went about their day, caring for themselves and their loved ones and not being bothered with things that didn't involve them, like a woman in a green dress with silver buttons.

I slip on my sunglasses and look south. "The killer can just come and stand here every day, and no one's really going to notice them." This is a good spot to admire their work. Some serial killers like to relish in their job and return to the scene of the crime. It's a way for them to relive that fantasy, and Clark Park offers the perfect opportunity to do just that.

Rodriguez turns around and looks at the WMS Boathouse, named for WMS Gaming, a slot machine manufacturer that once had a seven-acre campus across the river but moved to River North.

"We'll check the cameras," he says, and I spot several black domes along the overhang.

It's Sunday, so the boathouse closed at 3:00 p.m.

"Kinda weird building," Rodriguez says as he shields his eyes from the sun.

"What you learn about the boathouse?" I ask.

Rodriguez reaches for his notepad and starts reading. "It has a sculptural roof, with sharp peaks and dips, a series of Vs and Ms." He points to the dips and spikes in the actual building to signify this. "It's supposed to express the rhythm and motion of rowing. There are a few other boathouses in the city: Ping Tom Boathouse on Nineteenth Street, the River Boathouse RiverLab on Francisco Avenue, and Park No. 571 Boathouse on Eleanor Street."

"Good research paper," I say. "You get an A so far. Why this one, you think?"

"The reason they like this one is because Ping Tom is miles south from where most of our victims were last seen. Then, the River Boathouse RiverLab on North Francisco and the Park No. 571 Boathouse on Eleanor Street, they're just way north. This one, the WMS Boathouse, gives them the best access point for viewing their work. If a floater is left untouched, it's gonna come right up through here."

"But no one has ever gone missing here. Why's that?"

"It's too important to our killer. They wouldn't want to damage this place by killing someone here. Don't shit where you eat kinda thing. If they killed someone here, that'd just bring suspicion here, and they'd lose their vantage point."

We walk down to the boat launch, a wooden platform strewn with geese droppings. None of the geese look happy to see us, flapping their wings and hopping back into the water. Well, we aren't pleased to step around their waste. This is a quiet, pretty spot, and it reminds me a lot of Anna's backyard, how you didn't really feel like you were in the middle of a city. I look down at the water, green and murky, the color so thick you can't really see past the surface. I wonder what is swimming just below, what has been dumped here, and what would soon flow down this path.

"What are you thinking for the suspects?" Rodriguez asks.

I take a deep breath. "Well, from what we know, all of our men are heterosexual. They're young. College aged. Attractive. So who might elude suspicion?"

"A woman. Another man that looks like them."

"Exactly."

"So you're thinking Jennie?"

"Could be. Or could be Peter. Both of them are looking a little suspicious right now."

We leave the platform and walk up a small nature path surrounded by tall milkweed. Mer likes to plant these in our yard. Our backyard is a butterfly magnet in summer. They don't seem bothered by our presence and continue flapping their wings from plant to plant as we walk by. We approach the larger paved path; the canopy of trees here shields us from the sun, and I take off my sunglasses and slip them into my shirt pocket.

It's then that I stop, confused and shocked all the same by what I see. "That a frog?" I say, and Rodriguez laughs.

"Looks like it," he says of the small green critter several feet from us in the center of the path.

With our next step, the animal hops left and scurries down the bank. We hear a whoosh of branches and leaves as it shoves its way down, and then it's gone.

We continue walking. We pass a group of teenagers sitting on a bench, likely students from nearby Lane Tech High School. There's that familiar scent teenagers gravitate to sometimes, but Rodriguez and I ignore it. I stop briefly and ask if they've seen a woman in the area with long black hair wearing a black dress.

One of the girls in the group bursts out laughing. "Sounds like you're looking for a ghost."

Rodriquez laughs at me, and we keep moving.

"What?" I say. "I tried."

We continue walking.

"What are we looking for?" Rodriguez asks. "We can't expect we're going to run into a woman with red hair wearing a green dress."

"Yeah, we can," I say, and point, and there she is, just as we turn down the path. She's sitting on a bench, a book in hand, and she's looking up and smiling, as if she's been waiting for us this entire time.

"This is really weird," Rodriguez says.

"These past few days have been really weird. It's like the universe making sure I see it all before I retire."

"Excuse me," I say, approaching the woman. She closes her book and sets it down on the bench beside her. She's smiling, a loud sort of smile. I don't like it. I don't like any of this.

I reach for my badge in my jacket pocket, present it, and Rodriguez does the same. "I'm Detective Adam Kowalski, and this is my partner, Detective John Rodriguez."

"He looks a little young to be a detective," she says.

"I mean, I didn't hire him, but he's what I'm working with." I put my badge away. "We were wondering if you saw a woman here today or yesterday. Long dark hair. Probably wearing a black dress. Flats."

"You're looking for Jennie Arbor," the woman says.

"How'd you know her name?" I ask, but she ignores me.

"You're not the only people looking for Jennie. Her sister is looking for her as well. It's very sad what happened. A tragic accident. One wonders what the Fates were thinking when they placed the thread of that story on the great spindle that is life and began to weave. They knew there would be a great fissure. One can't hold that pressure back, of wanting something so much, but then all of the forces on Earth are preventing it. It's like a geyser. It will erupt. There's no holding it back, and Jennie Arbor's story was designed for her, sadly. What a beautiful, beautiful girl."

The last case I'm on, and of course everyone's got to be so painfully strange.

"What's your name?"

"I'll tell you that, in time."

"You talk to Jennie much?"

The woman points straight ahead, and I'm not sure what she means by that. "I know her from here. I come here, and I talk to her. She tells me things about her life, the life that she wants and the life she dreams of, but unfortunately for many of us, there is only a broken compass failing to guide us. Jennie holds dread and fear, and I tell her that this is the way that things will be. She fears the blue bolts of lightning when they appear, and intense weather, the rain and cold and snow, but I tell her not to worry, because I can summon the storms, I can predict the future, and like her and her darling sister, my voice holds power to sway and manipulate."

I feel Rodriguez lean in. He whispers, "None of this feels right. I think she probably needs some help."

I sigh and speak low. "Nothing we can do about that." She isn't hurting or harming anyone. We just need to be able to piece together whatever it is that could be useful in finding Jennie.

"Jennie's sister is worried about her. Wants to make sure that she gets home safe," I say.

"Anna, yes. I know Anna."

"You do?"

Rodriguez and I exchange a look. "Didn't know that. I heard Jennie spoke of you, but not fondly, though. Said she was scared of you."

"I very much doubt that I scare anyone. People come to me when they need me. How could you come to someone you fear? As for Anna, I only know of her, what her sister told me."

"Did you give Jennie a reason to fear you?" I ask.

"All I did was tell Jennie the way the stars are stretched out across the great sky. I told her where to look when she wanted to see constellations."

"Do you have a sister?" I scratch my chin. "Because Anna isn't doing so well and just wants her sister home."

"I do have a sister. Her name is Morgana. She's very different than me, but similar." She laughs. "I suppose we are like Anna and Jennie, two pearls in a single oyster."

"I don't understand any of that," I say. "We just want to find Jennie and bring her home."

"I'll ask you this, Detectives: Have you seen Jennie Arbor? Have you really seen Jennie Arbor?"

I'm not going to answer that question, because I don't even know what it means.

Rodriguez cuts in. "Do you have a number we can reach you for any more questions?"

"No, I do not adhere to ways of this world or the next, but if you need to speak with me again, I'm sure you will find me. Just follow the water, and we will speak again."

The woman stands up, tucks her book under her arm, and looks at Rodriguez and then me. "I don't know if you'll find what you're looking for, Detectives. Maybe in some capacity there will be a shadow of what is needed to fulfill the story."

"What are your thoughts about all of these missing persons cases? Men turning up dead in the water?" Rodriguez asks, and I sigh to myself. I was hoping he could be smoother about this.

"I think they heard the right song and gave the wrong answer." She proceeds to walk down the path.

"Wait, you didn't tell us your name," I shout.

She doesn't turn around but says, "Ursula Eddy. Soon again, we'll speak, I'm sure, Detectives. Please stay dry." And then she's gone.

"Stay dry?" Rodriguez says, and above us the sky booms. Thunder cracks, and we're both caught in a sheet of rain that seems to appear out of nowhere.

"That didn't give us anything," he says, wiping his face.

We're both rushing down the path to get to the car. I stop, and he asks me what's going on.

I look all around me and can't figure out where Ursula went. "We completely lost her. In just a few seconds," I say.

"I have a feeling she'll be back," he says.

Chapter 27

My sister, my blood, the person I sat out on the banks of the river with and watched as swans floated by, who conjured up fantastic tales of birds and fairies, what happened to her? How could someone who enjoyed such sweet and fantastic stories slip away into the night and not return?

Why didn't she return? Was she cross with me? I never meant to hurt her this way. I knew pain, and the last thing I ever wished to do was increase the hurt that Jennie lived with each day.

I stand outside, watching as birds land on the surface of the water, cooling themselves. The heat has intensified with each minute. I hold my phone in my hand, willing a message from Peter. I told him about Jennie. I told him about the detectives, and as I told him these things, I heard him scrambling to leave work, a rush of "family emergency" he uttered to his coworkers, and as he approached the elevator, he said he would call me back as soon as he got to his car. I begged him to please drive safely and to please just call me when he arrived.

I pace the garden and I watch the swans.

I remember then what Jennie had told me one day about swans.

"Swans carry messages of love tucked beneath their wings from those that have drowned. They swim up and downriver each morning and dusk, and when they emerge from the water and flap their great white wings, out flutter messages whispered to them from the dead.

Those words, carried in the folds of their feathers across the pink and orange and golden sunsets, then soon find their way to loved ones in the form of spectral kisses."

Back then, as a young girl, it sounded quite silly. "That's utterly ridiculous," I'd said. "How can ghosts send kisses? How can ghosts feel love?"

Jennie plucked a full green leaf from a low-hanging branch and then cast it into the water. We watched together as it glided downriver. "What's ridiculous about it?"

"That the dead would give their messages over to some silly birds."

Jennie smiled, continuing to follow the movement of the leaf as it floated along the water's surface. "I didn't say the dead. I said the drowned. The drowned are different, especially drowned women. Drowned women are different.

> But you, if all your lovers' frozen hearts
> Conspired to send you, desperate, to drown—
> Your maiden modesty will float face down."

She was quoting Aldous Leonard Huxley's poem "Second Philosopher's Song."

I correct her. "That's not true. We both very well know that drowned women float faceup, for their faces are too beautiful to be turned away from the sun."

But now, here today in the present, I want to believe more than anything that love has the capacity to rip through reality. I want to believe that love can puncture a hole through time and warp reality's limitations. With love, there are no rules or confines. Love just is. It is our natural state of being. Love is the purpose of this all, of existing. We are meant to love and be loved, and once we find love, it is in our power to nurture it. I love Peter, and I love Jennie, and they are both my only reason for being here right now. Without either of them, I would dissolve into tiny particles that the fish out in the river could nibble on.

The phone rings.

It's Peter.

"My love," he says, "it's rush hour traffic. It's going to take me an hour to get to you. Do you want to stay on the phone? I'm here. I'm here to listen. I'm here to help. Just tell me what you need. What can I do?"

I don't know if there's anything he can do. The only thing that can be done is that the river must make its secrets known so I can move on, because I feel myself slipping into a past that does not belong to me.

"I'm fine," I lie to him. "Please just drive. I'll be here waiting for you."

As soon as I hang up, I know I don't have much time. I request a car to pick me up to drive me to Clark Park. I need to find the woman in green.

When I arrive, the sun is a blood orange in the sky. The summer air is pleasant and sweet, and there are not too many people here. A man passes me walking a large white dog. The dog happily struts with a large stick in its mouth. A young mother is pushing a stroller; she pauses to lower the stroller's canopy to shield her sleeping child from any remaining light, and perhaps strangers.

I walk down to the boat launch but do not see anyone. Just in case, I look at the water, begging and hoping the elements will be kind to me and grant me what I've been longing to find, but there is nothing. Just slow, gentle ripples. I remember what Jennie says: that the woman lives on the river. I had dismissed it as an aspect of her mood, because there were no houses here on this part of the river, just a public park. There was nowhere for someone to set up a living space, but then I thought, perhaps the parking lot.

I run down the path, passing the mother and her stroller and the large white dog who barks, perhaps because I startled it. I figure the woman will be at the far end of the park, away from where most gathered. She would be in the darkest part, among the thick trees and brush where she could not be easily seen or bothered.

And there she is, standing with the van door open as I approach. She holds her arms out. A gleeful, welcoming smile is on her face. She is expecting me.

"Anna Arbor," she says, clapping. "Oh, how it took you so long."

She directs me inside her van, and I know that if I enter, everything will be different, that all things will go round and round and topsy-turvy and that I may find unpleasant answers to the questions I have long been asking. I do not know if this woman is *the* River Killer, but I know, I absolutely know, that she is *a* killer, that she has taken lives and taken great pleasure in the suffering of others. I feel all this, yet I still enter the van and feel my body flush with worry as I hear the door lock behind me.

The interior of the van has been converted to a tiny home. In the rear, there are two seats that are folded down to make a bed. On the side, there is a countertop with an electric stove, a sink, and a pull-out table. In the far back, there is a small door, which appears to be where the bathroom is. In front there is the driver's seat and the passenger seat. The van is clean and bare except for the seashells. All along the walls and the ceiling, there are seashells of all sizes and textures and variations of color—peach, pink, purple, beige, and white—glued to the surface.

"They remind me of my home," the woman says as she sits in the driver's seat and swivels it around to face me standing by the sink.

"Where's my sister?" I ask.

"Which one?" she says.

"I only have one sister. Jennie."

"Are you sure about that, Anna? Are you really sure?"

"What did you do to her? And those men?"

"I didn't do anything to them. They came to me, and they asked me questions, and I answered them. That's what I do. I offer services in the form of advice. People come to me already knowing what they want to do, how they want their life to unfold. I help them. I offer them words, or"—she reaches and plucks out a tiny seashell from her wall—"I offer them instruction, encouragement, even. But everyone makes a choice when they come to me. First they choose to visit with me, and then they can choose to take the advice and the instructions I have set out for them. I do not force anyone."

"Where is Jennie?"

"Where is Jennie? What about Jay, Anna? Haven't you been looking for *Jay?*"

"I . . ." My head throbs.

Her voice is slow and hypnotic now. "Jay, Anna. What about your sister, Jay? That was her nickname, wasn't it? But her real name was Jennie."

It's a waterfall, and I don't want to see it. I don't want to think about it.

The woman holds the small seashell out to me and places it in the palm of my hand. "You need to end the story, and once you end the story, you will end the killings. Take the book your grandmother treasured to Clark Street Bridge downtown, and drop it there in the water. By doing so, you will put Jennie Evenhouse to rest."

"I don't understand. Our last name is Arbor. My sister is Jennie Arbor."

The woman holds a finger up. "Yes, your name is Arbor. You are Anna Arbor. Your sister is Jennie 'Jay' Arbor. The two sisters who lived in your house a very long time ago were also named Anna and Jennie, but their last name was Evenhouse."

"How do you know that last name?"

The woman smiles. "I know all of the things that belong to water. Both those girls died in the sinking of the SS *Eastland* on Clark Street Bridge a very long time ago. What has been in your house, what you think is your sister, is not your sister. It's the ghost of Jennie Evenhouse, who died in 1915."

"I don't understand any of this."

"The book in your house of Hans Christian Andersen fairy tales belonged to Anna and Jennie Evenhouse. Your grandmother found it shortly after purchasing the house. Leave the book in the river at Clark Street Bridge and the murders will cease, and I hope that you will find your Jay."

"Who are you?"

"You know who I am. I am Ursula. The witch in the bottom of the sea. The witch in your grand story. You don't have much time, Anna Arbor. If you don't stop it, the murders will continue, and she'll kill Peter too, because she's so lovesick. She's so angry that she never had the love of a living man that she will cycle through all of them and cast them all to the water if she must. Take the book and leave it at Clark Street Bridge. Put Jennie Evenhouse to rest."

The door to the van opens and Ursula waves me away.

I don't know what to say. I want to utter something, anything, but before I can pull some words together, the van door slides shut and Ursula arranges the seat, facing the windshield. The engine turns on, and she waves and drives away.

Chapter 28

Anna isn't answering her phone, but I suspect she's in back. When I spoke with her last, she expressed apprehension about being in the house alone. I understood that that could be very stressful, finding yourself in a space where someone was last seen.

I park the car and look at the house. The blue diamond is a bright spot against the black sky, a beacon, in a way, and there, at the second-floor window, I see the curtain move and there is a woman. I raise my hand but doubt she can see me, Anna's sister, Jennie.

I release the seat belt, push the car door open, and step outside. My right hand is held high, in the hope that Jennie will wave back, but she doesn't do anything. She does not provide a greeting or an acknowledgment that she sees me, but I know she sees me, because her eyes are cast downward, street level.

I cross the street and reach the sidewalk, never really taking my eyes off that second-floor window and those eyes that track me here. Anna has said her sister is not well, but she never did disclose what exactly her condition was. I know about the car accident, how her parents' car plunged into the Chicago River and they drowned. I cannot imagine the pain my Anna carries and how she grieves for them. My love continues to mourn, and I will forever be by her side, to offer her my comfort.

I also understand that the recent missing persons cases and drownings along the river have proven difficult for Anna, reminding her even further that her entire family died mere months ago. She tells me she is fine. She tells me she is moving on, but I know she says these things to be strong, to signal to herself that she is healing, but I assure her that I am here and that we can feel this crushing pain together. I will never abandon her.

I dial Anna once more, and again it rings and rings. I send her another message.

"I'm here." I wait and hope for her to answer, for her to be home so that she can soon open the door and I can embrace her and tell her I love her and that we will process this all together, but there is no response.

I lift a finger to ring the doorbell, but something inside me turns. I feel uncomfortable knowing that it's just Jennie here at home, and I would rather wait outside at the river for my Anna. Plus, that look, that strange and peculiar look. It was just so cold and distant and dead.

I reach the side gate and lift the latch, close the door behind me, and enter the wonderful gardens that my Anna had planted and cared for so lovingly. Everything about this green space reminds me of how sweet and special she is. There are string lights and pinwheels, colored stones, and decorative glass bottles and old doors collected, painted in bright colors, and serving as a fence on either side of the garden.

I walk toward the little bench in Anna's fairy garden. She's so kind, and my heart just aches for all she has suffered recently. I know our meeting and connecting was fast, but it feels right. This feels right, and I don't need to explain my love for her. We love each other, and I want to live with her and only her for the rest of my life. I never thought I'd love anyone, but that voice, the very moment I heard it, was as if it were a song written just for me, and I can hear her words in my head even now. It's the sweetest call I've ever heard, and I want to hear it every morning when I wake up and every night before I go to sleep. I want to be comforted by her, and in turn, I want to comfort her. I need her to know each and every minute she breathes that she is loved by me. She's lost most of her family, and I lost mine. Maybe we were drawn together by some great force. Maybe the universe recognized that our mourning was too great and that we deserved some relief.

I approach the bench and spot something there. A book. *Hans Christen Andersen's Fairy Tales*. The book is beautiful, leather-bound with gold lettering. I open it and notice a delicate script inside:

This book belongs to Jennie and Anna Evenhouse.

Evenhouse? My Anna's last name is Arbor.

"You shouldn't touch that," I hear a voice behind me say. I set the book down and stand up.

I spin around, and there is Jennie, Anna's sister. "I'm Peter," I say, and she takes a step toward me.

Her eyes flash from me to the book. "Where did you get that?"

I motion to the bench. "I'm sorry, it was here."

Her nostrils flare, and she holds her hands together in front of her waist. "My sister is very irresponsible, you see. She lives in dreams, in her head, believing and relishing in her ghost stories and mysteries. These are not the things for a young lady, but still, I keep quiet, because they bring her joy. It is unfortunate that the one time she proved responsible was the one time I wish she hadn't, and so we died, and so we're here."

I knew Jennie was ill, but this is my first meeting with her, and I feel even more heartbroken for my Anna that she had to tend to her sister as well as mourn the death of her parents.

"Why don't I call Anna?" I reach for my phone in my shirt pocket, but before I can dial, Jennie rushes toward me.

"There's no need for you to call her! There's no need for you to be in her life. Anna has me. I am all that Anna needs!" She turns to face the house. "Anna has our home. Anna has the river. Anna has me. These are all of the things that Anna needs."

"Jennie, why don't we get you inside. Perhaps we can get you a glass of water and wait until Anna arrives."

"Oh, you want to get me inside, I see. Just like the other boys who want to be inside but do not want to love me. None of them want to really love me. I see the way they look at me. Their eyes are full for me, but their hearts are empty, and so they'll drown and so they'll die."

Jennie continues to walk closer to me. Getting closer and closer. I feel a sharp chill as if the temperature has dropped twenty degrees.

"Each of them, each and every one of them, was worthless. I looked into each of their eyes, and none of them looked back at me with any capacity for love. And oh how I longed to be loved. How I longed to be adored. How I longed for a man to embrace me, to breathe me in deeply, devouring the scent of my hair and admiring me in my entirety. How I longed for that genuine, sweet, and simple connection then and now. I begged the universe to grant me a love. I begged the heavens above and the waters below to grant me a true love, but all I got were screams, were people clawing at my face and neck. All I was granted with was death, and so that is what I'll offer back."

I step back again, and again. Jennie draws closer and closer. Jennie's eyes, I see it now, how they morph and change. They're different. They're empty. Black pits. Brackish water begins to pour from her nostrils, streaming down her lips and her chin. She opens her mouth, and it hangs wide, water pouring down her front.

I hear her voice in my head. Ringing. Stabbing. "To love me. This is all I have begged for, is for a man to really and truly love me, but none of them are capable of love, and so to the depths of the water they go."

Just then, as the phone buzzes in my hand, my foot slips, and my other foot follows. I tumble, shielding my face and eyes, but it's too late. A surprise of cold. Ice. Water. I am instantly shocked. My nerve endings fire. Everything is so cold. My eyes sting. My nostrils burn. I try to scream, but water rushes in. It's foul, and I gag and I choke. I try to scream for help, but there's so much water. Everything hurts, and I'm just so cold. I think of Anna. I hold on to the face of the only reason I have to live, and I beg anything that is listening to my thoughts to help me hold on just so I can be with my Anna. I love her. I love her. I don't want to drown. She needs me. I need her.

I hear Jennie scream above me, "Any man who does not love me will die, and so you will too! That is how this works."

And then it is quiet.

"It's just not right," Rodriguez says as we're parking.

"What's not right is you not paying attention and leaving your cell phone there. She's going to think you did that on purpose. She already doesn't want to talk to us."

Rodriguez is looking down by his feet, waving his hand back and forth across the floor of the car. There's nothing there. He turns around, checking the floor of the back seat behind him. "It's not here in the car. It's got to be in the house."

"I'm sure it's in the house," I say. That's just our luck.

We approach the house and that familiar blue diamond. I knock on the door, but there's no answer. I ring the doorbell, but again there's no answer.

Rodriguez leans over. "Side gate's open."

"That's weird. She doesn't seem the type to leave it open."

Rodriguez enters the backyard and I follow, and that's when we hear it. Splashing.

"The river," he says as he rushes toward the water.

Rodriguez runs to one of the decorative doors in the garden with a life preserver hanging on it. He unhooks the life preserver and throws it into the water. We hear a man calling for help between wet gasps. Rodriguez is crouching down at the far end of the bank, then he shouts, "I'm going in," and I feel my face flush hot. I look around and start shouting. "Anna! Jennie!" This isn't an accident.

"Kowalski! Help!"

I'm worried about my back. I'm worried about my footing, but I'm going to do whatever the hell I need to in order to pull this kid out of this water. I'm thinking of Bobby. Did he scream for help? My chest feels like it's being squeezed together on either side of me. I can't even tell if I'm breathing. Control. I can control this. My heart is pumping fast in my chest, and I need to control this. I gasp for air. Again, I tell myself, it's all about control. I'm moving down the bank slowly, careful with each step. I see Rodriguez. He's got his arm around someone. It's Peter. I just know it's Peter. I reach out a hand, and Rodriguez grabs my forearm. He doesn't pull too hard. I can tell he just needs to steady himself.

We pull the man up, and he's coughing, gasping, begging for air.

Rodriguez is patting his back hard. "Get it all out! You're okay. What's your name?"

He's coughing, spitting. Snot and tears are rolling down his face. "Peter."

Rodriguez and I look at each other, and I already know. Here we go. Were we wrong about our suspect this entire time?

"Where's Anna?"

"Not Anna," he says, coughing again and now wiping his eyes. "It was Jennie."

Rodriguez is calling for an ambulance, and I'm looking at the back of the house, wondering when Jennie returned.

"Guess she isn't really missing," I say, and then I pat Peter on the back once more. "You all right here?"

Peter nods, and I motion to Rodriguez to move toward the house.

He follows me as I walk up the back stairs. I check the french doors and they're open. I step inside and shout, "Police!" There's nothing. It's quiet.

"It's Detectives Kowalski and Rodriguez. Anna? Jennie?"

We enter the only bedroom on the first floor. It's simple and bare, like the rest of the house. I spot a large dog bed. This is Anna's bedroom, I assume. Rodriguez opens the walk-in closet, and there's no one there.

We look in the first-floor bathroom and then we head up the stairs.

We open the first room to the left, and there's no one. This must be Jennie's room. The bed is made. There's a large workstation overlooking the river with various metal parts and pieces and equipment. All of the stuff looks like cranks and gears to me. I walk over to the desk, and it's covered in a thin layer of dust, as are the tools that are laid out.

We reach the next room. It seems like it hasn't been used for quite some time.

"Their parents' bedroom?" Rodriguez asks.

"Yeah," I say as I enter. The room is also bare, just a bed. A nightstand on either end is also covered in dust. Rodriguez checks the closet while I stand in the hallway.

"It's empty," he says.

The next room is where we gather the grandmother once slept. It's not as bare as the others. This one is full of bookshelves. There are books everywhere, all along the walls, stacked on the floor in corners, and beside the bed. It's organized chaos.

Finally, the last room looks to be Anna's office.

In here we find her recording equipment, headset and microphone, a computer, and a tablet. There's another workstation beside the computer, this one with more metal parts and pieces spread out.

Pinned beside her computer on a corkboard is a funeral announcement. I call Rodriguez over and point.

"What the hell?" he says, and then reads the names.

The muscles in my neck tighten. I open my mouth to say something, but my brain is still processing this. I need a minute. I need more than a minute.

"It's just the one sister, I thought." Rodriguez looks from the announcement back to me. His mouth is open now, and he's struggling to say something, stuttering over himself. Then he finally spits it out. "Anna only has the one sister, right?"

I think back to the river that night.

Jay.

I always thought that was her name too, Jay.

Jay was the sister who died in the car accident that night.

I read the names once more, aloud this time.

"Agatha Arbor. Jeremiah Arbor. Jennie 'Jay' Arbor."

"She's been making it up?" Rodriguez asks, hoping I can make sense of this somehow.

I take a step forward and raise my hand, trying to settle him down. "I think she believes that Jennie is alive."

Rodriguez tilts his head from side to side. "How? There's just no way. You said that car crashed in the river in December. That was four months ago. You all found her parents' bodies. There's been no trace of Jay's . . . Jennie's body. There's just no way she's alive."

"We both know that, but I don't think Anna realizes that. I think Anna thinks that Jennie has been in this house with her this entire time."

"So she's just making this up?"

I thought about Bobby and how losing him wasn't just sad but absolutely wrecked Mer and me. There's no getting over losing a child. There's no getting over losing a loved one. You go through the motions—funeral and burial, and people coming by for a time to share stories—and then things go quiet, and that's when it gets heavy, when it's still and you just want to pick up the phone and call them, but there's no one there to talk to. Life is never right after the people you love die. Life is just different.

"Don't think she's making it up on purpose. Our brains do strange things sometimes when we're grieving. I feel awful for Anna. She lost her entire family in one night. Part of her is trying to hold on to something to the point of making it up." I hear the wails of the ambulance in the distance.

"We have to find her, to make sure she's safe," I say.

"Then make sure she hasn't tried killing anyone else," Rodriguez says, heading for the door.

My gut still tells me it wasn't Anna who pushed Peter into the river. Peter knows his fiancée. He was sure it was not Anna. So if it wasn't Anna, and we know that Jennie, Jay, is likely dead, who shoved him into the water?

Chapter 29

SS EASTLAND PODCAST: EPISODE #1

I arrive at the house, and Jennie is still not there. I find the side gate open, which is strange. I enter the garden, walk down the path, and spot the book, the book Ursula told me to cast in the water at Clark Street Bridge, and I will, but first I need to do something.

"I hope you enjoyed my introductory episode on the RMS *Titanic*.

"Today we'll begin the main story. But first, I wanted to let you know that by the time you listen to this episode, I will be taking a break for some time from the program to attend to my family.

"Thank you for listening to *The Chicago Vault* for these past few months. It's been my way of connecting with you through the stories about this city that are important to me. I'm also grateful for this podcast because of your company, and also because it's how I met my soon-to-be husband, so again, I thank you.

"I live on the Chicago River, and for many years I have thought of this story, of the *Titanic* of the Midwest.

"Today's episode is the first part in a series, but this episode attempts to summarize the deeply tragic events of July 24, 1915.

"This is the story of a river.

"This is a story about Chicago.

"This is the story about how people reacted when the floor beneath them fell, and their world turned.

"This is a story about heroes and cowards.

"This is a story about the heavy weight of our past, and that no matter how hard we try to forget, memories remain through family legacies, histories, or even embedded in creaking, old houses.

"First, let's start off where all stories begin: at the beginning.

"The Western Electric Company's Hawthorne Works employed thousands of people in Cicero, Illinois, just outside of Chicago. They made parts for one of the most innovative technologies of the day, the telephone. Just imagine, nearly all the telephones in the US at one time were manufactured at the Hawthorne Works.

"At its peak around 1915, the Works employed nearly fifty thousand people. Many lived in Cicero and were first- and second-generation immigrants: Czechs, Poles, Germans, Swedes, Norwegians, Italians, and Irish. Many also commuted from Chicago, like my grandfather, who commuted from the Ravenswood neighborhood in the city.

"You have to know that many of these people were factory workers. These weren't the extremely wealthy or the elite. These were working-class people. These were the people who built this city, and unfortunately, working conditions then were certainly not like they are today. They worked in the cold, in the heat, in unsafe and unhygienic conditions. They worked long hours and for very little pay. Most people worked long hours, and a six-day workweek was typical, and a reprieve for a break or a vacation was a rare luxury.

"So when the time for the annual company picnic arrived, many were excited for the opportunity to spend a day away from work.

"I try to imagine what it might have been like, say if I worked there, and unlike many other places at the time, the Works employed many women. It was progressive in that sense. Many families worked at the Works: husbands and wives, their older children, siblings, and cousins. The owners of the Works took pride in the community they built and the services and activities offered: night classes, a gym, a company store, and behind many of these types of activities were women. It was an innovative and forward-thinking workplace for that day and that time.

"Women were valued at the Works, even before the days of women's suffrage. They played key roles in all aspects of life at the Works, including the manufacturing areas, from critical roles dealing with intricate detail, such as coil winding, to key roles in engineering and even overall company culture.

"The Works even integrated their Women's and Men's Club, progress for that time, and that group, the Hawthorne Club, organized the massive annual picnic to Michigan City, Indiana.

"Ticket prices were not cheap. An average salary for a manager at that time was seventeen dollars a week, and tickets were one dollar each. But it was deeply encouraged that employees attend the picnic, and in 1915, over seven thousand tickets were sold to the fifth annual picnic. Before 1915, attendance was kept to just the employees, but in 1915, attendance was expanded so employees could invite neighbors, friends, and other family members as well.

"The picnic was a grand affair at the perfect location in Washington Park in Michigan City. The park had various attractions, including a dance pavilion, amusement park, bowling alleys, baseball diamonds, picnic grounds, the lakefront for swimming, and more. The workers brought food with them. Bands played, and people organized friendly and competitive games between each other's departments.

"Beyond the music and the dancing and the food and the games, this day offered manufacturing workers a serene few hours away from the monotony of their day-to-day lives.

"To accommodate the thousands of attendees, Western Electric chartered excursion ships to take its workers across the lake to their picnic destination, and one of those ships was the SS *Eastland*.

"The SS *Eastland* was built in 1902, and it was designed and built for speed. It was nicknamed the Speed Queen of the Great Lakes. The ship was narrow and sat high in the water, which caused it to be unstable. It was a fast ship, but it wasn't fast enough to do two round trips a day, which its owners wanted to do to make it profitable. So it was retrofitted in order to make it faster and increase passenger capacity, which only increased its issues with stability.

"The ballasts—massive tanks below the water level of the ship—would be filled with water to help with stability. The water levels in the ballasts would vary, but still it often leaned to one side or the other, and many passengers commented on this list throughout the years.

"On July 17, 1904, it almost capsized with nearly three thousand people on board. It developed a serious list on one side later that year.

"In 1912, after the sinking of the RMS *Titanic*, President Woodrow Wilson signed the Seamen's Act, which not only offered protections to various aspects of a seaman's life but also demanded that boats and ships carry more lifeboats and life rafts on board as ways of getting people off a sinking ship. The Seamen's Act mandated that there had to be lifeboats for seventy-five percent of the people aboard a ship.

"On July 2, 1915, the *Eastland* got its new supply of lifeboats and equipment.

"On July 24, 1915, it was scheduled to make its first fully loaded trip with all of that new equipment.

"People rushed to board the *Eastland*, as it was the first to depart. It was one of five vessels that was chartered by Western Electric to take employees to the picnic at Washington Park across the other side of the lake from Chicago, but it never left the dock on the river that drizzly morning.

"The ship started to tilt as people boarded. It's estimated that about fifty passengers boarded per minute. People searched for seats on the upper deck, and when none remained and as standing room became tight, many moved downstairs to the lower levels of the ship.

"People squeezed on with their belongings. They carried with them swimsuits and toys, rolled-up blankets, and baskets full of food. The baskets were full of Allegretti chocolates, honey rice salad, Zu Zu crackers, cold Smithfield luncheon meats, homemade pickled cucumbers, and mason jars full of sweet tea.

"The passengers dressed in their absolute best. Many had never even been on this type of ship before, with mahogany stairways and stained-glass doors. This was complete luxury for them.

"The men wore fine vested suits and straw hats. The women carried parasols that looked lovely against their layers and layers of white silk, crepe, linen, or taffeta. The ladies wore skin-clinging girdles, corsets, chemisettes, slips, black stockings, and petticoats, and then over that they wore bodices, blouses, tuckers, pinafores, flounces, socks, and overskirts.

"The women then added their finest jewelry, corsages, broaches, and pins. They topped this all off with their high-heeled Colonials or calf-high eyelet-laced boots.

"They wore their most beautiful fabrics, their weight as heavy as an anchor.

"Many of the passengers held the hands of their children, keeping their most important possession close by. The ship was full of babies, children, teens, and young women. In fact, the average age of the passengers was twenty-five.

"They weren't the elite. They were the real Chicagoans of that time. They were the people who worked in this city. They were the immigrants of that era, who came from different countries, who spoke different languages, but who all had a wish—to be happy. They were beautiful young people, from countries far away, trying to create and maintain magical lives and legacies spread before them, until everything went downcast and cold.

"Witnesses reported seeing water gushing out from the ship, the ballasts—the system meant to keep the ship stable—was being emptied.

"It's estimated that the boat reached a capacity of over 2,500 passengers by 7:10 in the morning.

"Musicians played aboard the ship as people continued to board, music filling the boat and the river. Passengers danced, and many laughed and brushed aside the boat listing from side to side as it did. They assumed this movement was normal. A thoughtless assumption.

"The list increased. The ship rocked from side to side in the river that was no more than twenty feet deep. Eventually, the ship groaned, leaning towards the water.

"A hush fell over the crowd as the vessel tilted closer and closer toward the Chicago River. When the SS *Eastland* reached a tilt of forty-five degrees, the Bradfield's Orchestra ceased playing. Their chairs slid out from beneath them. On the main deck there was a great crashing of shelves and dishes breaking as they smashed against the floor. A quiet panic settled over the crowd as many reached for something or someone to steady themselves. And as this happened, many of the crew members, instead of instructing the passengers to leave, in an act of great cowardice, abandoned the ship altogether.

"A piano detached from its hold and skidded across the floor, crashing into a young man and crushing him to death.

"The weight of the moment caused panic as the passengers stormed to the port side.

"Perhaps the lean was caused by the lack of water in the ballasts, the previous modifications made to the SS *Eastland*, the weight of new lifeboats and life vests—as mandated after many international laws had taken effect after the RMS *Titanic*'s sinking—or the mass of people that inspectors had approved, a capacity of people that the ship had never carried before nor had ever been intended to carry. The amount of people on board overwhelmed the structure's limitations.

"After swaying back and forth several times, the *Eastland* rolled completely port side, its side crashing into the Chicago River at 7:18 a.m. The morning was punctuated by a great crash and a roar of humanity being crushed, fighting to cling on to something, finding themselves trapped in the hull or falling into the river below.

"The ship was still tied to the dock.

"It all happened so fast that there was no time to deploy any of the life jackets or lifeboats that had been added to save lives."

"People were swept off the deck like ants into the water.

"Many who did not know how to swim drowned immediately. Others clawed at each other, desperate, gasping for air, trying to hold themselves up above the river's surface.

"Of those on the ship, men dressed in their finest suits trampled over women, babies that had slipped out of their mother's hold fell into rooms turned upside down, and many did not understand why their world had been flipped on its side. Just like with the RMS *Titanic*, many people died not knowing what was happening to them and why. As water gushed in, what was once the floor became the wall. What was once a side porthole became their only light above as they begged and screamed for help from those at the street level above as water continued filling the ship.

"Desperate people reached for whatever they could to keep them steady. They grabbed at legs, chairs, bannisters, hair, or the hems of dresses. People rushed to the stairs but were crushed to death in the stampede or struck and knocked unconscious by falling benches or furniture.

"Hallways and stairways were clogged with the bodies of men, women, and children. Those who reached outside leaped into the water, or, for some, they were in a prime position to jump onto the dock.

"In a matter of minutes, the SS *Eastland* settled on the mud of the river bottom. Despite the best effort of nearby ships and onlookers desperate to help, 844 people perished in the incident, including 22 entire families.

"Now, some say the ghosts of the doomed passengers linger on. According to reports, pedestrians strolling past the site of the disaster sometimes hear screams and splashes of water. However, when they stop to investigate, the river is calm, and no one appears to be in any distress. Other passersby reportedly see hundreds of ghostly faces peering up at them from the water at night.

"It seems the disaster site isn't the only place haunted by *Eastland* victims. The Second Regiment Armory had to be used as a temporary morgue. There are pictures of rows and rows of bodies wrapped in blankets and sheets, with people lined up, walking past to identify which body belonged to their family. For many years there had also been reports from that area of apparitions, until that building was torn down.

"Some people claim, too, that their houses are haunted with the ghosts of victims from the SS *Eastland*. There's the belief that many died so fast that they don't even know that they're dead, and so many of those ghosts returned home, unaware of what truly happened.

"Many of the people who died did not come from families that could immediately manage funeral costs. The American Red Cross, churches, and other civic and aid organizations helped at the scene of the accident and afterward in order to help families make funeral arrangements.

"So many people died on the same day that almost seven hundred funerals took place on a single day in Chicago on July 28, 1915.

"There's a picture of seven white coffins stacked on top of one another that I've found myself staring at while researching this story. A crowd of people dressed in black and holding umbrellas surround the coffins of the Sindelars, a family of seven that had been on board the SS *Eastland*. George and Josephine and their five children drowned. Their bodies were found at the bottom of the stairs the crowd had rushed to. The Sindelars were one of those twenty-two entire families that were killed on that tragic day. An entire family—more, their history and their possibility—ended there at the Chicago River.

"A civil suit dragged on until 1933, but its terms limited the payout to the salvage value of the SS *Eastland* minus the cost to raise it up from the river. So the families of the deceased wound up receiving almost no compensation for the disaster.

"No one, absolutely no one, was held responsible for the deaths of 844 people—mostly immigrant, poor, working-class women and children.

"Two salvage vessels owned by the Great Lakes Towing Company, including one named the *Favorite*, righted the ship. Cables were run from the *Favorite* underwater around the *Eastland* and secured to the starboard side of the ship. The entire process of righting the ship took two weeks and included clearing away the inside of the hull, tearing out the bulkheads, removing the coal and mud, and pumping several hundred tons of water out of the ship.

"The SS *Eastland* was then purchased by the Illinois Naval Reserve and refitted as a training vessel. It was renamed the USS *Wilmette* and performed well up until it was decommissioned in 1946. In 1947, it was sold and broken up for scrap, and the Speed Queen of the Great Lakes ceased to exist.

"After the funerals and the burials, life returned to normal. For the working class, there was no choice but to return to work, to the very place they last saw many of their friends and family. The annual picnic was moved from July to August. It was also moved from Michigan City,

Indiana, to Riverview Amusement Park in Chicago. All in an effort to not associate that annual picnic with the horrific loss of life.

"Two years after the sinking of the SS *Eastland*, six thousand people attended the picnic in 1917, already contributing to the healing and, in some way, suppression of the trauma and terror experienced by so many.

"The SS *Eastland* disaster is Chicago's worst tragedy. It killed more than twice as many people as the Great Chicago Fire, but it's as if it has been forgotten. The entire city suffered together for a moment, but then over the years it became a citywide repressed memory.

"We went about our day, to the next media event, to the next tragedy, but this tragedy was real.

"This tragedy happened.

"These people were with us, and in a moment, it was as if a black hole was punched into the collective consciousness of this city, this country.

"The average age of a passenger on the *Eastland* was twenty-five, but the average age of the deceased was twenty-three. It was mostly women who drowned in the river that day, inhaling water full of sewage and waste as they tried to cling to their babies, children, husbands, brothers, fiancés, and sisters.

"I wanted to tell you about the SS *Eastland* because while much of the city forgot and much of the world forgot, I refuse to forget about them.

"On next week's show, I will tell you more about the families and of the aftermath."

I stop the recording and clutch the book to my chest, knowing it's time to make it to Clark Street Bridge.

Chapter 30

We get off on Clark Street from Lake Shore Drive. Traffic crawls along as we approach Kinzie Street. It is a beautiful day where it isn't too hot or too humid. The temperature is mild and makes for a perfect day to be outside, to be recharged by the power of the sun.

Today feels like a resurrection, a day of possibility when all things can be refreshed and renewed, and we can bask in the splendor of our sparkling city on the lake. Pleasure reads on everyone's faces outside. Today is a good day. Today is a special day.

"Actually . . ." I say to the driver. "It's so nice out. I can walk the rest of the way."

He gapes at me in the rearview mirror.

"You sure?"

"Yes."

I start walking down Clark Street still clutching the book to my chest, ignoring the looks I am getting. I cradle this book as if it holds the key to life and death, because it does. I need to put Jennie Evenhouse back to rest; if not, her tortured and vengeful spirit will continue to hurt and harm.

I think about the Little Mermaid, and how after she died, she was given the gift to continue existing as an air spirit, as opposed to dissipating into the ocean as sea-foam. I hope and pray that for Jennie Evenhouse, she can find peace.

I walk down the concrete steps to the Riverwalk. A yellow Chicago water taxi is ferrying passengers along from one point to another.

A couple holds hands and smiles as they walk past me.

I approach a platform that extends out slightly over the river. I put my hands on the railings, and several kayakers pass by me. One waves, and I smile to return the greeting but am startled by a group of swans floating inches from the platform and flapping their great wings.

I feel my phone buzz and reach for it.

It is Peter.

"Where are you?" he asks.

"I'm at Clark Street Bridge," I say, walking down the platform along the river.

"Please stay right there. I'm on my way."

I stop. Pausing at the sight where the ship went down. "Peter, I'm safe."

"I'm worried about you, Anna."

I take a seat on one of the steps in front of the water, setting the book down beside me. "Wait, where are you?"

"I'm at your house. Getting out of an ambulance."

"What? What happened?"

"I don't even know how to explain it, but, Anna, listen. I was talking to the detectives and . . . Anna, do you remember Jay? Jay, your sister. She was in the back seat when your parents' car went over into the river. Jay was able to release herself from the seat belt. She got out of the car. She had rolled the back window down as water came rushing in, and once she released the seat belt, she swam out. The authorities believe she tried to save them by opening the passenger door to free your mother but was unable to. The same with your father who was in the driver's seat. She probably tried to swim back in through the rear window, and there she tried again to release your mother but was unsuccessful. Jay tried, she really did try to save them all. Your parents were recovered but not Jay. And that's why you've grown so invested in the missing people and bodies that have appeared in the river, because you've been waiting for a body to make an appearance, your sister, Jay. Anna, listen to me—Jennie, the Jennie you see in your house, is not Jay."

"I know that. I know all of that now," I say. "But you don't have to worry about that anymore. I'm putting Jennie to rest."

"Anna, what are you doing?"

"I'm fine and safe, but I have to go now, Peter. They're boarding."

I hear the music now.

I do not want to slip back into that past, but I know it is the only way. I close my eyes and listen for that past that is always there, waiting for us to pick up on its frequency.

"Remember," I hear Jennie whisper. I can now feel the weight of my dress, my corset pinching me too tight at my sides and digging into my skin.

I open my eyes now, not as Anna Arbor, but as Anna Evenhouse, who stood on this river, in this city, over a hundred years ago.

This is the flicker, the memory I was trying to recall. The only memory. My last memory. Or was it mine? Or hers? What does it matter how we merged, Anna Evenhouse and I, but we did. Two sisters across time, with the same name, who lived in the same house, and who had suffered so much.

"How?" I say.

"Time. Memory. Synchronicity. This is a story of two sets of sisters who lived years apart. Jennie and Anna Evenhouse and Jennie 'Jay' and Anna Arbor. Jennie and Anna Evenhouse lived in a beautiful manor along the Chicago River. They were raised by their loving parents and an adoring grandmother, but they all died by drowning one dreary summer morning in 1915 when the ship they boarded to take them to a picnic rolled over on its side. The house sat empty for a time, mourning this terrible loss. It exchanged hands in the family, but they didn't have small ones, and the house missed the laughter and magic of little children. Then one day, your grandparents purchased the home. They had a daughter, your mother, whom the house loved very much, but then years later, two sisters were born who coincidentally shared the names of the two sisters who lived there and who died very long ago, Anna and Jennie. Synchronicity. Two simultaneously occurring events that seem connected but are not, not really. Only in the similarities they keep. When Jennie went missing in the river, Anna Arbor came to the house and mourned so intensely that the wound was reopened and I appeared, because I wanted to comfort you, my little sister."

"But I'm not your little sister Anna. Your little sister Anna died a long time ago, here in the water."

"Yes, she died, and I died in the sinking of the SS *Eastland*. And now it's your turn to join me and my sister, and your sister too, in the water. They all wait for us in the water."

"What about the missing people, the men who have drowned?"

"I am the siren of this city. I am the gust of wind that pushes too hard, that throws one off balance, and that kills. They deserved to die, for they did not and could not love me."

"I don't understand. What happens now?"

"We will be forgotten. The forgotten sisters. You will board the SS *Eastland* with me, as my sister and I did that morning in 1915. The boat will roll over to its side, and hundreds on the deck will lose their balance and slide into the water. Hundreds inside the ship will be trampled. Hundreds in the water will struggle. And hundreds will die, and you will die too."

I can now smell burning coal and sense the sky above us growing cloudy and gray.

"Anna," I hear my sister say behind me. Jennie places her hand on my shoulder.

I admire her in her finest dress, a long, white, flaring A-line skirt and a tight bodice. Her hair is pinned up in curls, and she wears a lovely wide-brimmed hat. She is singing the words to her favorite song, released just that past year in 1914 by the Heidelberg Quintet.

> By the sea
> By the sea
> By the beautiful sea
> You and me, you and me
> Oh, how happy we'll be

She laughs. "Well, it's not really the sea, but the river and on to a lake, but it's as good as we can get. Still, I was hoping to find you here. How unfortunate that the ship is already terribly packed." She glances over my shoulder. A young man runs past us, ticket in hand, and gives it to the attendant ushering passengers on board.

"Well, shall we?" Jennie hoists up a day bag containing our swimsuits and towels. "Mother and Father are already on board."

I feel like I should be doing something in this moment. I stare into my empty hand and then across to the river. I had been holding something. Where did it go?

"Anna!" I hear a man shout somewhere in the distance. Calling my name over and over. "Anna! Don't!"

I feel Jennie's arm on mine. She laughs. "Are you all right? It's as if your head is in the stars."

"I thought I heard someone calling my name. It sounds like . . . I think his name was Adam."

Jennie presses a finger to my lips. She leans into me, the tip of her nose touching mine. She whispers. "Don't say that name."

My head feels in a daze, and it sounds like my name is still being called, a warbling echo as if being shouted at the far end of a tunnel. "I thought I was talking to someone," I said.

"You are, my dear and silly sister. You're talking to me. Well, do you have your ticket?" She motions toward the ship that is now crowded with people we work with and their friends and families.

"I . . ." I study my empty hands, certain I had been doing something just moments before Jennie distracted me.

She draws a ticket from her purse and hands it to me. "What would you do if I didn't take care of you?"

Jennie takes my hand in hers, and we look at the redbrick clock tower that looms over us at the Reid Murdoch Building.

"Tickets, please!" the attendant calls, directing us to board. "There's no longer space on the top deck. You'll have to go below, young ladies."

Jennie whispers into my ear as soon as we step on board, "I feel like we'll find love on the river today."

Jennie and I squeeze past passengers, ignoring the suggestion to go belowdecks. She pushes us through to the top deck, to the river side. We slip in between a family and get hold of the railing and gaze out over the water. A light drizzle begins to fall.

"We fought so hard to find this spot, and now I fear we'll get wet with the rain. I doubt we can make it belowdecks now," she says as she adjusts her hat over her head. "It's certainly not the type of day for a picnic. It's more like the perfect day for a funeral."

"Anna!" My name is being called once again from the tunnel. I look around, searching for whoever is calling me, and then across the way at the street level, I spot an older man waving his arms. He is dressed most peculiar, not like how we are dressed.

Jennie takes hold of my chin with her thumb and pointer finger. "Do not look at him." She turns my head.

We can see the other ships lined up behind us on the dock. All around us, early-morning risers are tending to their small shops, and customers are purchasing fresh fruits and vegetables or selecting freshly butchered pigs or chickens that were brought to the area from the nearby stockyards. People all along the river wave to our ship, the first to set sail today for the Western Electric picnic.

The band plays. People try to dance in the cramped space. There is laughter and the sounds of children playing.

"Oh, he is handsome." Jennie directs my attention across the river.

I see a young man with a dark suit and red hair. His cheeks grow equally as red when he looks in our direction. I look away before meeting his eyes, too shy.

"He's smiling at you," I tell Jennie.

"He's still looking." Jennie continues to wave. "How I wish he were on this boat and not up there."

She laughs and throws her arms around my neck.

"I love you so much, dear sister. I do hope we'll always be together like this. You and me."

Jennie lays her head on my shoulder and begins to hum her favorite song again.

I sing along too.

> I love to be beside your side, beside the sea,
> Beside the seaside, by the beautiful sea

"Jennie," I say, "I'm scared."

Jennie wraps her arms around me. "Don't be. I'll be there." She holds me at arm's length and studies my face. "You and me and your Jennie and my Anna. We'll all be together again. Just close your eyes. The song will stop playing, and it'll all end soon."

"Anna!" The voice in the tunnel returns. It is closer now. The older man, and now I remember—he's looking for Jennie. My Jennie. Jay. He's also looking for the men who are missing.

"Where are they?" I ask Jennie. She ignores my question. "Shhhhhh," Jennie whispers in my ear. "John can't save us. No one can."

My stomach turns as we lean toward the water. The band stops playing. There's a loud groan from the crowd. I hear plates fall. Women scream. Babies cry. And through all of this, Jennie hugs me even tighter.

Bodies slam against me, and together in a tangle of limbs, we fall. First, I feel wind and then water. Arms and legs and faces. There's splashing and water slapping against me. I reach out and try to wipe at my eyes to see.

"Anna! Anna!" I hear Jennie call, and then she is gone.

I reach around me, calling and crying for Jennie. My hair is plastered to my face, and as I push it away from my eyes, I can see children and babies bobbing in the water around me like corks. Choking and gasping and gagging. The surface of the river is nearly covered with men and women and children desperately trying to hold themselves up and fighting to keep their faces above water. All of their belongings are floating around us—hats and shoes, baskets and towels.

People from the nearby shops rush to the river's edge. They throw down crates and boxes, pieces of wood, and whatever they can get ahold of in hopes that we can float on top of it. There are just so many of us covering the surface. Objects fall from above and hit people below, knocking them unconscious. I see a wooden crate fall and strike a woman's head in front of me. Blood spurts and sprays and then she is gone.

I scream for Jennie. My Jennie. "Jay!" My legs are growing tired. Kicking. My arms are growing weak splashing and striking against cold limbs. Water rushes into my mouth, and it's awful and sour and tastes of bitterness and putrefaction, and I spit it out. My eyes sting, and the smell is all-consuming. Dead fish and dead animals and human waste. Water clouds my vision, and then I see her, a pale, faceless woman. Her dark hair sticks to the sides of her face. She wears a white dress that clings to her body. She's swimming toward me, and before I can scream, she sinks beneath the water.

And then the voice from the tunnel is here, beside me. "Anna, it's Adam. Can you hear me? Help! Somebody!" I feel his arms around me and see this world begin to dissolve, water pouring down a watercolor painting. The past and the present.

"Give me your hand!"

John. I remember his name too. I reach for his hand, and he pulls me up to the Riverwalk.

A crowd has formed around us. Everyone is staring, but no one can see what I see. No one can see the great ghost ship on its side and the surface of the river covered in a layer of people, screaming, pleading, splashing, and begging to be freed.

"Kowalski! You all right?"

Kowalski's on his back. Rodriguez rolls him onto his side. He's coughing now.

I search around me. The book. I had set it down and spot it on one of the steps. I run over to it, press it to my chest, and run to the edge of the Riverwalk.

Kowalski points at me and shouts, "Don't!"

Rodriguez is on his feet, approaching me.

"I'm fine. I'm not jumping."

There are splashes and cries. My eyes are still burning, and my ears sting from the screaming and shrieking. I feel a great crash and then see the man from above leap into the water. He's swimming, pushing against crates and objects tossed from above to help people stay afloat. He approaches Jennie, and in that moment, I see their eyes meet, and I look at the way they look at each other, and I know—that is what Jennie has been searching for. That look of true love, in an instant, and that is the look that none of those men she encountered were ever able to give to her.

He pulls her, but he seems caught on something, and it's in that moment I know what it is.

The faceless woman.

My fairy.

My mermaid who has come to protect me.

"But she can't come back!" I scream. "She can never come back!" It's then that I toss the book into the water and hear a great wail as the side of the boat finally crashes and settles into the bottom of the Chicago River. The entire city is rocked.

The water is violently churning and spinning, and in that last moment, in which all of the past is pulled down into the watery depths, I think I see it for just one second: the splash of a great fishtail.

"Oh my God!" someone screams. And there's another and another scream. People are panicked, and I hear Rodriguez shouting for Kowalski.

"Kowalski, do you see this?"

There's silence on the Riverwalk as we all take in with our eyes what our minds cannot comprehend.

I turn back to the water, and there they are, bodies of drowned men. So many. Dozens of them. All of them. Jennie Evenhouse's victims. The river has returned them home.

Chapter 31

Peter is at home waiting for me.

On the way home, Detective Rodriguez and Detective Kowalski remain mostly silent. They pull in the drive-through at Portillo's and buy themselves some food. They ask if I'd like anything, but I can't eat. They eat silently, and once they arrive at my house, they park, and both lean on the car, looking up at the blue diamond on the roof peak, knowing that none of this made any sense.

"We'll head back to Clark Park and check if Ursula's van is still there. We might have enough to bring her in for questioning. We've got a witness saying a woman in a white van was asking men if they wanted a ride. It's not much to go on, but maybe we can get her to cooperate."

I laugh. "She's gone. I'm sure. Plus, it seems like Ursula is the one who does the questioning and not the other way around."

I wonder if any of it even matters. It will take days to identify all of the bodies, but I feel as if one of them is Joshua Martin. I'm happy that he will soon be reunited with his family, as well as the others. Their families will grieve, but at least they'll have some closure. I at least will have the closure of knowing that no more deaths can ever be attributed to Jennie Evenhouse.

"Will you call me if you hear of anything about Jay?" I ask.

Detective Rodriguez turns around from the passenger seat and looks me in the eye. "I promise you, we'll do everything we can to bring her home."

Inside I find Peter. He's on my sofa with an ice pack on his knee and cuts and bruises on his face. I motion for him to please stay seated. I sit down beside him and lean my head on his shoulder and cry. "They still haven't found Jay," I say.

"But they will. She'll return. And I was thinking, I'm not taking that job back home. I'm staying here with you, because this house is your home. Well, if you want me to stay here, that is."

"I never want you to leave," I tell him.

Clover and Thistle paw at the back door. It's time for their walk. I tell Peter to remain on the sofa in comfort. I gather the dogs, and we walk down the path together, admiring how the setting sun has cast a sheet of gold across our beautiful garden.

We pass the bench and pause at the fairy garden. I say a quiet thank-you to my fairy for protecting me.

I hear a loud splash at the river, louder than any fish I have ever encountered. I walk to the edge of our garden, to that space where land meets water, and there she is, radiant, luminescent, a piece of the sun that's fallen to Earth. It's her. My sister, Jay.

She's finally come home.

Acknowledgments

Thank you to Jessica Tribble Wells, Grace Wynter, Lane Heymont, Becky Spratford, Hailey Piper, Karmen Wells, Gabino Iglesias, Brian Keene, and Brandi Guarino.

Finally, thank you to my children and to Gerardo Pelayo. Ger, we stood at the Riverwalk and stared at the Chicago River one night many years ago. It was there that I thought I spotted the shape of a woman floating beneath the surface, looking up at us. It was then that this became a story I needed to tell.

About the Author

Cynthia Pelayo is a Bram Stoker Award–winning author. Her novels include *Children of Chicago* and *The Shoemaker's Magician*. In addition to writing genre-blending novels that incorporate elements of fairy tales, mystery, detective, crime, and horror, Pelayo has written numerous short stories and the poetry collection *Crime Scene*. The recipient of the 2021 International Latino Book Award, she holds a master of fine arts in writing from the School of the Art Institute of Chicago. She lives in Chicago with her family. For more information, visit www.cinapelayo.com.